Barbara J. Hancock ...... Ridge Mountains wher... edge of the wilderness ..... isn't writing modern g..... shadows with a unique .... heat and heart, she can be found wrangling twin boys and spoiling her pets.

Also by Barbara J. Hancock

Brimstone Seduction
Brimstone Bride
Brimstone Prince
Legendary Shifter
Darkening Around Me
Silent Is the House
The Girl in Blue

Discover more at millsandboon.co.uk

LEGENDARY SHIFTER

BARBARA J. HANCOCK

MILLS & BOON

First Published in Great Britain 2018
by Mills & Boon, an imprint of HarperCollins*Publishers*
1 London Bridge Street, London, SE1 9GF

Legendary Shifter © 2018 Barbara J. Hancock

ISBN: 978-0-263-26677-1

49-0418

MIX
Paper from
responsible sources
FSC **FSC™ C007454**
www.fsc.org

Printed and bound in Spain
by CPI, Barcelona

For the warrior in us all. Because she rocks.

Prologue

All he could do was watch and wait.

He found pleasure in it, surprisingly enough. Anticipation made the torment sweet. Elena Pavlova's mother had slit her wrists to protect her daughter ten years ago. Her sacrifice hadn't kept him from visiting her daughter's nightmares with delicious visions of the future they'd have together. He couldn't physically have Elena, yet. Her mother's blood had bought her a reprieve. But the protective power of the spilled blood was running out.

As a witchblood prince of the Dark *Volkhvy*, Grigori was used to getting what he wanted. He was part of the royal family in a culture that condoned Darkness. He stood just inside the open window of Elena's bedroom and watched her toss and turn in her sleep. The soft sounds of her fretful sighs were mere whispers compared to the noises she would be making in the nightmare that disturbed her sleep. Because he was in control there, unbound by her mother's rough folk magic.

What a shocking surprise that had been.

The voluminous curtains on the window billowed outward to brush against him, stirred by a midnight Saint Petersburg breeze. He'd seen the girl dance. He'd decided to have her. But her mother had been raised to believe in the old ways. She'd died so her daughter could live.

Or so she'd thought.

The curtains continued to flutter around him like white wings on either side of his tuxedo-clad body. When he was finished here, he would make other clandestine appearances throughout the city. He was a royal among Dark *Volkhvy* circles and the Dark *Volkhvy* ruled from the shadows. Their power was rising, bubbling to the top of a world rent by betrayal and hunger.

The mother's blood had run out before he was bound forever. At best, she'd bought her daughter time. Time to be stalked. Time to be hunted, night after night in her dreams. Elena had been a lovely swan as a teen. She'd only grown more graceful and more alluring as she'd aged into a prima ballerina. His anticipation had grown with every passing year. Every time she donned the pristine white feathers and pirouetted across the stage.

Then an injury had interfered with her dancing, and her vulnerability had inflamed his desire to even greater heights. He had fought against the binding. He'd done everything to try to break it, to no avail. She still had a grandmother who lived and watched over her with all the old folk magic most modern-day Russians had forgotten. He could only send more violent and vivid visions to Elena each night, fueled by his frustrated passions.

Finally, her grandmother had died and he'd sensed the power of Elena's mother's blood fading. She'd sacrificed every last drop to fuel a protective barrier spell around her daughter, but it wouldn't last. She might have known some of the old ways, but she was no *Volkhvy*. Lately, he'd been able to approach Elena and speak to her. He'd added to the torment of the visions he sent to her nightmares by telling her that they were true.

She would be his.

When the protective spell her mother's blood had created ran out.

Grigori watched his delicate swan whimper in her sleep. He couldn't even approach her bed to get a closer look at the rapid rise and fall of her chest, the flush on her porcelain cheeks, the heat rising off her sweat-dampened skin.

Love was abhorrent to him. The residual love of her grandmother was infused into every object in this house and, combined with her mother's sacrifice, continued to hold him at bay…for now.

Power was everything to one of his kind. Once a witch turned to darkness, the taint was passed down through the generations—growing stronger with every birth. And his family was the oldest and darkest of all the Dark *Volkhvy*. He gloried in subjugating innocence. His conquest of Elena would be more satisfying because it hadn't been instant. Her fear and his anticipation fed the dark taint in his blood, making it—and him—stronger.

The breeze from the window must have soothed her. She quieted as he watched, and he knew it was time for him to leave.

But soon. Very soon. He would be free to make her nightmares come true.

Chapter 1

Wind blew stinging clouds of icy dust from the jagged gray rocks on the side of the mountain. The snow was so white the exposed rock glistened darkly against it in the fading light of the sinking sun. Every surface was coated with a fine sheen of ice. Elena Pavlova had only been outside the full cab all-terrain vehicle that had brought her this far for a half an hour, but in spite of the preparations she'd made—her ski suit, insulated boots, gloves and scarf—the protective clothing didn't prevent her face from feeling as cold and hard as the frozen rocks.

Mountain tours never came this far in winter, but it had been imperative that she get as far as possible before she sent prying eyes away. She'd insisted that the driver leave her, but only a substantial bribe had finally persuaded the man, who obviously thought she was on a suicide mission.

And maybe she was.

Night was falling in the Carpathian Mountains in

Romania and she would never survive the elements if she didn't find the shelter she sought. Refuge. Redoubt. Haven. Her eyes teared against the biting wind and the moisture froze on her eyelashes until her lids were heavy and her vision obscured.

She'd heard the tales since she was a child. She'd listened, rapt, as her grandmother had read from the worn but beautiful book Elena currently carried in a small pack on her back. Her childhood had been two things: dancing and the Slavic legend of the Romanov wolves. Bloody toes and even bloodier stories of the fight against evil.

Hundreds of years ago, the Light *Volkhvy* had chosen a younger son of royal blood to stand against their dark brethren. They'd spirited Vladimir Romanov away to become their champion. He'd been given enchanted wolves and a castle enclave deep in the Carpathian Mountains. In return, he'd been bound to an endless fight. Grim fairy tales to read to a child, but, looking back, Elena realized her grandmother had been preparing her to fight the darkness herself. The old ways were wise ways, but knowing them wasn't only a defense. Playing at the edges of *Volkhvy* power by telling the tales and practicing the small hearth magics with charms for luck and wellness ran the risk of attracting the attention of true witches. Ones from the dark as well as the light.

Too much dabbling could lure an ordinary person into a *Volkhvy* world they weren't prepared to face. *Perhaps her family remembered the Old ways too well.*

Elena was living proof. She was stalked by a witch-blood prince and her fascination with the legend had turned into a call she couldn't ignore. She'd been pulled across thousands of miles from Saint Petersburg to Cerna, and the call only became stronger the closer she came to the mountains.

It was almost physical now. In spite of the cold, she was aware of a strange pulse beneath her skin that compelled her onward. Her choice had seemed so clear—heed the call or stay within Grigori's grasp.

By the time she came to the pass, her lungs hurt with every frigid breath and her weak knee was on fire. She wouldn't have made it this far over the ice and rugged terrain if she hadn't spent years pushing past physical pain to achieve the optimum performance from her muscle, sinew, heart and will. Prima ballerinas weren't born. Or made. They were forged in the fire that was the Saint Petersburg Ballet Academy.

Elena paused. She wiped her eyes with gloved fingers, but they weren't so hindered by icicles that they missed the castle she'd come to find. She couldn't see it because it wasn't there.

She'd chased help that only existed in a book of legends. No more. No less. She'd followed landmarks in the illustrations and carefully tried to sleuth her way to the right place. But her beautiful book crafted of intricate, hand-painted and cut designs that leaped from the page in three-dimensional depictions of a castle, the Romanovs and their enchanted wolves was nothing more than a storybook.

Her grandmother had blamed Elena's nightmares on the book, but ten years of bad dreams hadn't prepared her for the true horror of the witchblood prince who stalked her. She'd been haunted by the loss of her mother, only to learn her death had been a heroic sacrifice and not a suicide. Her mother had spilled her own blood to protect her daughter from a Dark *Volkhvy* prince. Her blood had fueled earthy folk magic. Nothing compared to the power it faced down and held back, but her mother's fierce love had strengthened it.

He had stood out from the other patrons even before he spoke—tall, lean and beautiful to the point of being unnaturally perfect as if he was a mannequin, not a man. Not a hair of his glistening gelled hair had been out of place. There hadn't been so much as a speck of lint on his tailored tuxedo. He'd moved like oil into her path with a flow to his gestures that was less grace and more fakery. His appearance was a charade. One meant to obfuscate his true nature. Yet one that revealed all, if you looked closely enough.

The sun was almost gone. Suddenly the white glare of ice and snow turned russet as it reflected the orange glow of the sky. Elena had nowhere else to go. The guide in his all-terrain vehicle was gone. He had taken his money and followed her orders: *Don't wait for me. I won't be coming back.* The dire economics of the region precluded any squeamishness over what she might do once he drove away.

It was true. She would freeze to death rather than go back and give in to Grigori's demands even though she hadn't found the help she'd hoped to find.

You'll be utterly mine. Your mother only ensured I would require even greater satisfaction from our time together because of the delay.

A sudden sound dispelled the ice in her veins. A long, echoing howl—both mournful and triumphant—filled the air and conquered the wind as the king of sound on the mountain. Adrenaline rushed lifesaving vigor to her limbs. Her heart pounded. Her breath poured from her lips in vaporous puffs of fear and hope. The call that had brought her all the way from Saint Petersburg seemed to respond to the howl. It rose in her throat as if she should cry out a reply.

But her head was more rational than her heart.

Freeze or fangs?

Probably both, yet the possibility that the legend was true sent her scrambling farther along the pass in spite of her terror and the pain in her leg. The Romanovs controlled powerful wolves that were trained to fight the Dark *Volkhvy* witches. The alpha wolf was her last, best chance to defeat the witchblood prince. Another howl swelled up and out from the unseen chest that gave it birth. Paired with the decreasing light, the howl seemed to raise hungry shadows to consume the world. She hadn't brought a flashlight. Or a tent. She didn't own a weapon of any kind. Weapons were useless against the witchblood prince, and mortal shelter would only protect her from the elements long enough for him to find and claim her.

Perhaps she'd been seeking death after all. If the call that had drawn her here was a lie, death would be preferable to a life spent as Grigori's captive.

Even sleep hadn't given her peace in years. Every night she suffered horrible nightmares in which she was caught by Grigori and unable to escape. She'd thought they were only nightmares. Now that she'd seen her tormenter in real life, certainty had settled into her bones. Death wasn't the worst fate she could suffer. As his stalking had escalated, so had her resolve to escape.

The snow was deeper and softer where drifts had accumulated in the protected lee of the pass between mountainous ridges. Her legs weren't very long. At twenty, she was thin and graceful, petite and powerful. In spite of her knee, her body responded to the desperate pounding of her heart. *Go. Go. Go.*

She was all muscle, tendon and sinew. It didn't matter that the ligament in one knee had required surgery to repair. All the rest made up the difference, fueled by adrenaline and fear. But if the howl had spurred her on, the sight of the creature who had opened its maw to create the sound caused her to freeze in place. A white wolf had climbed to the top of the ridge on her left. He was immense, larger than any wolf nature could have made. He stood on the peak, a ghostly silhouette against the darkening sky, and he howled again.

Elena's legs—her stock and trade, the one thing between her and oblivion—gave out beneath her. She collapsed to her knees in the snow. She cried out when her right knee made contact. An unnoticeable deformity in the shape of her femur had caused her to land from jumps with incorrect form. Over the course of a decade, after millions of repetitions, her knee had been stressed by the imperfection. She'd recovered well from surgery and spent over a year in physical therapy, but the snowy hike had aggravated her injury.

Another howl answered the first. On the left peak directly across the pass from the white wolf, another wolf appeared, as russet as the sunset had been moments before. Even if she could get to her feet, she would never outrun them in the deep drifts of snow. There was no castle. There were no Romanovs. As hard as she squinted against the icy wind, she could see nothing to refuel her hopes. There were only two giant wolves whose echoes sounded hollow and hungry as they bounced off the icy walls of the pass. *This is better than Grigori*, the blood seemed to whisper as it rushed in her ears. The ice on her eyelashes had melted as fresh hot tears filled her eyes. They shimmered there, making the gloaming world mercifully indistinct, but even now she refused to let them fall. She closed her eyes to will them away, but then it was an effort to lift her lids against her weighted lashes.

She did it anyway. If she had to meet a grim fate, she would do it with her eyes open.

Only her nightmares made her cry. On waking, when she was alone with no one to see, she often found her cheeks damp. She'd grown to be terrified of enclosed spaces and the sound of frantic, fluttering feathers— the two elements of her nightmares that never changed. She'd never cried over bloody toes or aching muscles or the harsh practices meant to perfect the curve of her arms and spine. The nightmares were far worse than any real-life trials. It had been horrible to discover that Grigori was real even more so because it meant that he had witnessed the tears she'd thought were shed in private. He'd seen her weak and terrified. That knowledge and his pleasure in it caused bile to rise and burn her throat. She wouldn't cry now that she'd found only a part of what she'd been looking for, even if the wolves turned out to be her salvation in a darker way than she'd intended. She wouldn't season their meal with tears.

The illustrations in her book hadn't done the wolves justice. They were more monstrous. Far above her, she could see the power in their limbs and the glint of their eyes. She could also see the flash of white that indicated deadly teeth against their damp fur.

It was only the movement of the wolves' attention from her to elsewhere that caused her to lower her attention from the ridges back to the pass. She blinked against icy lashes as an approaching form swam into focus. A tall, muscular man clothed all in black walked purposefully through the deep snow. He came out of the swirling white clouds of flakes as if he materialized before her eyes. He wore a cloak with a fur mantle that covered his broad shoulders. Its voluminous folds whipped around his powerful strides. But it was another sight behind him that caused her to gasp in stunned surprise.

Before she'd fallen, there had been nothing but ice and snow on the cliffs of the pass. Now, in the last hazy hint of twilight, ramparts and towers seemed to solidify from the shadows high above. Behind the man, the castle had appeared as if the mountain itself had decided to morph its rocks into the shape of a king's home. Around the highest tower, ravens circled in and out of storm clouds that clung to its pointed peak. The structure was surrounded by a stone wall that enclosed the entire keep and a small village around the foot of the castle. She could see thatched rooftops peeking over the wall. Wind swept over her in a new way. The sudden appearance of the castle and the enclave its walls created had diverted the air. This new breeze rushed over the man, and his long, tousled hair was blown into a riotous black mane around his face.

He held a lantern in his hand. Its light suddenly flared to life and its glow illuminated the man's face. The world fell away—castle, mountain, wolves and snow—until only his face shone before her. The call had brought her to the right place and the right time. The compulsion to come here hadn't been a lie.

"Romanov," Elena said. Her lips were stiff with cold. Her voice was muted by the wind. The white of her breath dissipated in wisps blown away from her face, taking most of the sound with it. The snow had claimed all feeling from her legs, and the numbness climbed steadily up her hips to her waist.

He heard her. He stopped and lowered the lantern so its light shone in her eyes and on her face, leaving his in shadow.

"Whoever you are, I'm not the man you seek," he said.

The wolves had leaped down from the peaks on either side of the pass while the castle and the man had distracted her. Their large, powerful forms had eaten up the distance much sooner than ordinary canines might have done. They came to the man—one on each side—and he chided their eager prancing without taking his attention from her face. She'd been right about the wolves' size. Both came to their master's chest, and he was no small man.

The wolf she'd come to find would be even larger.

She needed larger-than-life legends to help her escape Grigori's clutches.

"I'm not here for a man. I'm here for the wolves," Elena said. The wolf she needed was the alpha of the Romanov pack and he would be as black as midnight. The old legends said that only the alpha wolf could defeat the strongest of the Dark *Volkhvy*.

The creatures paced toward her, but the man called them back to his side by name.

"Lev. Soren. Heel." Though his face was shadowed, she could see the stern set to his lips and jaw. "Then you have come for nothing," he said to her bluntly.

He gestured and the two wolves churned snow as they spun around to rip back toward the castle in the distance. Oddly, she felt abandoned rather than spared. Her stomach hollowed within her as if she'd fallen from a great height. The cold reached relentless icy fingers into her heart. Its thumping had slowed as if the muscle that pumped her blood was beginning to freeze.

"You risked your life," the man said. "For nothing." He didn't follow the wolves. He stepped closer. His clothes were fashioned with tooled leather and thick stitches. The wool of his cloak was thickly woven and the fur of his mantle blew this way and that in glossy chunks. There was a richness of texture to his entire appearance that made her frozen fingers twitch. Though she'd come for the alpha wolf, a being more fantasy than reality, this man looked solid and strong. Against the backdrop of ice and snow and plain gray rock, he was sudden, vigorous and very alive.

Far from *nothing*.

Only his eyes kept her from reaching out to him. They were green. A frigid pale green. Ferocious and intense. Bright against his black hair and the deepening darkness, but also intimidating.

"I risked my life to escape from a nightmare. I've accomplished that. At least for now," Elena said. His words had caused the pulse beneath her skin to fade. She was left on top of a mountain in a snowstorm with nothing to anchor her there. No certainty. No song.

"You won't find escape here," the man said. But he knelt down beside her. Elena was so cold, the heat from his lantern seemed to warm her, or maybe it was the heat of his large body so close to hers.

This was the right place. She wasn't mistaken. Even with the physical pulse of the compulsive call to climb diminished, her instincts to trust the old legend wouldn't fade. She was here for a reason. The book in her bag had shown her the way. Her grandmother had told the old tales as if they were true. They might have fueled her nightmares, but they might also prove to be her only hope against Grigori once the protective binding her mother had bought with her blood ran out.

"I won't go back," Elena said.

Her body was done. Frozen. If he refused to help her, she would die. But it was force of will, not bodily exhaustion, that caused her to take a stand even as she knelt in the snow.

"Not tonight anyway," the man said. "The storm is only getting started. I won't leave you here to die." She cried out when he reached to pick her up, but she quieted when his hold turned out to be surprisingly gentle for such a large man. He stood easily, trading his lantern for her body in one smooth, easy move. "But this isn't an invitation to stay," he continued.

"You are a Romanov," Elena murmured against his windswept hair. He turned to walk back through the deep snow. The ache in her knee throbbed in time with the thudding of her heart. Her weight in his arms didn't slow him down and neither did the drifts of snow. He left the glowing lantern behind them, so every stride carried her closer and closer to the dark where his wolves had disappeared. She'd seen his face earlier. She'd recognized his features—the square jaw, the sculpted nose. She'd seen their like in the book that had brought her here, but her book's illustrations had been fanciful compared to the actual man.

"I am Ivan, the *last* Romanov," the man replied. "You came for a refuge, but you found nothing but cursed ground."

When she'd fallen to her knees, Ivan Romanov wanted to rush forward to her aid. That very human reaction had slowed his response. It wasn't the fall that caused his heart to swell and his chest to tighten with concern. It hadn't been the pale blue of her lips or the porcelain of her skin or her thick dark lashes crusted with a dusting of white. Her sapphire eyes, vivid against the blowing snow, and the stubborn light that intensified in them even as darkness fell, had compelled him forward. Whatever had driven her up the mountain in winter hadn't faded with the fall or the intimidating appearance of the wolves.

She would rise.

She would press on.

And if he didn't do something to prevent it, she would die at Bronwal's great gate. Her eyes revealed a different person than her slight form suggested. When he picked her up, she weighed nothing in his arms. He had trained for centuries, but it wasn't until he felt her delicate, mortal burden that he had the insane idea he had trained for just this moment.

For centuries.

She reached to hold around his neck. In spite of the stubborn light in her eyes, her arms surprised him with their strength. Only the wisps of respiration that came too quickly from her lips betrayed her fear. She was bundled in insulated clothing of a make and design he'd never seen. It had been many years since anyone other than the *Volkhvy* had ventured close during the Romanov materialization. The glimpses he'd seen of the modern world as it progressed had created an incomplete picture in his mind, always changing.

Her clothes told him little about the woman who wore them, but her determined journey through the pass should have alerted him. Her size was deceptive. Her eyes and tight hold as well as the tension in her body against him—those things revealed the woman to him.

Her limp did not define her.

She wouldn't be frightened away. Not easily.

"You can shelter here for the night out of the storm, but when it passes, you leave," Ivan said. He'd left the gate open. Lev and Soren stood on either side to guard the entrance. He'd seen them do so thousands of times before. The momentary electricity that had claimed his limbs when he'd lifted the woman in his arms drained away. He recognized the numbness as it returned. He was beyond weary. More worn by the years of coming and going from the Ether than he'd ever been worn by battle.

His father, Vladimir Romanov, had betrayed the Light *Volkhvy* queen centuries ago. He hadn't been satisfied to be a champion. He'd wanted to rule. The queen's punishment had been unrelenting. She'd cursed Bronwal and all the people in it to be bound to the Ether for eternity. Every ten years, the castle materialized for one month. It was taken into the Ether after the month was over, again and again. Each materialization, fewer survivors materialized. His father had been the first to succumb.

The quickening Ivan had felt in himself when he'd rushed to the fallen woman wasn't respite. It was torture. The years had piled on until his soul was crushed by too many losses to bear. And yet there was always one more.

Not always.

His enchanted blood had prolonged his life as had Vasilisa's curse.

But he wasn't immortal.

He said a prayer of thanks for that small mercy before he carried the woman inside.

Chapter 2

Even though she had the snowstorm and the frigid mountain pass for comparison, she didn't find the great hall of the castle welcoming. It was nothing like the illustrations in her book. Dark, gray, unlit by torches or firelight, it seemed more a massive cave than a place where people would gather. A fireplace several times larger than any she'd seen before yawned cold and dark. Wind whistled down its chimney like a banshee. A frozen banshee.

In the shadows, the elaborate tapestries hanging on the walls were lifeless and dull. In her book, they were painted with vivid detail that never seemed to fade. Romanov had carried her through the outer keep without greeting or comment from a dozen or so dreary-looking denizens going about half-hearted work. The gamboling of the giant wolves had seemed cruelly vigorous in comparison. The wolves were playful when all else was doom and gloom. They must have been protected from the gloom of the villagers by their simpler, animal comprehension.

Something was wrong with Bronwal. The wrongness permeated the people and the atmosphere, including the man who held her to his chest.

Inside, the great hall was deserted. Elena tried to speak, but her teeth chattered together and shivers racked her body. The trembling meant her nerves hadn't been frozen, but the pain of her skin coming back to life caused her to moan.

"We have no accommodations for visitors. Not anymore," Romanov said. He turned around as if he was looking for somewhere to put her that wasn't dark and damp.

"I s-see th-that," Elena replied. Welcome or not, she was here. She'd made it. Once she warmed up enough to face the challenge, she would find the alpha wolf even though this last Romanov was determined to send her away. She'd be much better off facing this man's determination not to help her than she'd been facing Grigori in Saint Petersburg alone.

"Fetch Patrice. To the tower room," Romanov ordered. The russet wolf jumped to attention. He stopped his leaping and stared at his master for several seconds as if his wolf brain had to interpret the command. Then he was off. The white wolf sat on its haunches and looked at them.

"I know there are plenty of empty rooms. Don't look at me like that. Anyone who would have an opinion about where best to put her is long gone," Romanov said.

He tightened his arms when she tried to press her palms against his broad chest for release. He didn't place her on her feet. Inside the castle, even in the lofted great hall, he seemed much larger. He was well over six feet with muscled arms and legs that matched his intimidating frame. His hold was overwhelming. His embrace swallowed her petite body. He held her close against his chest. Odd, since he had ordered her to go away. His heartbeat was clear and strong against her cheek.

Suddenly, he was too real. Her respiration quickened and her fingers curled into the damp material of his cloak. He felt her increased tension and paused. His whole being became alert. She could sense the intensity of his attention on her face. Her focus was on the fur of his mantle, but she forced her gaze from that safe haven to more dangerous territory.

In the shadows, his eyes were lighter than his dark brows and hair, but they were hooded against her. She couldn't read his emotions before he looked away. He betrayed nothing of his inner feelings yet she sensed them beneath his stiff demeanor. She noted his tightened hands and his unwillingness to meet her eyes. They waited for a long time, made longer by her fatigue and fear.

Finally, at some unspoken signal, he turned again and headed from the room in a decided direction. They came to a circular stone hall that eventually changed to stairs. She held him as he carried her up and up the never-ending climb. She was accustomed to athletic artists and dancers. Sophisticated and polished businessman and patrons were her usual companions. She wasn't used to storybooks come to life from legends that originated in the Dark Ages.

Romanov's scent was one of wind and snow, leather and fur. His hair had enveloped her with stinging strands outside on the mountain. Now it dried around his face in a riot of damp waves. By the time they came to an open door at the top of the stairs, Elena had seen Romanov's face by the light of a thousand torches. The impact of his appearance wasn't diminished by the increased time to study him. His face was as bold as the rest of him, with a strong brow and patrician cheekbones. His lips were sculpted and sensual against his hard features and there was a shadow of beard growth on his jaw that only served to highlight its perfect, sharp angles. The contrast of his green eyes continually startled her against his dark hair and pale skin.

Not that he looked at her again. He kept his gaze on the stairs. He didn't have to look. She could feel his attention zeroed in on her every blink and sigh. She'd followed a call she couldn't define to a strange place she'd only heard about from a storybook, but she was afraid she might have found more danger than she'd left behind. The wolves had been terrifying, but Romanov was in some ways more intimidating than his pets. In trying to escape Grigori had she placed herself in even greater danger?

The glow of a small fire met them when he stepped inside the room at the top of the long, spiraling stairway. A round woman in a faded apron bustled around and the russet wolf stretched out by the fireplace, soaking up what heat it provided in its infancy. Romanov had carried her up into the tallest tower she'd seen from far below in the pass. The windows were obscured by ancient stained glass, wavy and dense with imperfections. Occasional shadows seemed to swoop by, hinting that the ravens still circled outside. The room was furnished sparsely with a plain wooden bed draped in thick velvet textiles against the cold. There were two sturdy chairs on either side of the fire. There were no lamps or electric outlets. No technology of any kind.

Had she expected modern amenities in a castle made by magic hands centuries ago?

The woman didn't speak. She quietly straightened a woven throw on one of the chairs by the fire and Romanov responded by placing Elena on it. The move was hurried, as if he couldn't wait to put her down, but also gentle. He was being careful with her leg. His size and strength and gruff manner made his courtesy that much more surprising.

"It isn't a new injury. My name is Elena Pavlova. I'm a dancer. The stress of the climb aggravated an ACL condition I developed from my years in ballet," Elena said. "I'll be fine with rest and another knee surgery." She didn't tell him she'd never dance again. An additional surgery might give her a greater range of movement, but she would never reclaim the grace she'd lost.

She could no longer focus on dancing. It had been a necessity to help support her family. It had saved her when her mother died, but now all of the drive she'd used for the dance needed to be focused on survival. Never mind there was an empty place left by the loss of her dance deep inside of her. It had given her purpose for so long even though it had been a cruel taskmaster more than a heartfelt occupation. The call had seemed to fill the void for the last several days, but she tried to ignore it now. She was here. Why did it still seem to compel her toward something she couldn't see?

"Thank you," Elena said to the woman, who tucked another throw around her legs. Patrice didn't reply.

"It's been several Cycles since she's spoken. You spoke of the wolves. You must know of the curse that binds us. The Queen of the Light *Volkhvy* punishes us for my father's betrayal of her trust. Every ten years, Bronwal materializes from the Ether. At the end of the month, we disappear into the Ether once more. We all change each time we're lost in the Ether," Romanov said. "When the enclave dematerializes, we're left with an awareness that makes the Ether a purgatory. It drains our souls away, little by little, time after time. For some there's a sudden vanishing. For others, a slow fading away. Vladimir Romanov hasn't been seen since the first Cycle."

The legends about the Light *Volkhvy* champions had always seemed magical and romantic to her, filled with heroics and daring. She hadn't known about the curse. No wonder there seemed to be something wrong with her storybook castle and all the people she'd encountered in it. The thaw she'd been experiencing seemed to pause as ice reclaimed her heart, but if Romanov noticed her chilling realization he betrayed nothing. Elena slowly shrugged out of her backpack as her host ignored her, and Patrice took it from her only to drop it on the floor as if she wasn't aware she had taken it. The chubby woman had crinkles around her eyes and merry red cheeks, but her silence negated who she'd once been. Her features seemed to indicate that she'd once been a jolly soul, but she wasn't fully with them. Her eyes were distant and her movements were automatic. It wasn't only that she didn't speak. She didn't seem to hear them well. The backpack landed near the russet wolf and the giant creature nosed it and then ignored it as if it had proved of no interest.

"You're here after all this time," Elena said. She'd come looking for champions. She'd hoped to find enchanted wolves and their masters. She'd never imagined she'd find the original Romanovs themselves. "You're the oldest son of Vladmir Romanov. One of Queen Vasilisa's champions. Fully awake and aware." The heat from the fire began to warm her again. Her shivering had stopped. Her teeth didn't chatter. Romanov filled the room with his restrained energy. He'd let her go, but she could still feel his hold. He was powerful, but his power wasn't merely physical. There was no way he had faded from what he had once been. Why did he want her to think otherwise?

"In time I'll fade away too," he said. "In one month, Bronwal will go back to the Ether. Maybe this time I'll stay there, vanished, like the rest of my family." He shrugged, but the light gesture didn't match the shadows that haunted his eyes. *He's not sure what each materialization will bring. Who will remain and who will be gone forever.* Elena's body was beginning to adjust to the heat from the fire, but Romanov's circumstances left her heart permanently chilled. It must have been torture through the decades to lose his loved ones, one by one.

He sat in the opposite chair and stretched his long legs out in front of him in a deceptively relaxed position. The white wolf, Lev, had found them. He came into the room reluctantly and slumped at his master's feet as if he had grown unused to such comforts. The russet wolf, Soren, stretched out on the other side. Without saying goodbye, Patrice left the room. Would she wander the halls aimlessly until the castle went back into the Ether? Would she even exist during the next Cycle or would she be lost to nothingness, never to be seen again? Elena had come looking for help against Grigori, but she had found more darkness here than she'd expected.

"I need the alpha wolf. My grandmother said he was the Light *Volkhvy*'s greatest champion. Are you his master? Will you help me find him?" Elena asked. It made her nervous to see her bag so close to the subjects of the book inside of it. It might seem childish to Romanov even though it had served as a lifeline to her. But her knee throbbed and that was the more pressing problem. She stood and leaned to unbuckle her boots. She carefully took them off without jarring her knee. Then she reached to unzip her ski suit and pull it down. Beneath its down-filled pale blue polyester, she wore simple white silk thermals. Gooseflesh rose on her skin at the sudden rush of air against the thin material. Finally, with some painful maneuvering, the damp suit was peeled away. She draped it over the back of her chair and she sat again, free to massage her troublesome knee. There was a scar where the first surgery had extended her use of the knee. Without that repair, her walk through the snow would have been impossible, not merely excruciating.

It wasn't until her pain eased that she noticed the tension in the air. Elena stilled. The fire had caught and it blazed brightly, bathing her in a flickering spotlight. She understood her mistake even before she lifted her eyes. Romanov wasn't a modern man and she had basically stripped in front of him. She was a ballerina. Her body was an instrument, a tool. Her every movement was a deliberate placement of everything from her spine to her toes, but she was completely disconnected from the sensuality of her lithe limbs. The theater had no patience for modesty. They hurried to change from one costume to another in hallways amid a rush of similar nude forms.

But this man wasn't a dancer. He didn't even belong to this century at all. He'd been born in the Middle Ages. Her book was very old and it told a tale much older than its pages.

She'd always thought of the Romanovs as legends. Larger than life and not quite human. But this Romanov was a man. One she didn't know, from a time she couldn't understand. And he was a man tortured by a cruel curse. When she did look up and her gaze collided with his, he looked stunned, as if shedding her wet clothes in front of him was more shocking than his cursed castle, monstrous wolves and disappearing people. He also looked even more real. The leaping flames reflected in his eyes seemed to reveal the emotion he'd tried to hide before. His glance dropped to sweep her body. There was color in his cheeks and his lips had softened. Her stripping might have surprised him, but he was appreciative of what she had revealed. His lingering perusal made her cheeks heat. The flush was a tingling pleasure in the cool room.

In time, he might fade as he predicted, but he was fully here now and she must seem nearly naked to his old-fashioned standards. He didn't look away, but he did raise the direction of his gaze from her breasts to her eyes.

"You won't find help here. Loss. Despair. Resignation. Those you will find. But not help," Romanov said. His hands had grasped the arms of his chair with a white-knuckled grip and his voice was strained. His accent was exotic to her ears. His vowels and consonants were slowly uttered with deeper inflections as out of place and uninfluenced by current civilization as his leather and furs. He must have had contact with the outside world each time he materialized. She could understand him, but it was as if he was a time traveler speaking a language that wasn't his native tongue. It was a visceral experience to have to listen to him so carefully and watch his eyes and his lips move as he spoke. She had to attune her entire body to him in order to communicate.

Elena trembled again, but not from the cold. She didn't see resignation in Romanov's eyes. The waves of black hair around his face were highlighted by a halo of firelight. From that glowing frame, his green eyes shone with repressed passion…and anger. Beneath his dramatic brows and offset by pale skin, the emotion in his irises caused her heartbeat to kick in her chest and her breath to quicken.

He didn't want her here.

In her nightmares, she had wings, but they were always clipped. She was flightless. Caged. Kept at the whim of Grigori for reasons that caused her to beat against the bars of her cage until her white-feathered breast was stained with blood. She'd danced Odette many times—the swan tormented by a sorcerer. Her performances were as prophetic as her dreams. Grigori had seen her dance as a young girl. He'd vowed to have her. Her mother had used every last drop of her blood to bind him away from her daughter.

She'd never known why her mother had killed herself. Only a few months ago, Grigori had revealed the truth. Her mother had traded her life for her daughter's and it had only bought Elena's safety for a limited time.

"I've had my share of despair and loss," Elena said. "Resignation? Never."

She wouldn't be frightened by his anger. Or not cowed by it anyway. She had done nothing but search for a way to survive. She was going nowhere until she found it.

Suddenly, over Romanov's shoulder, she saw bars on the door to the tower room. They were artistically twisted in patterns of vines and flowers, but they were iron bars nonetheless. Romanov had drawn his legs back and he'd straightened. His wolves had also straightened to sit at attention by his side.

Three sets of eyes stared her down.

She had nowhere else to go, but that didn't matter. Not if she was trapped in a tower of a cursed castle and kept from finding the alpha wolf she sought.

I am the last Romanov.

He hadn't said it in a tone of resignation. He'd said it like his soul stood rooted in its last stand for eternity if need be. Had she disturbed his lonely vigil? Was that why he was looking at her with anger in his eyes?

This man ruled here. There were no councils or committees. He was a king and she was a trespasser. For some reason, he had decided to stand between her and the alpha wolf she needed to find.

"The Romanovs were given great power by the Light *Volkhvy* to fight against the dark. You were given powerful enchanted wolves to fight by your side. A Dark *Volkhvy* is my enemy," she said.

Romanov stood. She wasn't certain if it was a conscious move or if it was an automatic response to her mention of the Russian witches who had cursed his family.

"My father betrayed the Light *Volkhvy*. He wasn't satisfied with leading a pack of champions. He wanted Vasilisa's crown. His actions brought the curse down upon us. There are no champions left here. Only the dishonored and the walking dead. My father doomed himself and all of his people to this endless punishment. You've wasted your time," he said.

"You're not dead yet," Elena whispered. He was anything but dead. He shone with life. That was what captured her attention when lantern light, torchlight or firelight illuminated his face. She'd seen many dancers glow on the stage, backlit by spotlights and painted scenery. With only the gray of his cursed castle's backdrop, Romanov glowed—with anger, frustration and restrained passion—but he was definitely alive.

"All I ever held dear are dead. Gone. Vanished into nothing. My time will come. It *must* come. And soon," Romanov said.

His hands were fisted. This man was part of the legend she'd sought, but he was also more—more human, more fallible, more tortured than the tales had led her to believe. She'd been an innocent child fascinated by the three-dimensional paper images that had popped up from the pages of her grandmother's book. What had she known of love and loss? Since then, she'd lost her mother and her grandmother. And, finally, she'd lost the dance. Everyone she'd ever loved and her lifelong purpose. But that didn't mean she was ready to give up. She'd been called here for a reason. She refused to be turned away before she understood the tingling in her veins that said this was where she was meant to be.

If he wouldn't help her find the alpha wolf and fight Grigori, she would have to find the wolf and face the witchblood prince on her own. Romanov was a living, breathing legend, but he was finished. Fed up with the love and loss of this world and all the people in it. He wanted her gone because he wanted to die.

She jumped up when he turned toward the door. She couldn't be caged. It was too much like her nightmare. But instead of running for the door, she rushed to her backpack. She unzipped the top and rummaged until she pulled her precious book from its depths. Instinct drove her now as instinct had driven her to follow its stories into the mountains. Her grandmother had been a wise woman. She'd treated the legends with respect. Romanov was at the door when she turned to show him the book. He needed to be reminded of what his family had been in the fight against the Dark *Volkhvy*. Of what he could be still.

"Stop," Elena commanded. She held the book toward him and opened it as if she was the witch casting a spell. But in this cold, dark stone fortress, the book had lost its magic. It seemed small. Its colorful pages were more worn and faded than she remembered. It opened on her favorite scene. A lush forest of dozens of paper trees popped up from the page, and from between the trees three wolves ran. The white. The red. And the black. But they paled in comparison to the real wolves in the room, and they were so crumpled from use that they didn't leap from the page as they had when she was a child.

Romanov looked from the book as the trees fluttered in her trembling hands up to her face.

"This is what brought you here?" he asked. The whole hollow castle seemed to still around them. His soft, pained voice echoed down the quiet stairs.

"My grandmother's stories brought me here. She told them while we looked at this book," Elena explained. The book itself wasn't as impressive as her grandmother had been. In the same room as the last Romanov and his wolves, it wasn't impressive at all.

But she couldn't explain the pulse beneath her skin that had drawn her to his castle as if it were magnetized and she was raw ore dug up from the earth by an unseen hand.

He turned away again, from her and the legend, and Elena closed the book and dropped it onto her chair. She wouldn't be locked in the tower. She would fight if she had to. The wolves led the way. They disappeared down the stairs in front of their master. Romanov's large body blocked the door. He turned back to face her when he crossed the threshold. He slowly reached for the door to swing it closed.

"No. Wait," Elena said. She rushed forward, but he shut the door too forcefully for her to prevent its closing. The lock clanked home as her hands gripped the iron vines. She pressed her face to the space between the bars. Romanov stood inches away from her, separated by the thick oak of the bottom of the door and the scrolling iron at the top, but also by centuries of experience that had left him jaded and untouchable.

Roses. She saw them closely now. Dozens of iron roses "grew" along the vine-shaped bars. The door was an ancient artisan's masterpiece and a horror at the same time. She was trapped. The only thing that kept the scream from rising up from her gut was the absence of bloody feathers. As long as she was still herself, she could fight.

"You can't keep me in here," Elena protested.

Romanov leaned down. The firelight illuminated his face once more. He leaned so close that his raven hair brushed her cheek through the bars. He was older than she could imagine, even though he looked barely older than she was. He was more savage than anyone she'd ever encountered with his leather and furs and several white jagged lines from battle scars on his face, but he was also fiercely handsome. His rough, masculine beauty caused her to gasp at the sudden intimacy of his closeness. The door was between them but it felt like nothing at all.

She'd come looking for a legend, but he was *real*. She breathed in the scent of wind and snow held in his hair. And then she held her breath to keep from appreciating the wild bouquet. Of its own volition, her gaze cataloged every scar, every dark eyelash that lushly rimmed his eyes and the oddly vulnerable swell of his sensual lips. His eyes were hooded and hard, but the tenseness in his jaw eased when he noticed her catch her breath and hold it. He must have seen her sudden surprise at the physical attraction she felt for him in spite of her desperation. His gaze tracked over her face. She held her body still. She bit a lip that suddenly tingled because his were so kissable and so close. His attention dropped to her lips and then to her tight-knuckled grip on the bars. When he spoke, his voice was quiet.

"I'm not locking you in the tower, Elena Pavlova," he said softly. His voice still vibrated against her even though they weren't touching. It was deep, low and raw with some restrained emotion she couldn't name. He looked back up, into her eyes. His gaze held her for long moments so that when he lifted an iron key scrolled with tiny vines and roses that matched the bars, she released her breath in surprise. The key dangled from a delicate silver chain and it bumped her hand again and again through the bars while he waited for her to move. She released the bar to open her hand for the key. Her fingers were shaking. Rather than dropping the chain, he lowered it slowly down into her palm to pile on top of the cool key in a slow, lazy coil of precious metal. For several seconds, his large hand rested over hers. His touch was light and warm. He stilled her trembling. She'd thought she knew his story, but his tale was still unfolding right before her eyes. She'd become a part of it, and it was a tale rife with danger.

She'd responded to the call. She'd come to the mountains for a legend and his wolves.

She'd found a man.

"The tower is for your protection. You hold the key while you're here. Don't be fooled by your pretty book. This isn't a fairy-tale castle. Bronwal is cursed. Those who come and go from the Ether are forever changed and even while we're in this world the Ether isn't fully dispelled. Whatever you do, don't consider this a refuge. The *Volkhvy*, both Dark and Light, aren't to be trusted *and neither am I*. The Romanov curse is real…and deserved. Don't forget that while you're here," Romanov said. He was warning her away. He wanted her to keep her distance. But he uttered the warning only after he'd leaned down until their lips were even closer together—nearly touching—between the iron bars. The door was nothing. It didn't seem to exist at all. She looked up into his eyes and rather than repel, they caught and held her more thoroughly than any cage.

Perhaps it wasn't the castle that was the magnet.

She'd been wrong. He was worn, not jaded. And he was touchable. Very touchable. It took all her self-control not to touch him now when he seemed to invite it.

"Sometimes the month passes in the blink of an eye and sometimes it stretches on in an endless trial. But however our time passes, it ends with a *Volkhvy* Gathering. If you came here to escape a *Volkhvy* prince, it was a mistake. They all come to dance on our graves. Or wasn't that bit a part of the tale you were told?" Romanov whispered. "The *Volkhvy*, Dark and Light, are drawn to power. And Bronwal glows cruelly and seductively with power to their eyes. You'd do well to stay locked in this tower until the storm passes and you're strong enough to leave." His voice had dropped even lower and one sigh would have brought her to the taste of his lips. She held very still. She didn't move. He dared her to greater intimacy, but she refrained. Because she could see that he was only torturing himself. He had no intention of kissing her. She wondered if he knew how much he tortured her too. His body was pressed to the outside of the door and hers was pressed against the inside. She could have sworn their body heat mingled even as they were kept apart.

"When you've caught the attention of a witchblood prince, there isn't any place safe on earth," Elena said. "I thought I was looking for refuge, but I'm not. I'm looking for a fighting chance."

She straightened back from the bars and lifted her chin. She hadn't come here to tempt a legend to kisses. She'd come to find a wolf and she didn't intend to give up.

Chapter 3

Elena placed the key's chain around her neck and let her means of freedom dangle down between her breasts like a pretty bauble. She couldn't leave the tower immediately to hunt for the black wolf. She didn't want to follow Romanov and the other wolves down the stairs. After the moments of intimacy through the bars of the door, she thought it best if she avoided the alpha wolf's master. He wanted her to go away…and he didn't at the same time. His actions didn't match his words.

She found herself wanting to prove to Romanov that he was still alive. As if he could be woken from his stubborn vigil of despair by a kiss or a touch or an embrace. She hadn't expected to find that sort of temptation at Bronwal. Romanov was a dangerous distraction she couldn't afford. The pain in her knee was also a distraction she couldn't afford. She always carried supplies to deal with her injury. In her backpack, she had first-aid cold packs, pain medication and a neoprene sleeve to offer support when she overdid.

Mountain climbing definitely qualified as overdoing.

She needed to treat her knee before she tried to do more. The strange compulsion that had called her to Bronwal now seemed to urge her on the hunt. She needed to resist that compulsion until she was sure that Romanov was farther away from her room.

Patrice surprised Elena before she could pull on the orthopedic sleeve. She opened the door with a key on an iron ring that hung from a braided leather belt around her waist. She led the way in front of a haphazard team of servants. They carried a large hip tub and a seemingly endless supply of steaming pitchers and pails full of hot water. Two large men in mismatched livery placed the wooden tub beside the fire. They both nodded in her direction before they left the room. Patrice gestured and the other servants walked forward one at a time to pour the water they were carrying into the tub.

Observing the procession was like watching time pass before her eyes. The people had hair and garb from varying centuries and all of them looked worse for wear. Elena's chest tightened in sympathy. The curse had punished all of the Romanovs' people, from the head of the powerful family to the tiniest chambermaid. It looked as if anyone who was able chipped in to do the work that had to be done even if it hadn't been his or her original specialty. The liveried men had obviously been something other than maids in the past.

Once the tub was filled, Patrice pulled a corked vial from one of the numerous pockets in her shabby apron. When she opened the vial and upended it over the water, a light, fresh scent filled the air. Mint. Elena breathed deeply as the aromatic steam rose.

"That'll warm your bones, Miss," a pretty young girl said. When she smiled, a dimple graced her cheek alongside a sprinkling of freckles. "If you need anything while you're here, they call me Bell." She was last in line and emptied her chipped pitcher with a nod of accomplishment before turning to leave the room. Her dress was nicer than most. It had been patched and mended. And her brown curls were clean beneath a faded cap. The cap and her boots looked like she'd borrowed them from a boy twice her size. Elena supposed there was no one left to protest if a maid chose unconventional attire.

As before, Patrice didn't say a word. She followed the last servant toward the door.

"Thank you. Thank you all," Elena said.

She was surprised when the older woman paused at the door to look back over her shoulder. There was a crinkle in her forehead as if Elena's thanks and the steaming tub confused her. Poor Patrice. Not all there, but still present enough to perform old duties long expected of her. She must have been a housekeeper to the Romanovs before the curse descended. Elena ached for her confusion, but then the puzzled look eased and Patrice turned back to walk out of the room. She closed the door behind her and the lock engaged.

So if the lock on the door wasn't to protect her from Ether-addled servants, what did it protect her from? The *Volkhvy*, the Romanov wolves…or Romanov himself?

Elena reached up to grasp the iron key Romanov had given her. She closed her fingers around it, easily remembering the brush of his hand and the closeness of his lips as he'd warned her to stay locked in the tower of her own volition.

Those that come and go from the Ether are forever changed.

She'd seen dishonor walking with the witchblood prince. Romanov seemed its opposite in every way. Yet she couldn't help if an insistent thrill of fear electrified the blood in her veins. He wasn't what she'd expected. He was cursed by a dark enchantment she couldn't imagine having endured for so long, but he was also undeniably attractive. Her urge to hunt that wouldn't ease might well be blamed on the memory of the almost-kiss. He'd seemed so hungry for contact and so determined not to succumb. Still, she had to focus on the black wolf, not his master. She could fight Grigori without Romanov, but she couldn't win without the alpha wolf.

A wolf hunt loomed, but Elena's knee throbbed and she was cold to the marrow of her bones. She released the key and ignored it and her memories of Romanov's nearness as she took off her long underwear. She was alone. The door was locked. She couldn't resist soaking her whole body, including her knee, while she waited for the right time to leave the tower. There was no doubt that she would. She had come to Bronwal for a wolf champion. She wouldn't leave without finding him first.

It was probably not wise to wander around a strange castle after midnight looking for a witch-eating wolf. Sometimes wise wasn't an option when you were hunted by a witchblood prince and running out of time.

Elena had dried herself with rough towels the servants had left near the tub. She'd pulled on the one change of clothes she'd packed—underwear, jeans, a T-shirt and a loose-knit sweater. Soft-soled sneakers completed a look that was practical and completely out of place. If the servants had presented a hodgepodge of passing centuries that had briefly influenced castle life, she was fairly certain she would be the first person to walk Bronwal's halls in jeggings.

Even after the bath, her body was exhausted. She might have opted for a quick nap before she left the tower to refresh herself if it wasn't for the possibility that her sleep would be disturbed as usual by nightmares.

She wasn't a swan.

She was a woman.

And hiding in a tower wasn't going to solve her problems.

Her knee still ached, but she washed several pills down with a bottle of water she'd also packed in her bag. Patrice hadn't thought to offer her food or drink and Romanov hadn't returned with a tray. Thank God. She couldn't handle another tête-à-tête with or without bars between them. Eventually, moonlight filtered through the wavy glass that must have been an extravagance when it was installed in the narrow tower windows. Had it been placed by magic before Vladimir's betrayal? The whole castle was evidence of enchantment later darkened by the curse. The wavy stained glass glowed beautifully by the light of the moon while hungry ravens circled perpetually outside.

When Elena decided it was relatively safe to leave the room, she pulled the chain over her head and used the key to unlock the door. The sound of the tumblers moving in the lock echoed down the stairs with loud metallic clinks. She placed the chain back around her neck while she paused to wait for a reaction. No one came to stop her. From the top of the winding stair, she could only see torch-lit shadows flickering on the walls. Distant sounds came to her ears. Singing and sighs and soft sobbing from somewhere far away. The castle didn't sleep. The atmosphere was one of restlessness and regret. Patrice wasn't the only one who wandered. Romanov had warned her that it wasn't safe. She risked running into Light or Dark *Volkhvy* or humans caught up in the curse and driven mad by their endless returns to the Ether.

Yet it was running into Romanov again that she most feared. His magnetism was at least as strong as the original pull that had drawn her to the mountains, but the curse had changed everything. She had to be careful about the darkness she'd found, in Romanov and in his castle. He was right. She had to resist her attraction to her host, but she also had to find the alpha wolf. Her resolve to resist Grigori was useless with no power to back it up.

Elena Pavlova would leave tomorrow. The training courtyard was the emptiest, most hollow place he had to endure during a Cycle and tonight it was rapidly becoming covered in a frigid blanket of snow. Nevertheless, Ivan had trained in it for hours. He rarely wasted a Cycle with sleep, but this time his restlessness had another cause. He would be haunted by her small, perfectly formed breasts for the rest of his days on earth. Her nipples had been hard from the cold and damp. Their rosy darkness had been vivid against the thin white silk of her unusual undergarments. He'd had to force himself to look away. And now he needed the snow and exertion to keep him sane.

She had been completely innocent of her inadvertent seduction. Not in the manner of a child, but in the manner of a woman who had more urgent matters than seduction to attend to. She had said she was a dancer. It showed in her every move. Even her limp was graceful, a careful shifting of weight and form. He was captivated by her manner of movement and her urgency. She'd flushed when she'd noticed his reaction to her disrobing. It had been a simple, practical removal of wet clothes not intended to shatter him completely.

But it had.

And then to pile torment on top of torment, she had paused in her desperate bid to ask for his help to tremble and stare. Her eyes had widened. She'd held her breath and captured the soft swell of her lower lip in her perfect white teeth. He'd been alone for a long time, but he knew the signs of desire when he saw them. Especially when he was burning with it himself.

First, she'd looked at him like she was searching for something he could never be. Then she'd looked at him as a woman looks at a man, and he'd wanted to respond to the hunger that had risen in her eyes.

He'd been blissfully numb before she came. He couldn't remember the last Cycle where he'd felt anything but the growing wish to fade away. He'd gone through the motions. He'd cared for Lev and Soren. He'd endured the "honor" of the *Volkhvy* Gathering that was, in fact, a celebration of his eternal torture and the aura of power released by the Ether every materialization. But it had all been done in a haze of endurance as if he ran a marathon of epic distance with one stride more, then one more, then one more before the final finish line.

His haze had been cruelly lifted.

He struck again and again at the scarred oaken practice figures in the moonlit courtyard with the sapphire sword. The gem in its hilt was flat and plain. It was an enchanted sapphire, but it was only moonlight that occasionally caused its surface to glow. The Light *Volkhvy* queen, Vasilisa, had given the sword to his father as a gift for his mate. When Ivan's mother had wielded the blade, the power in its gem had been dazzling. Now it was dulled by the curse.

The dead stone was doubly cruel because its moonlit dark blue reminded him of Elena's serious gaze leveled on him with expectation and hope.

He couldn't help her. He couldn't revive the sword. His blows rained down on the oaken cross that had once been used to train the Romanov guard. Clouds of white burst into the air as every blow shook the wood and kept the snow from settling. They were all gone now. The Ether had eaten them. *A devora.* It had taken his father first. Perhaps justly, for it was Vladimir Romanov who had tried to betray the Light *Volkhvy* queen, Vasilisa. It hadn't been strictly a political betrayal. It had been a betrayal of the heart. Ivan's mother had been killed by the Dark *Volkhvy* king. Afterward, his father had become Vasilisa's lover. But his father had craved more power. He hadn't wanted to be a mere champion. He'd wanted to rule.

In retribution, Vasilisa had punished him and his offspring and all of his people.

Sweat poured down Ivan's face like the tears he'd never allowed himself to shed as a teen when the weight of the world had fallen on his shoulders. Steam rose off his heated skin as the salty moisture hit the night air. He'd been raised to fight the Dark *Volkhvy.* As the oldest, he'd assumed leadership. He'd become the alpha. Even as a teen, he'd already been a battle-scarred warrior in those days. But he'd been unprepared to fight against dishonor, nothingness and despair. He'd carried on. For years, he'd tried to earn redemption while one after another after another of his people and loved ones faded away, Lev and Soren by his side.

He hadn't been able to hold back the darkness. The Ether won, again and again. The curse was triumphant. Bronwal had been under siege for centuries and it wasn't until Elena arrived that Ivan had realized, for him, it would never be over.

Because in that moment, at the door of her room, he'd known he had no intention of succumbing to the beast as his brothers had done. Neither would he vanish quietly into the Ether. He was the last Romanov. He would stand. Alone. Forever. *To ensure that the curse ended with him.* If he allowed himself to disappear into the Ether for good, the castle, the wolves and the sword would be undefended against anyone who might try to claim them when they materialized each Cycle. His brothers, Lev and Soren, had given up their humanity to escape permanently into their wolf forms. Either they couldn't remember how to be men or they didn't want to. The shame of their heritage was too great.

He would never abandon them, but would never join them.

He wasn't free to help Elena Pavlova in his wolf form because he had to maintain his control and his human faculties. He had to defend Bronwal and keep possession of the sword. Until his unnaturally long life finally came to an end in death and dust.

He also wasn't free to be a man with Elena. He had to resist the mutual attraction that had flared between them. The only way to break the Romanov curse was to guard against passing it on.

The cross he attacked with powerful blows finally disarmed him. With one last swing, he buried the sword too deeply to retrieve and he released its hilt. The dulled sapphire seemed to mock his resolve in the moonlight. Snowflakes immediately began to adhere to its surface now that it was stilled. Let it be there, buried deep in the oak, when the Dark *Volkhvy* came to try to steal it. Every

Cycle, they came. And he was always ready. This time would be no different.

He was the alpha wolf that Elena Pavlova sought. But he wasn't free to be wolf or man with the woman who needed his help.

Chapter 4

The lighting in the castle was as haphazard as the servants who had helped her the night before. With servants influenced by their time in the Ether, it was no surprise that jobs such as maintaining torches and lanterns went undone or half-done. The entire castle had an air of hushed neglect, but there was also a sense of expectation as if dust and cobwebs and candles waited and waited for care that never came.

Elena walked quietly on her sneakered feet. She placed her weight on her toes, unconsciously tiptoeing down gloomy halls. There had to be hundreds of empty rooms. She explored them, one by one. But the weight of what she found settled heavily on her heart. Her chest constricted and her breathing turned shallow. Again and again she found knitting laid to one side and never taken up again. She found dusty books marked with faded ribbons. There were chessboards waiting for next moves that would never come and clothes laid out that would never be worn. Toys abandoned.

And paintings of generations of Romanovs lost to the Ether.

The curse had been a terrible punishment and a horrible fate for the legends she'd loved as a child. Ivan Romanov lived in a haunted home. Bronwal was a majestic graveyard filled with the discarded remains of lives interrupted never to resume.

Finally, Elena came to a large portrait hall lit only by the scant light of sunrise filtering through heavily draped windows set high in the stone block walls. The scarlet of the thick velvet drapes gave the light a reddish glow. She moved along the edges of the room, avoiding the center of the floor filled with a forest of sheet-draped statuary.

Instead, she looked at the people. Especially an oversize painting that dominated the room. The subject of the painting was Ivan Romanov and his family—mother, father, and two younger brothers. She stepped close to the base of the portrait to stare. There was warmth and familial affection captured by some long-gone artist's deft hand. Ivan stood behind and between his younger brothers with his hands on their shoulders as if he held them still. She could see the twinkle in the boys' eyes and the patience of a wiser older brother in Ivan's. The younger Romanovs weren't identical twins. One favored his father with reddish brown hair. One favored his mother with pale, unblemished skin and platinum blond hair. But all of them had the Romanov nose and the tall, fine forms of aristocratic warriors.

Had he lost them all to the Ether?

His mother had leaned toward all three of her boys. Her body language conveying that she preferred their company to her husband's. The eldest Romanov looked more proud than warm, but she was certain it was her knowledge of his failures that diminished him in her eyes.

She'd come for the alpha wolf, but she couldn't help being drawn to the Romanov tragedy, as well. No matter what their father had done, the boys had been innocents caught up in the curse through no fault of their own. Elena had to force herself away from the painting. It was too easy to be transfixed by the younger Ivan and the warmth and ease that was now absent from his green eyes.

She saw the shapes first beneath large sheets in the center of the room. She walked to each and pulled them off, first one and then the other. She found stone carvings of the two wolves she'd already met—the red and the white.

But there was one larger covered form behind them.

Its sheet came off in her hand in a sudden flourish and dust filled the air with motes that rained down over the black marble she'd revealed. The alpha wolf was the size of a great stallion. It wasn't a pet of the Romanov family. It was the greatest champion just as her grandmother had said. Its purpose was evident in every stone sinew and in its marble teeth.

Where had the alpha wolf gone?

Surely he hadn't disappeared into the Ether. Not the largest and strongest of them all. She looked into his ferocious maw and her flight instinct kicked in. The sheet dropped from her numb fingers and her breath came quickly.

She risked her life in this place where'd she'd come to try to save it.

Hunting such a creature without its master's blessing was as suicidal as climbing up the mountain looking for a fantasy castle. She should leave as Romanov advised and never return.

Elena lifted her hand and her fingers hovered near the black wolf's face. She noted the tremble of her digits and forced herself to touch the cold stone. She cupped beneath the great snarling mouth as if she held the wolf's head in her hand. She couldn't leave. The hollow place inside of her where the dance had been wouldn't allow it. She was here for a reason she didn't yet understand, but the search for the black wolf was a part of it.

Her silent communication with the statue was interrupted by a clicking sound behind her.

She recognized what made the sound even without turning around.

Slow, stalking claws click, click, clicked on the tiled floor. They approached her from the way she'd come. Elena didn't turn around. She looked into the alpha wolf's stone eyes. They were as black as the rest of him, but the midnight glinted in the soft glow of filtered sunlight. Even as her heart pounded and her spine froze, the sculpture's eyes seemed compelling.

She braced herself. The clicking came closer and closer from two distinct directions. One to her left and one to her right. When the massive creatures she'd met earlier came into her peripheral vision, flanking her on either side, she had the crazy sense that the two other wolf sculptures had come to life. Of course they hadn't. These were the wolves from last night. And this time their master wasn't around.

There was no one to call them off.

"You know where I can find the alpha wolf. Take me to him," Elena said. Her voice didn't waver. She spoke firmly. The flutter was hidden from view deep in her stomach and her knees. The wolves moved to stand beside the sculpture of the alpha wolf, on either side. They loomed over her and they were no longer acting like gamboling giant puppies. Their eyes blazed with predatory intent. Had they been hunting her while she searched the castle? Had they followed her from room to room at the bidding of their master or for some hungrier cause?

"I came for the alpha's help," Elena said. They weren't ordinary wolves. Perhaps they would be able to understand. "A Dark *Volkhvy* stalks me. A witchblood prince. No friend of yours. Help me against him," she urged.

She had no idea if they understood her words, but she had to try. She hadn't come this far to stay locked in a tower.

First the russet and then the white stepped toward her. Elena lowered her hand from the marble wolf's jaw. The trembling in her fingers was more noticeable, the better to show the wolves the terror she tried to hide. It was the russet wolf with coppery eyes who lowered his head to her hand first. She cried out softly, certain he would bite off her hand, but then the silky hair on the top of his head tickled the palm of her hand. The white wolf stepped forward to lean and lower and nudge her other hand until it too rested on a monstrous wolf's head.

"Does this mean you'll help me?" Elena said. "Will you lead me to the alpha wolf?"

The courtyard was churned into ruts and packed dirt by frequent use. Considering it was only materialized a month every ten years that meant the sweat that ran down Ivan Romanov's half-naked body had been well-earned time and time again.

The wolves hadn't understood her after all.

They'd led her to their master. A betrayal for sure, but she couldn't blame them. Especially when she was grateful that they hadn't eaten her for breakfast. They left her and bounded onto the field, chasing each other beneath the rising sun. It was cold in spite of the sun. Snow drifts lay all around. Elena wrapped her arms around herself. The castle walls protected the inner courtyard from excess snow accumulation, but Romanov's practice field was dusted with white and edged by icy foliage on evergreen bushes. It glistened and dazzled her eyes because they'd grown used to the dimness inside.

Ivan lowered his arms. He'd left a sword embedded in the cross-shaped practice form. It was buried deep in the scarred wood. So deep that she wondered at the force required to leave it there. He didn't turn around. She could see streaks of sweat on his muscled back and his labored breathing as his broad shoulders rose and fell. A leather cord wrapped the wild hair she remembered from the night before. The thick queue hung midway down his spine.

She didn't like his hair bound. She wanted to free it. The crazy urge took her by surprise, as did the sudden feeling that everything she'd been looking for was here, in this courtyard, for her to see.

She hugged herself tighter as she waited long heartbeats for him to turn and face her. He expected her to leave today. She hadn't found the alpha wolf. Grigori would find her, alone and defenseless. There was nowhere she could hide from him. Ivan Romanov couldn't be her only hope because he was a man who didn't believe in hope. Not anymore.

"Did you send the wolves to find me?" Elena asked.

Though she'd braced herself, she wasn't prepared for Ivan to suddenly turn around and pace toward her. She backed away several steps from the ferocity that tightened his face before she stopped herself and stood her ground.

"You weren't in the tower," Ivan said.

He came close enough to touch her, but instead he reached for the key between her breasts. He didn't pull it from her neck. He only held it in his large, calloused fingers. She looked from the key up to his eyes. He loomed over her, but it wasn't fear she felt at his sudden nearness. No. The thrill in her veins and the rush on her skin was something besides fear. Awareness. Expectation. In the meager sunlight, she noted that his irises were brighter than the snow. His pupils had retracted, allowing lighter green and gold flecks to glow. The lightness softened his otherwise forbidding expression. His hair had been loosened around his face by his exertions, and glossy chunks of it threatened to come free from the leather cording.

If he sought to intimidate her, he succeeded, but only because she was intimidated by his accessibility. Why did she notice indications of softness that were probably a lie? And why did she feel as if she was missing a truth she needed to see?

"You gave me the key. And I chose to unlock the door," Elena said. She still didn't mention the call that made it impossible for her to hide. There was something here she needed to find. Something more than a man and a wolf, but they were part of it, she was sure.

"I can't decide if you're brave or foolish," Romanov said. His gaze was intense. His hold on the key between her breasts was tight. She couldn't back away. She was caught and held—both by his hand and his eyes.

"Careful and brave rarely go hand in hand. Brave is doing what has to be done, no matter the risk," Elena said. "My mother was brave. She gave her life to call forth an ancient binding spell so that I could live free. I'm only just learning how to be brave for myself."

He leaned slightly, bowing his head toward her face. At the same time, he pulled the key slightly toward his chest. It was an infinitesimal movement. But the chain definitely tightened against her neck. Her neck and his hand were engaged in a silent tug of war that mimicked the tug of war she was battling between the magnetic pull of his broad chest and her trembling body.

Why did the courtyard seem like the final destination in the long journey she'd taken? And why did she look for softness in this legendary man? Because she wanted him to tighten his grip on the key and tug harder. He was powerful. He could narrow the gap between them without her permission. It would absolve her of the bad decision she suddenly wanted to make.

Because in spite of the talk of being brave, all she could do was lower her attention from his angry eyes to focus on his mouth. Somehow, the truth was there for her to see. The swell of his sensual lower lip belied his talk of her foolishness. He wanted her here. He wanted her close. Deep inside, a liquid tightening coiled and a hunger rose. She wanted to kiss him. Never mind that he was an angry warrior who claimed he wanted her to stay locked away until she could leave. He held her for a reason. He stood tense as their bodies paused in the nearly touching position. Her breasts were inches from the warmth of his chest.

She lifted her gaze quickly to see what he would do. But his eyes were shadowed now by a thick fall of wavy black hair that had escaped its confinement. His irises glittered with an emerald sheen behind those snow-dampened locks. But his expression was obscured. She could only take in the rise and fall of his chest—

it seemed slower than it should be, as if he controlled his breathing or even…did he hold his breath? Her own breath was shallow and quick. Her body held still as she waited to see what he would say or do.

"You are brave. Braver than I hope you'll ever know," Romanov said. It was almost a growl, uttered past a tense and tightened jaw.

"What is it I should be afraid of? What could possibly be worse than being captured by the witchblood prince who stalks me?" Elena asked. She closed her eyes and willed away the hot moisture that threatened to rise behind her lids. She'd already betrayed too much of her vulnerability to him and he refused to be moved. She wouldn't give him her tears too.

"I don't know the prince of whom you speak. And I know many monsters. Some man, some truly beast. The Ether claims more of my humanity with every Cycle. And you ask what you should be afraid of as if a threat doesn't stand before your very eyes," Romanov said. His voice had dropped to a low, agonized whisper. It seemed confessional. Yet he told her nothing she didn't already know. He was dangerous. She could sense it. She could see it. But he was also so much more. Compelling. Alluring. Seductive. More attractive to a civilized woman than he should be.

"I will not give up. I will not go away," Elena insisted. A sudden persistent pull on the silver chain caused her eyelids to open quickly. They were closer. There was only the slightest brush of contact between them, but the tips of her breasts burned. She did hold her breath then because respiration caused an agonizing allure of friction she couldn't resist.

But she didn't pull away.

And she didn't close her eyes again.

There were no tears now. Only a giddy heated pleasure radiating from her distended nipples to the rest of her body. The glittering intensity of his gaze was locked on hers, but he must have known the chain was indenting the nape of her neck because he allowed the silver links to go slack. Now it was up to her to stay close or move away. He no longer held her in place.

She stayed.

And the attention of his eyes fell to the key in his hand. She watched him as he focused on placing the key against the hollow of her neck. The heat of his hand had warmed the iron. Nevertheless the contact sent shivers down her spine, especially when he allowed the key to fall. It slid down until the hollow of her cleavage caught it. The warmed iron between her breasts caused her to gasp. But then when he lifted his free hand to touch her, the sudden weight of his calloused fingers and palm cupping the back of her neck was so much hotter. Her gasp became a trembling sigh and then a whimper when his fingers brushed under the chain as if to soothe the mark it had left on her skin. He was moved, but she wasn't sure what to expect. She suddenly feared she'd woken a sleeping giant, one that might consume her body and soul if he decided to stay awake.

"I won't send you back out into the snow. But you won't find what you seek at Bronwal. There are no champions here. Only heartache and defeat. Only darkness and danger," Romanov warned.

Elena breathed freely now. Her whole body burned and she didn't care. For so long she'd been harassed and harried. She'd been injured, physically and emotionally. Plagued by nightmares and loss. Desperation hadn't been the only thing that drove her to climb the mountain, but it was desperation—a different kind—that caused her to lift her arms. She placed her palms against Romanov's sweat-dampened chest. She felt the thudding of his heart, his powerful muscles and his heat. He jerked at the contact. *But he didn't jerk away.* He stilled as she slid her hands up inch by inch, measuring his height and his solid reality, until she held a broad shoulder in each hand. She didn't understand what had called her to Bronwal, but she understood this.

Her hands had been trained to be a graceful expression of her art, but in that moment they were strong. They held a legend. And he was the one who trembled beneath her fingers. His mighty form reacted to the delicate intimacy of her touch.

His hand tightened on the back of her neck. She was held again. And she didn't mind. For the first time in a long time she focused on pleasure instead of pain. It was warm and immediate and all else fled from her thoughts.

"One word and I'll let you go. I'm not so Ether-addled that I have no self-control. I will be a man, not a monster, for as long as I'm able. For now, I'm able. Walk away from me," Romanov said. But as he spoke he pulled her close and it was gentler than she could have imagined. He didn't crush her against him. He pressed and her curves complied until they were melded together.

She tilted her chin to meet his descending face. And still he paused. Their lips were only millimeters apart. His warm breath tickled her slightly open mouth.

"I'm a dancer. I've spent more time as a swan than as a woman," Elena said softly. The tears were back, burning her eyes. She ached to kiss him. And more. He was big and powerful, and when his other arm came up to press against her lower back the sensation of being held, safe, away from all that had come before, left her light-headed.

But she was at a loss off the stage. She didn't know how to claim a new life now that her old life was over.

"No. I'm holding the woman. Without a doubt, it's the woman's mouth I'll taste," Romanov said.

Elena drew a shuddering breath of air as he traversed the last distance left between them.

Their lips touched and his mouth moved with eager hunger against hers. In nightmares, she'd endured depravity. This was pure, human and real. She tightened her hands on his shoulders as her stomach swooped and soared and her legs went weak. She also opened to the masculine seduction of his rough, slick tongue teasing between her lips.

Living off the stage was more instinct than practice. She swooned into the kiss without thought to form or precision. Romanov was all heat and pleasure and he consumed her easily. The thrill that rushed beneath her skin echoed the call she'd followed up the mountain. She couldn't separate the sensations. She'd wanted his hair unbound because she wanted this wildness. He'd seemed to offer it with every glance, with every move, even though he'd withheld it.

Her tongue hungrily licked past his lips and twined with his. He held her tight as if he hadn't been offering to let her go seconds before. She didn't want to go anywhere. Her search seemed to be over. The call was silenced because it had been answered, somehow, someway, by his lips and teeth and tongue.

"You risk much. This woman is protected by her mother's spilt blood and claimed by Grigori, the witchblood prince. You might be Vasilisa's plaything, but that won't stop him from torturing you for eternity if you despoil his prize."

Romanov tore his lips from hers and whirled around

to face the interruption. A man had entered the courtyard from the keep. Elena immediately found her footing as she was shoved behind the warrior she shouldn't have been kissing.

Her life wasn't a life free to indulge in sensual assignations. Especially with the legendary master who refused to help her engage the help of the alpha wolf.

The man who had entered the courtyard cautiously approached them. Of course, he was no man. He was *Volkhvy*. And judging from his intimate knowledge of her tormentor, he was Dark, not Light.

"You've come for the Romanov blade, but you'll find it buried deep in a cross purified by generations of my honorable men. It won't come to you easily, and the sapphire has long lost its glow," Romanov said. He'd placed himself between her and the *Volkhvy*. But he had no weapon in his hands.

The Dark witch was dressed in black leather from head to foot. He shone like obsidian in the winter sun. His white hair was braided in a thousand plaits and piled on top of his head, and his movements were young and quick. He was at least as tall and strong as Romanov himself. Elena's heart pounded, overwhelmed with the rude transition from passion to fear. The wolves would come. Surely, the wolves would come.

"Grigori will kill you for taking the taste he hasn't been able to take himself. He will cut out your bold tongue," the man said. He laughed when he said it. And he attacked.

Elena was startled by another sudden shove that sent her sliding backward in the snow away from Romanov as he pushed her several feet before he and the *Volkhvy* collided. She didn't fall. She kept her balance as only a woman with years of physically demanding training could have. Her knee screamed, but it didn't give way. Her arms flew out to automatically aid her equilibrium, and anyone watching would have thought she had merely been landing from a smooth pirouette.

"You grow weaker with each materialization, old man. The stone can be recharged. I'm not sure the same can be said for you," the witchblood man said.

"Try and try and try again. But always empty-handed in the end. Right, Dominique?" Romanov taunted in return.

"You know this man?" Elena asked. She'd immediately recovered and gone to a weapons rack where practice swords and daggers were hung in a rough array.

"Him. Many others. They're all the same to me. They come for the sword Vasilisa gave my father," Romanov said. "They leave without it." His blows connected powerfully with the *Volkhvy*'s abdomen, chest and jaw. The witchblood man recovered from each blow much more quickly than a mortal man would. But after one particularly hard connection, he did spit blood into the snow. "Sometimes they don't leave. Perhaps it's your turn to die, Dominique."

"Romanov!" Elena shouted. She threw a short broadsword high into the air. It flew in a wide arc and then down into Romanov's hand. She grabbed two daggers for herself, but as her hands closed over their hilts, something drew her attention across the courtyard. Her eyes fell on the sword Romanov had buried deep in the scarred practice form. Her feet carried her closer to it of their own volition. One step and then another. The sapphire didn't look that dull to her. It seemed to sparkle in the sun.

"No. Go inside," Romanov ordered. She ignored him. The *Volkhvy* had drawn a blade from a sheath on his back. His leather trench coat whirled around his legs as he brandished it. It wasn't jeweled, but the metal itself glowed in his hands.

Elena had gone for the easily accessible weapons because that's where she'd ended up when Romanov had shoved her away. Now she tucked the daggers in her back pockets and went for the more powerful blade. It was buried deep in the wood of the cross. So deep that it held her entire body weight, such that it was, when she grasped its hilt and tried to pull it free.

"I'm not running away. Not anymore," she said through clenched teeth. She refused to let go even when the hum of power in the sword caused her arms to go numb. Romanov was wrong. There was power left in the blade. It hummed like bees beneath her skin, vibrating her body as she pulled. She braced her feet against the practice form. Her knee screamed, but she used all of her strength to push with her legs and pull with her arms at the same time.

"It won't matter. Running, hiding, making a stand. He'll have you in the end. There are many that claim to be *Volkhvy*, but only Dark *Volkhvy* royals can trace their lineage back to Baba Yaga herself. The witchblood prince won't be denied. Oh the pretty tales he's told about his future plans for you, my pet. Or I should say *his* pet," the *Volkhvy* said. His laugh was cut short by a sudden fierce attack by Romanov. The powerful warrior hacked and hacked until the muscles on his back stood out in bunches and the witchblood man was driven to his knees. The *Volkhvy*, Dominique, parried as many blows as he could, but others connected with him until his white hair was painted with crimson flecks of blood.

"You should have given up. This will be your last attempt," Romanov said.

Elena suddenly fell to the ground as the Romanov blade came out of the practice form. She cried out as the fall jarred her knee and she closed her eyes against the pain, but she didn't drop the sword. She landed on her back with the sword grasped in both hands. It took long seconds to catch her breath and regain her feet. Seconds Romanov didn't have. As she opened her eyes and stood, the *Volkhvy*'s hands glowed. His blade had been knocked from his fingers, but he looked prepared to unleash some kind of spell against the man she'd been kissing minutes before.

"No," Elena shouted. She ran toward the men with the sapphire blade held high.

But there was no time for spells or the Romanov blade. Romanov plunged the dull practice sword into the *Volkhvy*'s chest. The rusty metal must have penetrated the witchblood man's heart. Thick black blood bubbled up from the wound and from between the man's lips as he fell to the snowy ground.

Romanov fell to his knees beside his old adversary and grasped him by the lapels of his leather trench coat. He jerked him up toward his face. Elena stopped dead in her tracks and lowered the Romanov blade before the gruesome scene.

"Take Grigori a message. Tell him Elena Pavlova belongs to no one but herself," Romanov said. "And that Bronwal is defended. For eternity."

Elena started and dropped the Romanov blade when the bleeding man hazed before her eyes and disappeared leaving nothing but a puddle of steaming black blood on the ground. The sword fell with a solid thud that caused Romanov to rise to his feet and turn as if he was prepared to face another challenger.

"It's a defense mechanism. *Volkhvy* fade back to their

home when they're gravely injured," Romanov explained. There was black blood on Romanov's sculpted cheek. From it a slow curl of steam rose in the air. His hair was loose now. It had come unbound during the fight. Long black waves framed his face. His hands were clenched. His chest rose and fell from the exertion of defeating a magical foe. But it was his eyes that caught her attention. They tracked from the sword on the ground to the practice form, to her face and back again.

"You tried to bring me the Romanov blade," he said.

"You warned Grigori away," Elena replied.

He stalked toward her looking battered and bruised, but the confident look in his eyes and the puddle of *Volkhvy* blood on the ground made him seem invincible. Why had she been so desperate to help him when he had refused to help her?

The answer came from the things he'd said to the witchblood man.

She thought he would pick up the blade she'd dropped, but he stepped over it instead. He'd already recovered. His breathing was no longer labored. As she watched, the black blood completely evaporated from his face. He ignored the sword and came to stand directly in front of her, his attention fully on her. His penetrating gaze caused a flush to rise as she remembered her hungry response to his kiss.

"I'm no longer Vasilisa's champion against the Dark *Volkhvy.* I'm no one's champion. But I am the last Romanov and I stand to defend Bronwal. Forever. I warned Grigori away for that reason and that reason alone," Romanov said.

"Why didn't the alpha wolf...or any of the wolves come to help you?" Elena asked. The courtyard was empty. The sunlight was hidden behind clouds that had drifted in sometime during the fight. New snow fell in soft silence. Fluffy white flakes contrasted against Romanov's dark hair for brilliant seconds before they melted. The black waves released from his queue grew damp once more.

Romanov laughed softly and the snow globe the world had become suddenly crystallized and warmed at the same time. Elena hugged herself to keep from reaching out to him because his laugh was hollow rather than happy.

"I don't need wolves to fight a *Volkhvy* of Dominique's degree. Only the lesser witches come for the Romanov blade in its current state. Its power has faded. It holds no attraction or appeal to greater witches," Romanov said.

"Grigori would never fall to a common sword. Even if it pierced his heart," Elena guessed. Deep down she'd already known. That's why she'd sought the help of the alpha wolf.

"This blade is far from common. But it is also far from what it was when it was given to my father," Romanov said. He turned away to bend and retrieve the jeweled sword. The sapphire in its hilt winked dully in the cloudy light.

Elena reached to touch the sapphire. She wasn't sure why. The dark gem was cool and damp beneath her fingers.

"It's very old," she said.

Romanov had frozen and she was reminded of her first glimpse of him last night. He stared at her face as if he saw something in it that caught his attention and wouldn't let him look away. The snow was falling more heavily and it swirled around the place where their bodies kept it from the ground. But when she looked from the gem up to his eyes he was no longer a legendary fig-

ure come to life. He was a complicated man. One who
swore he was no hero while at the same time warning
her greatest enemy away.

"It isn't age that diminishes the stone. It's dishonor,"
he said. "It wasn't meant to be brandished by a traitor."

Elena withdrew her hand and Romanov blinked and
looked away from her face. He lowered the blade until
its tip pointed to the snowy ground.

"You've carried the weight of your father's mistake
for a long time," Elena said. "But I can also see that you
aren't bowed beneath this burden. You might doubt that
you're still a champion, but your body knows. You don't
fight like a man with nothing to lose. You fight like a
man with everything to lose. I can see that the stone
doesn't shine," Elena continued as she turned to walk
away through the accumulating snow. "But I can also
see that you still do. You shine. And you could help me
if you would."

He didn't reply and she didn't pause. She left him and
his dishonored blade in the whiteout of falling snow. She
wouldn't kiss him again. She would avoid him while she
sought the alpha wolf. The ferocity of his unexpected
needs drew her, as did the skin-to-skin electricity between them. But she hadn't climbed the mountain to find
a seductive lover. She'd answered a call that couldn't be
denied and she'd come to find a way to defeat the witchblood prince.

Chapter 5

She'd tasted like honey cakes and her scent had been feminine and minty sweet. The combination had gone to his head like a mead brewed for maximum potency and pleasure. Romanov sought out his rooms and the cold comfort of a bath to wash away the remnants of his long training session and his battle with Dominique. He used a rough cloth to sluice icy water over his skin. Crazy that he should kiss her. But it was a crazy inspired by sizzling attraction that clouded his thinking and burned in his blood. She should have been frightened away by his brothers, by the castle, by his tales of Ether-mad people wandering the halls.

Instead, her body had melded against his chest in his arms. She'd reached for him. She'd held on tight. She'd eagerly welcomed the thrusting of his tongue. She'd tasted him. She'd moaned and sighed as if her body craved more intimate contact with his than could be had in a courtyard in the snow.

The cold water was useless against the onslaught of sensations his mind insisted on recalling—one by one in slow, torturous succession. He hardened with the memory and he was glad he'd filled his own tub. He didn't need an audience for his body's reaction half an hour after Elena Pavlova had allowed—nay, participated in—an embrace and kiss that shouldn't have happened.

Once again, he'd been surprised by how powerfully muscular her seemingly delicate dancer's body could be. He'd wanted to rip her clothes away so he could explore and appreciate every taut line, every smooth curve. Not to mention the soft, full breasts that contrasted with her spare frame and the warm, hidden crevices he could only imagine.

Oh damn, how he could imagine them.

Many Cycles had come and gone since he'd been alive enough to feel like this. And even more since he'd been foolish enough to act on the feelings. He was cursed. He wasn't free to crave and savor and…

His body was reddened from its rough washing when he stood to allow soapy cold water to run off his skin. He wouldn't indulge his erection. He left the bath instead, wrapped in a sheet that was tattered and faded. No one had been prescient enough to mend or replace linens in a long time.

He walked to the window and pressed open the stained glass that had been added centuries after the castle was constructed. Throughout the castle there was evidence of the passage of time. People had tried to carry on. Some still did. The window's iron hinges protested, but the cold air rushed in, bathing his moist face and chilling his body temperature. He needed the blast of winter air.

Dominique wasn't dead. A normal blade would never kill a *Volkhvy*. His bold message would be delivered to Grigori. He'd told Elena he wasn't a champion. He'd told her the alpha wolf wouldn't help her. Both of those things were true. But he was a defender of his family's enclave and he would be here when Grigori came for the dancer he had claimed.

If he assumed wolf form to fight the witchblood prince, he might lose himself to it as his brothers had. Bronwal would be deserted and the Romanov blade would be up for grabs. The Dark *Volkhvy* might gain a foothold that couldn't be dislodged without a clearly sentient person to stand against them.

He couldn't risk the shift even for Elena Pavlova.

From where he stood he could see the ravens that circled around Elena's tower. They soared like feathered shadows around her room. It seemed a dark foreshadowing of what was to come.

His only option was to force her to leave Bronwal.

Cruel that he should continue to taste her and recall with perfect clarity the bold strokes of her tongue.

He wasn't sure how he would drive her away when everything in him wanted her to stay.

But he had no choice.

She'd fallen to the ground when she'd pulled the Romanov blade from the practice form in the courtyard. It had been a hard, bone-jarring fall. The blond waves of her hair had tumbled into her face and her eyes had closed. She hadn't seen what he'd seen as her body flew backward. It hadn't been the weight of the blade or the momentum of her jerk that had sent her to the ground.

The dormant, fading sapphire in the hilt of the Romanov blade had flared in her hands. A powerful force had radiated out from the awakened gem. It was that force that had sent her petite body to the ground.

The stone had dimmed immediately after and it hadn't glowed again when she rose to her feet and picked it up. But it hadn't been his imagination. The sapphire had reacted to Elena's touch. He shouldn't be surprised. He'd felt the same awakening in her presence. Not to mention what her touch did to him. An hour later, and the blood in his veins still thrummed from the fleeting kiss they'd shared.

As the ravens swooped and soared, he lifted his hand to feel his lips as if he would be able to feel the ghost of her heat on his mouth as well as he did within.

The wolf he kept buried howled deep in his chest, but not as deep as it had been before Elena arrived. She tested his control. She tempted him to give in to the passions he'd denied for so many Cycles with ease.

He had no choice but to send her away when the weather allowed it. He'd almost shifted when Dominique had taunted him in the courtyard. He couldn't risk what he might do if Elena was still at Bronwal when the *Volkhvy* came to gloat at the Gathering.

Almost as if he'd willed it to show its face, the sun burst from behind the storm clouds that had eaten its light earlier in the day. The mountains were covered in snow, but the clouds were gone and no more flakes fell from the sky.

He couldn't help remembering the stories of how the Romanov blade had chosen his mother. He remembered her as a ferocious warrior well able to wield it, and yet she'd died with the blade in her hands in spite of its power. She'd fallen against the Dark *Volkhvy* king.

Vasilisa had created the blade for the alpha's mate.

He refused to accept what its wakening in Elena's hands might mean.

The curse changed everything. It twisted all of the old enchantments. He was doomed to stand alone forever. The sapphire's glow only illuminated his pain.

Chapter 6

Evening came early as the sun set once more behind the rocky ridges of the snow-capped mountains. Elena figured out how to open one of the stained glass panels in her room so that she could see the brilliant red sphere as it sank. It turned the entire world to crimson and gold, while ravens continued to lazily patrol the skies around her tower. After the kiss and the fight, she'd retreated to the tower. She'd slammed the door and turned the key. But no one had followed her. She was alone except for the ever-present birds. Their constant revolutions occurred silently, with only the occasional flutter of wings.

Once the sun went down and the world went dark, Elena took one last deep breath of the fresh air and then closed the window against the night. With the snowstorm clearing, it was only a matter of time before Romanov decided to send her away. She didn't have long. The unwound clock in her room didn't tick. It didn't have to. She felt the seconds counting down with every heartbeat in her chest. The call beneath her skin had become a continual sense of urgency rather than a pulse.

It compelled her to be brave. She didn't have much time. She unlocked the door and left the tower to search for the alpha wolf. The long winding stairway was deserted, but when she left the tower to travel into the main part of the castle, she wasn't alone. Lev and Soren appeared behind her. Romanov had ordered his wolves to stalk her. Their claws could be eerily quiet when they wished. But not as eerie as how loud they could be seconds later. The *click-click-click* that occasionally sounded behind her caused her heart to pound. She bit her lip so often against the fear that her lower lip became swollen and sensitized.

She was already more conscious of her mouth than she'd ever been.

She'd been kissed before. She'd enjoyed it. That pleasure was pale in comparison to what had flared between her and Romanov when their mouths had come together. He could have crushed her, easily. His arms were massive and not in that showy way that bodybuilders attained. Romanov had real, ropey muscles that flexed and released when he moved, in the same way that a dancer's muscles stretched and released. Not for looks. For utility. It so happened that muscles built for utility were the most attractive of all. Her stomach went all molten liquid when she remembered his embrace—his calloused hand on the back of her neck, his other splayed on the curve of her lower back. He'd pulled her close, not as if she needed to be held, but as if he was hanging on for dear life.

She'd felt solid and necessary. So real and seductive because he seemed to crave her warmth and solidity.

And all because a man kissed her. Not a mere fantasy. Ivan Romanov was a legend, but that wasn't all he was.

The stories were dust, blown away by muscle and heat and friction and the hungry penetration of his tongue.

Elena Pavlova belongs to herself.

His words had been echoing in her head for hours. He was wrong. She had never belonged to herself. The dance had owned her for two decades. She'd loved her grandmother and her mother, but the dance had ruled her world. Every move she made from dawn till dusk had been to serve the dance. All of the masters who had driven her to try to achieve perfection had demanded her obedience and her complete dedication, but it had been the ballet that they'd all served.

Back in the apartment she'd shared with her grandmother, dozens upon dozens of pointe shoes hung from their ribbons on nails driven deep into the wall. They were dingy pastel satin, stained with years of her blood, sweat and tears. They were also prize trophies that proclaimed her servitude, not her independence.

What did the servant do when the master freed her from obligation?

Elena shivered as she continued her self-guided tour of Bronwal.

Even if Grigori had never seen her and never claimed her as his own, she would be in crisis now that her career was over. She was a prima ballerina, but an injured athlete's future wasn't guaranteed with surgery. At best, retirement could be held off as a dancer was forced to accept lesser and lesser roles. Where she went from there was always going to be a question she had to answer.

Lev and Soren seemed to have infinite patience with her wanderings. Only the occasional sound of their claws on tile interrupted her thoughts. The clicks were discordant against the ticking clock of her heart.

She'd wanted to dance and the dance had consumed her. Now she longed for a chance at something more.

Elena Pavlova belongs to herself.

There was a possibility that Ivan Romanov, the last Romanov, had voiced her true desire. If she survived Grigori, she would be free for the first time. It would be up to her what she decided to become with her freedom.

The castle seemed to be utterly empty except for her lone human form followed by two giant wolves. Only distant sounds indicated that her solitude was a lie.

As Elena searched for the alpha wolf, she thought about Romanov's lips. She'd kissed him even though she shouldn't, but it felt like the first real choice she'd ever made. She'd been driven to dance by a natural affinity, but the dance had subsumed all of her passion years before it ruined her knee. It had stopped being a choice and become an obsessive obligation. She danced because she had to. To provide for her grandmother. To honor her dead mother's memory.

Seeking the alpha wolf was also something she had to do. It wasn't a choice. It was survival.

But kissing Ivan Romanov had been *her* decision. He had given her ample opportunity to run away. She had to take responsibility for the consequences. The weakness in her knees. The warmth in her belly. The heat of shame when she acknowledged she would make the same choice if she could go back and relive that moment again, even though the kiss had been a mistake.

She hadn't gone back to the tower room to flee Romanov. She'd fled from her desire until she could be certain that she would come out only to seek the alpha wolf and not her host.

The castle was as poorly lit as it had been before. She walked by the sparse light of flickering torches and a small flashlight she'd packed in her bag. On the walls she caught occasional glimpses of the wolves in the form of hulking black shadows. She'd grown up with tales of these wolves. Their shadows were very like the paper cutouts that leaped from some of the pages of her grandmother's book. Ferocious yet lovely. Mysterious yet beloved and familiar.

"My, what very big teeth my childhood stories have," Elena said. Her voice echoed down the empty corridor. It also trembled. Because no matter how nostalgic she was for her grandmother and the old tales she knew, the wolves that trailed after her were deadly and real. They didn't walk by her side as friends. They followed suspiciously and cautiously as she searched their home for the alpha.

And their master ignored her desperate efforts.

She was glad he was nowhere to be seen.

Once again she roamed from room to room. She didn't expect to suddenly turn a corner and run into the alpha wolf, but she did hope for a clue to his whereabouts. The Dark *Volkhvy* and his talk of Grigori had only increased her sense of urgency. Before the witchblood prince found her, she had to have a champion to face him down. If Romanov wouldn't help her, she had to help herself.

Her chest grew tighter and tighter with every room she searched. Every breath seemed to require more and more effort to take.

It wasn't only time constraints and her failure to find the black wolf that caused emotions to knot around her heart and crowd out her lungs. It was the fate of the people who had once called Bronwal home. She'd yet to encounter a single soul wandering in the halls. She heard them far off—laughing, crying, calling out the name of a loved one again and again with no reply. She braced for a possible encounter around every corner, behind every door.

But she found only dust and desertion.

She was a living trespasser rifling through the belongings of the lost. She tried not to disturb personal effects. She limited her search to books and papers. Some bit of knowledge about the alpha that might add to what little she'd learned from her own book of Slavic legends.

There was nothing. The people of Bronwal had lived with legends. Their personal tales had been told over tables and cook fires. On dance floors and battlefields. The books they'd kept on shelves had nothing to do with the *Volkhvy* or the legendary wolves. The dusty papers were love letters or ledgers. Diaries about mundane daily events. Not tomes devoted to the alpha wolf's summoning.

Lev and Soren paced restlessly when she paused in a room and then they followed her on to the next. They didn't make a sound until she stumbled upon a large chamber that had obviously been a family suite.

Elena pushed the heavy door open wide and walked into the room. One of the windowpanes had cracked. Snow had disturbed the sanctum created by abandoned neglect. It swirled icily when she opened the door. Her breath fogged from her parted lips in the unheated air. The bed was a curtained masterpiece of carved mahogany. But it wasn't the snow or the bed that caught her attention.

There was a small cradle beside the bed. The winter breeze from the broken window caused it to sway with the tiniest of creaks, a sad and empty sound far from what must have been ages ago when a mother rocked a sleeping infant in his or her comfy bed.

Elena's eyes burned. She walked toward the cradle even though the tightness in her chest had spread all the way up to her throat. She grasped the flushed skin of her neck with a trembling hand when she was close enough to see the crumpled blankets and an abandoned toy on the floor.

She knew what it was before she bent to pick it up. It was grayish in the dim light of her flashlight, but she recognized its shape. It was Lev. Or a hand-sewn likeness of the great white wolf made from a fluffy white cloth that had grown dingy with neglect and age.

It was the first evidence she'd found of the wolves beyond the sculptures in the portrait gallery.

She turned the toy wolf around and gasped when she saw the finely rendered face. Blue embroidery thread had been carefully employed to represent the wolf's eyes. This had been the baby's toy and it had been left behind when the baby—disappeared into the Ether for the last time?

A tapestry hung behind the cradle, softening the cold stone wall with muted colors. She raised her flashlight to illuminate the intricately wrought piece of art. Then she gasped. How had someone created so much life and movement with a needle and thread? The compulsion that had brought her to Bronwal suddenly became a thrill of recognition. Thousands upon thousands of tiny stitches glimmered beneath her flashlight's beam. They composed a portrait of a woman dressed in medieval style, but she wasn't some simple maiden. Over her long dress, bronze thread had been used to depict a breastplate, and she wore a matching bronze helmet. From beneath it, a riot of red hair swept out from her face and shoulders in a wild halo created by an unseen breeze. The expression on her face was both ferocious and serene. Purpose was evident in every line of her body and in the sword she lifted into a sewn sky filled with embroidered clouds.

She didn't recognize the woman, but she recognized something in her—an emotion she felt within her own breast.

At first, Elena mistook her sword for the sapphire blade, but once she pulled her eyes from the fascination caused by the woman's seeming serenity in spite of whatever unseen danger she faced, she realized her mistake. The stone in the hilt of the sword wasn't a sapphire. It was a blood-red ruby. The massive tapestry seemed an odd choice to hang over a baby's bed, yet Elena could almost imagine the woman in the portrait watching over the tiny baby as he or she slept. With that thought, it suddenly didn't seem out of place at all.

She held the toy wolf in one hand and the flashlight in the other, but she reached with the hand that held the flashlight to gently touch the gem on the sword with one extended finger.

A low growl suddenly interrupted her fascination with the tapestry.

Elena whirled toward the hall, wildly painting the walls with an unsteady beam of light. Once her eyes could focus, she saw the wolf toy's living likeness blocking the door.

One of her wolf shadows was no longer content to follow in her wake. He'd come forward. And he didn't seem happy at all. He was much more ferocious than the toy in her hand. As her flashlight steadied and her beam illuminated the doorway, Lev's legs were braced and his hackles were bristled along his giant back. Worst of all, his teeth were bared in a snarl. The trembling in Elena's hand returned and transferred itself to her entire body in an instant. If the wolves had been suspicious of her before, that suspicion had transformed into outright aggression.

Lev paced one stiff-legged stride toward her and then another.

"I mean no harm. I didn't mean to…disturb the baby's room," Elena said. And it was true. She wished she'd walked by this door. It was too horrible. Her understanding of the torment that must have plagued these people was complete. Here had been a tiny baby only beginning his or her life, but now gone. This was worse than death. A baby ceasing to be. Had the mother gone first or had she followed later? And what of the father? Had he mourned, had he grieved? The *Volkhvy* divided themselves by Dark and Light, but this curse had been the work of the Light *Volkhvy* queen. Which meant there was really no distinction between Dark and Light at all.

Elena turned slowly and carefully to place the wolf toy in the cradle. Lev growled louder, but she withdrew her hand to show what she had done. She raised her empty palm toward the wolf that had allowed her to pet him before. He didn't seem soothed. In fact, he took another step toward her while Soren stood tense at the door.

"I'm sorry, Lev," Elena said. She meant for everything. Not only that she'd disturbed the chamber, but for all the loss and the pain. She was sorry that her presence disturbed the entire castle. Bronwal was a tomb. Every footfall in the dusty passages was a desecration. And yet it was a desecration she must commit to survive.

Soren had disappeared. But the distant castle and the room suddenly hazed as her perceptions narrowed down to her and the lone wolf that remained. She was alone with the white wolf and he seemed seconds away from tearing her throat out. Elena edged back inch by inch until the cradle was between her vulnerable jugular vein and Lev.

"I need the alpha wolf's help. I can't stop looking. I won't. But this room is obviously off-limits. I understand. Let me leave and I won't disturb the baby again," Elena said. Even as she said it, she was glad she'd seen the tapestry. There was something important about the warrior woman. Her senses tingled with potential revelations that seemed just out of reach. Something about the tapestry captured her. She'd been searching Bronwal to unlock the secrets of summoning the alpha wolf. The tapestry seemed to hint there was more to the legend than she'd been told.

With a start she noticed that Lev's giant paws were already in the snow that had come in the cracked window. His breath came in white clouds between his bared teeth. She wouldn't be able to fight him off with nothing but a flashlight. She was trapped as she was trapped every night in swan form in her nightmares. Her only consolation was that Grigori wasn't here to see her die. He would get no more pleasure from her pain. The trembling in her body transferred to the light in her hands. The beam wavered on the floor. She faced her death. She wasn't sorry she'd tried. She didn't regret listening to the call that had brought her here. If anything, the discovery of the tapestry made her fiercely glad. She didn't cower. She braced her legs and waited for the white wolf to pounce.

"Lev," Romanov said from the doorway.

Elena's attention flew from the shivering light to the man who had suddenly appeared from the shadows.

He didn't shout. He didn't have to. His firm tone rent the silent, chilly air as commanding as it needed to be without him raising his voice. Romanov was part of the mystery. He, too, caused a thrill in her like the tapestry on the wall. Even in danger, she recognized the pieces coming together—Romanov, the missing alpha, the warrior woman, the swords.

The white wolf froze. His breathing was labored as if he expended great effort to halt his attack midspring. Sure enough, his haunches were compressed as if his master had interrupted seconds before he left the ground.

"I didn't mean to upset him…" Elena began.

"You can't possibly understand what you've done," Romanov said. "Lev. Leave. I'll take her away. She won't bring you here again. She didn't know."

"You weren't always his master," Elena guessed. "This was his family."

"He isn't a dog. Or a pet. He has no master, Elena. He's never had a master. But, yes, this was his family," Romanov said. His tones were raw and subdued as if his chest was as tight as hers.

"I'm sorry," Elena said.

The white wolf blinked as if he'd been woken from a berserker trance. He backed away from her until he bumped into Romanov's legs. Then he yelped as if he was startled. Romanov reached and placed his hand on the side of the great wolf's face. But Lev jerked away and ran into the corridor. Elena watched as the wolf disappeared. Soren, who must have gone to fetch Romanov, stood in the hallway. He blinked at her several times, slowly. Then he ran after his companion.

Elena's face was wet. She stumbled away from the empty cradle toward the door.

"You wander a cemetery looking for salvation. Yet nothing exists here beyond invisible bones," Romanov said. He stopped her at the door with two large hands on her upper arms. He held her at arm's length and looked down into her eyes.

"Is the alpha wolf gone? Is that what you're not telling me?" Elena asked. She searched his gaze, but her flashlight was pointed at the hallway and they were left in cold shadows.

"You'll never find him," Romanov replied. "He isn't gone, but he's buried. That's all you need to know."

He was wrong. She needed to know much more. She needed to understand. She'd been compelled to come here, but she was confused by all she'd found. Elena pulled away from her reluctant host. Romanov was a mystery, but she understood one thing: Grigori was coming. He was ten times as dangerous as Lev.

"Then I'm cursed, as well," she said. "Lost like all the people of Bronwal. Without the alpha wolf, I'll die."

He didn't go in search of his brother. Lev would have run far from the castle to try to escape the grief he wasn't able to leave behind as easily as he'd left his human form. His memories might be muddled. So hazy that he'd followed Elena as Ivan had ordered without knowing he would step into a room that would penetrate the senses of the beast he'd allowed himself to become.

It must have been like losing Madeline and Trevor all over again.

He hadn't thought that far ahead when he'd ordered the wolves to trail after the woman he had to avoid himself. There were portions of Bronwal he refused to visit even though he didn't allow himself the luxury of retreating into wolf form. Near immortality was a heavy weight to bear. He couldn't blame Lev for running away. Not now. And not when he'd given up his human form for good.

Elena didn't understand the forces she tampered with

or the simmering pain she threatened to unleash. He clenched his fists against hundreds of years of love and loss. He stiffened his spine against the weight of it. Lev would recover. The farther he ran, focusing on the churning of his powerful legs in the snow, the better he would be able to fully become the white wolf again. He would forget. Ivan didn't have that luxury. He could only endure.

Perhaps Lev's pain would at least serve a purpose.

Elena had been terrified. It had been a fresh hell to see her in danger and frightened. When Soren had come to his rooms to find him, he'd understood his brother's unspoken urgency. But he hadn't expected to find Elena in such dire circumstances after the red wolf had led him to her. Lev might have killed her without completely understanding what he'd done. Ivan had interrupted just in time.

He'd warned her that the castle wasn't a safe place. Now she'd seen for herself. He should be glad.

Instead, it was torment to recall the fear in her eyes.

In his wolf form, he was much bigger than his brothers and much more savage. He was the eldest brother and the leader of their enchanted pack. And the black wolf was so close to the surface of his skin this Cycle that its ferocity was a part of him even when he walked on two legs. He hadn't needed to assume wolf form to defeat Dominique. He'd done it with human hands.

Lev wasn't the only danger to the determined dancer.

Bronwal was no haven for Elena. It was a monster's lair.

Lev had terrified Elena, but her fear was nothing compared to Ivan's horror as he'd seen the white wolf stalk the woman he'd kissed hours before. The scene had seemed like a premonition of what might occur if he gave in to the alpha wolf clawing its way out of his heart.

But it had also been a revelation.

Whether she knew it or not, she'd held the flashlight in the exact same way that his brother's wife, Madeline, had held the ruby sword in the tapestry on the wall behind her. Elena had been frightened, but she'd also been magnificent. In her simple modern clothes, she'd seemed as much of a warrior in her own way.

He cursed the fickle universe that would bring him a potential mate now, when he was doomed and disgraced. The sapphire might flare for her. The Romanov blade might come to her hand. She might be a warrior at heart, all determination and perseverance and steadfast resilience, but the time when he might have gloried in discovering her was long, long past.

He would never bind her to his horrible fate.

The Light *Volkhvy* had chosen the Romanovs as champions. They had gifted the Romanov sons with the ability to shift into supernatural wolves that could stand against the dark. And they had crafted the swords to aid in the fight. Lev's wife had claimed Lev's sword before she had claimed his heart. She'd fought by his side from the first day they'd met, and it had been obvious the sword had chosen her as its mistress.

But he couldn't allow the sapphire blade to choose Elena Pavlova.

Chapter 7

On the way back to the tower, Elena was puzzling over the tapestry when she ran into Bell. The young servant was struggling to pull a trunk up a flight of stairs. Her burden was bigger than she was, and Elena paused to watch as the other woman doggedly refused to give up. Her lack of makeup and her size had caused Elena to misjudge her age the first time they'd met. This time, Elena could see that she was curvier than she'd appeared while she'd been carrying water. She probably wasn't much younger than Elena herself, and that wasn't even taking the curse into account.

A shock shivered down Elena's spine when she acknowledged that the young woman might look eighteen or nineteen years old, but she'd been born centuries ago.

Bell paused and stood against the trunk so it wouldn't slide backward. She used her weight to hold it while she straightened to stretch her back. Elena wasn't sure how many more flights she had to tackle, but she was only halfway up this one and the brown curls on her forehead were damp with sweat from her exertions.

"I can help," Elena offered. She was sorry she spoke without clearing her throat when the other woman dropped down in a defensive crouch as if she braced against an attack. The move allowed the trunk to slide back one jarring step with a loud boom that echoed off the stone walls of the stairway.

"I'm sorry," she apologized as she stepped forward to place her weight against the trunk too. "I didn't mean to startle you."

"Can never be too careful in Bronwal. Not now. You never know if someone Ether-addled or worse is going to come at you without really seeing who they're attacking," Bell said.

"Someone or some *wolf*," Elena agreed.

"There's only one wolf you have to worry about at the moment. Soren would never hurt you," Bell said.

"You don't worry about the black wolf?" Elena asked.

Bell had leaned to pick up the end of the trunk she'd been tugging before, but this time Elena leaned to pick up the handle on the other side. They hoisted together and, even though it was heavy, they were able to climb up the stairs without much trouble.

They were both stronger than they seemed.

"I worry about everyone and everything in Bronwal. It would be a mistake to lower my guard. But the red wolf is usually not far when bad things happen. He keeps an eye on those of us left behind," Bell said.

"Isn't the black wolf a guardian too?" Elena asked. She followed Bell's lead from the top of the staircase down a short hall and up another flight of stairs.

"Romanov is our guardian," the other woman said.

She acted as if she'd answered Elena's question even though she hadn't. Where was the black wolf? Had it disappeared into the Ether or was it wandering around the mountain like Lev, Ether-addled and dangerous?

After several more flights of stairs that left even Elena winded, they came out of a narrow door and onto the ramparts of the castle. Bell was probably used to the view, but she paused to take in the endless stretch of craggy mountains anyway. They must be too spectacular to ever become commonplace and maybe she missed them when she was in the Ether. Enough to need to soak in the view when she could.

"The Mountains of the Sunset...you need to come up one evening to see the colors. I never tire of it when we're materialized," Bell said. She really was surprisingly pretty. Her hat shadowed her face and hid her good looks until her bowed lips and dimple flashed when you least expected it. "That's why I've made my room up here. And because no one wanders up this high. Romanov was right when he said you should stay in your tower. To survive, we have to be careful, all the time."

Bell tugged on her handle to show Elena which way she wanted to go. They wound around the main body of the castle on a walled walk with openings that allowed a person to see for miles. Elena supposed the openings had once been intended for guards to keep watch. Now, she took advantage of them to gauge the weather on mountains as they walked.

No snow fell. The sky was clear.

Finally, when her arms seemed like they would scream in protest, they came to an abandoned aviary. The stone structure was circular with a high, domed roof made of copper. The scrolled iron cage that had once surrounded the aviary on one side was in rusty disrepair, but the mews was intact. Someone had lifted the top fastening window shutters and propped them open so that they fanned out all around the aviary. There were no birds inside to keep contained. Instead of birds, the floor had been swept and mopped clean and covered with colorful rugs. There was a bed and several chairs, as well as shelves full of books. There were other bits and baubles that shone or sparkled throughout the room so that Elena revised her opinion.

There was one bird who inhabited the aviary—a cheerful magpie just over five feet tall.

"Thank you for your help. It's been a while since anyone has lent me a helping hand," Bell said.

Elena was glad to set her side of the trunk down when Bell indicated the spot where she wanted it placed at the foot of the bed.

That's when she turned and noticed the russet fur that covered one of the rugs near the door. Did Soren keep vigil between the door and the bed when Bell was sleeping?

"But not so long since someone lent a helping paw?" she asked. She leaned over to pick up a strand of red hair and lifted it to show the other woman.

"I don't sleep a lot while we're materialized. I hate to waste a minute. But needs must, and sometimes I can't help myself. Once, last Cycle, a Dark *Volkhvy* found me here in my aviary. They're always a danger, but they usually confront Romanov. I don't know how or why one came for me. But Soren intervened," she said. "He saved me."

She opened the trunk while she spoke. Nestled inside was a jumble of clothes and possessions. Elena noticed that the clothing was meant for a man. No doubt more practical than some of the clothes made for women when the people of Bronwal were born.

And Bell did seem to favor practical clothes. Her boy's hat was always placed firmly on her head.

"He seems to do that a lot," Elena said. "He fetched Romanov and saved me from a very angry Lev a half an hour ago."

Bell dropped the lid of the trunk and straightened.

"Was Soren okay? I worry sometimes that Lev will turn on him. He's so far gone," Bell said.

"He was fine. The last I saw of him he was chasing after Lev and he didn't seem frightened," Elena said. "You grew up with them?" she asked. She already knew the answer. Bell was younger than Elena but not by much in actual physical years, although the curse had doomed her to "live" much longer.

"I came to Bronwal when I was a baby. I've never known any other home. But I wasn't always a servant. That happened after the curse, when more and more servants disappeared," Bell said. "I was put to work and I didn't mind. Not when the Romanovs had taken me in and given me a safe place to live."

"What happened to your parents?" Elena asked.

"They were killed in one of the last battles between the Romanovs and the Dark *Volkhvy*. I don't remember them. Sovkra was the mountain village where I was born. It was decimated. Vladimir Romanov found me in a field of burning bellflowers. He carried me out of the village as a wolf would carry a pup."

"And he brought you home," Elena said.

"Yes. The nanny and servants who cared for his children raised me. They all called me 'Bell' because of the scorched flowers I clutched in my hands when the gray wolf lifted me from the flames. I was clothed and fed and basically allowed to run wild until I had to take up the tasks of running the castle myself," Bell said.

"If Vladimir had taken you elsewhere, you wouldn't have been caught up in the curse," Elena said. Bell had been an innocent babe rescued by the Romanovs when she'd been orphaned.

"I wouldn't change a thing if I could go back and if I had that power. This is my home. These are my people," Bell said. She stood tall and squared her shoulders. In spite of their serious conversation she still had a hint of a sparkle in her eyes. It might be moisture. It might be determination. Elena couldn't be sure. "One day the curse will be lifted and the Romanov brothers will be free. I won't lose myself before that. I want to be here to see…their faces."

Elena had the feeling there was a particular face that Bell might be pining for, but she shied away from further questions. There was no way to know if Ivan Romanov's brothers would return from the Ether where they had disappeared, but she had too many of her own foolish hopes to dash Bell's.

"I'd better go and find Soren," Bell said.

Elena took one last look at the view. It was a fairy-tale setting, but this was a dark, dark tale indeed, especially now. The snow that had bought her time to search for the black wolf had stopped falling.

Her book was tucked in the backpack she'd left in her room. The familiar object came into her hands as if her fingers were made to flip its pages. She'd looked through it so many times. It had been an escape from the dance when she'd thought it was a fantasy world. Later, after her mother's death, it had been a comfort. Then, later still, once Grigori revealed himself and his plans, it had been hope. But she hadn't turned to the book for comfort or hope this time.

The binding fell open to her favorite illustrations: one of the castle. One of three Romanov wolves running through a wintry wood. One of Vladimir. She paused on the illustration of Ivan's father. She traced the square angle of his jaw and the sharp line of his nose. So very like his eldest son's.

Ivan Romanov and his brothers weren't pictured. His mother was only shown on horseback with indistinct features. As she looked closely at each intricately crafted three-dimensional image that rose from every page, she scanned for something she'd never noticed—swords with enchanted gems on their hilts. The artist had created a complex world completely out of paper. The movement of the pages caused the paper to fold up and out and each image was seen as a silhouette against a backdrop of shadowy black.

There were battle scenes. There were many ordinary blades. None with the jeweled hilt she was looking for, but she thought to scan the vines and flowers, the skies and borders and all the other places in the book that had become so familiar to her that she barely noticed the details they contained.

That's how she found the sword from the tapestry. Its ruby was unmistakable once her eyes and tracing finger separated it from the leaves of the great oak in which it was hidden. After that, she redoubled her efforts to find Ivan Romanov's sapphire blade, but it eluded her notice. Page after page held birds and roses and scrolling designs, but no Romanov blade. Until finally she found another sword. This one was hidden in the twining briars of a wild rose that climbed the side of the castle's wall. Except the gem in its hilt winked with an emerald sheen.

She'd held the sapphire hilt in her own two hands. She knew she would find its like in the book. She'd seen the ruby sword in the tapestry. Now she knew there had been at least three Romanov blades. One for each brother?

But it hadn't been Romanov's brother wielding the sword in the tapestry. Who then? The missing brother, the abandoned room, the empty cradle... Elena closed the book before she'd found the sapphire sword. Her throat was tight and her eyes burned. The warrior woman in the tapestry had seemed so at home with the sword in her hand. Had she been married to one of Vladimir Romanov's sons?

She'd never known her favorite childhood story was a tragedy. She wondered which brother in the portrait she'd seen had disappeared with his entire family into the Ether. Had they all gone at the same time or had some or one been left behind?

There was so much she didn't understand. She didn't know if she'd have time to delve as deeply as she needed to into the past and the facts behind the legend in order to summon the alpha wolf. It was all much more complicated than she'd expected. She'd wondered if the legend would prove to be true. She'd never expected to have to search for a reluctant champion once she found Bronwal.

It was late. Most of the distant sounds in the castle had quieted to murmurs and indistinct scrapes and sighs. Bronwal never slept. But it did experience lulls in activity. Elena's stomach had growled for the hundredth time. Her encounter with the white wolf hadn't faded in her mind, but her hunger couldn't be ignored any longer. No one had brought food to the tower, and her energy bars were running out. She was forced to abandon the book and go looking for a kitchen.

This time she bumped into several servants on her

way down to lower floors in the castle. Each time they barely acknowledged her presence. Each time she was struck by their eclectic manner of dress. There were many different periods represented, as if coming and going from the Ether was a kind of time travel. Often they were disheveled and threadbare, as if they didn't have the cognizance necessary to take care of simple matters of hygiene and personal appearance.

One man tried to stop her. He grabbed her arm and yelled nonsense questions in her face. His bloodshot eyes rolled around in their sockets and his clothes were nothing but rags that hung on his emaciated body.

"I'm sorry. I don't understand. I can't help you," Elena said. She pulled away with all her strength and the man fell sobbing to the floor. She backed away as she finally recognized some of the syllables he was rolling together.

"Mywifemywifemywifemywife."

She had to leave him. There was nothing she could do. She couldn't break the curse or end his suffering. The inhabitants of Bronwal were wanderers. Drifting in and out of existence every ten years. Her heart beat rabidly in her chest as she continued down more flights of stairs. She noted many others she passed had similar wild eyes and uncoordinated, shuffling steps. For the first time, she wondered if Romanov had ordered Lev and Soren to follow her as guardians rather than spies. Alone, she encountered many more of Bronwal's mad inhabitants. Now that she didn't have the wolves' protection, how would she ever find the alpha wolf when she had to dodge the angry white wolf and navigate crowds of desperate, zombie-like people?

This was Ivan Romanov's world. How had he managed to stay sane for so long?

And what of the alpha wolf? The curse affected the

people of Bronwal, but now she'd discovered that it affected the wolves, as well. The white wolf's statue was smaller and less powerful than the black wolf. The alpha was larger in her book's illustrations too. If she found him, he might be more savage toward her than Lev.

When she reached the lower levels, the smell of freshly baked bread filled the air. It was a welcome change to dust and unwashed bodies. She hurried forward, propelled as much by her stomach as by the need for cheer, any cheer, especially the kind found in a warm kitchen on a cold night.

She didn't expect to find Ivan Romanov leaning on a scarred wooden table where Patrice worked. The older woman's arms were up to her elbows in dough.

"I thought you might make your way down here," he said as Elena hurried into the room only to stop dead in her tracks.

Unlike the rest of the castle, the kitchen wasn't deserted. There was a fire in the large hearth, and the ovens built into the stone on either side of it were filled with baking loaves. Besides Patrice and Romanov, there were several other servants bustling around. Elena recognized some of them as people who had carried bathwater to the tower her first night. Several were busily sweeping up the flour that Patrice didn't seem to notice she'd dusted all over the floor.

"Nothing like the smell of breakfast to get you out of bed," Patrice said. It was well past noon. Breakfast would have been hours before if Bronwal kept to a regular schedule. Elena had eaten nothing but protein bars since the light meal she'd bought in Cerna after her long journey south from Saint Petersburg to Romania. Her stomach gurgled audibly and Romanov straightened. He motioned her forward to a stool beside him. In front of it was a plate filled with freshly sliced bread. Near that was a stone crock of pale yellow butter and a wheel of fragrant cheese.

"The kitchen is the last living place in Bronwal. You can always be sure of finding someone here," Romanov said.

Why would he offer her comfort if he was determined she should go away?

She'd sworn to keep her distance from her host, but Elena couldn't resist the bread or the warmth of the fire. She tried to tell herself there was nothing else drawing her near him. Her hands were like ice from the chilled corridors and stairways. She stepped forward and perched on the stool. The scent of the bread and cheese caused her to nearly swoon, and her mouth watered as she used a knife to dip up and spread the thick, churned butter. It flaked in rich chunks beneath the knife's blade, as only real butter would do.

"I was going to bring you a tray," Patrice mumbled as she continued to knead and roll and punch the springy dough.

"Actually, I was," Romanov said.

He reached for a piece of bread from her plate and lifted it to his mouth. He took a bite as she bit into the piece she'd buttered. They both chewed slowly. As the butter and bread dissolved in Elena's mouth, she was light-headed with relief. Better that she'd come to the crowded kitchen than to have Romanov come to her room alone. But her relief was short-lived because a smudge of butter from the bread had smeared on Romanov's lower lip. Her mouth went dry and she couldn't tear her focus away. She watched the butter as he chewed. She stared, transfixed, as he swallowed and licked his lips clean. His enjoyment of the fresh bread was evident. His pleasure caused her to tighten and tingle, then liquefy in places best ignored in his presence. She had to force herself to swallow past the sudden paralysis in her jaw and throat as tingling desire rose up, refusing to be ignored.

It was torture to be physically attracted to the man who was standing in the way of her desperate goal. She'd never allowed sensual distractions in her life, even when her situation hadn't been life or death. But the chemistry that assailed her whenever she was around Romanov didn't ask for permission. In fact, it seemed to be heightened by her desperation.

How could he ignore her predicament when he obviously couldn't ignore her?

His large body leaned against the tall table closer to her than it had been before. She was certain he had imperceptibly shifted while she'd been focused on his lips. When she forced her gaze up from his mouth to meet his eyes, his intensity caused her breath to catch. His eyelids lazily hooded the gleam of his irises, but his interest was anything but lazy. Although his posture was relaxed, his body was taut. He radiated a heat that competed with the oven. He was gauging her reactions. He was tuned in to her response. He'd noticed her quickened breath and her focus on the mere flick of his tongue. And judging from the intensity of his interest he liked the way she had instantly kindled from such a simple, innocent move.

The liquid in her belly and lower seemed to bubble in response. She'd been famished for food, but now she was hungry for whatever his dark green eyes seemed to promise as they looked into hers.

"You say you want me to go away before the *Volkhvy* Gathering, but then you offer me warmth and comfort. The snow is piled high outside, but it's no longer falling," Elena said. She couldn't indulge the heat between them with flirtation or niceties. She needed his help to find the alpha wolf. She didn't need this desire that flared between them. Kisses wouldn't save her, even though her body lied and tried to tell her they would.

"We move toward oblivion with every passing second," Romanov said. "I can offer you a meal before you have to leave." He didn't back away. In fact, he reached to toy with strands of hair that had fallen free of the messy bun she had hastily created with her heavy blond waves before coming downstairs. Again, it seemed as if he tortured himself. His body was tense. Did he want to plunge his fingers into her hair and pull her into his arms? His powerful hand shook. *He would rather devour than toy.* That thought did nothing to help her ignore the heat that had radiated out from her bubbling stomach to claim her entire body. His hand might shake, but its trembles were contagious. Her whole being quaked. Her breath came quick through dry lips. And she held herself back with only the most determined control.

"Your oblivion will not save me. I have to stay here and fight. There's no escape but the one I make," Elena said. "I can't run away. Ultimately Grigori is going to find me. I need the alpha to fight by my side."

"And what if the alpha devours you instead? What then?" Romanov asked.

Suddenly, the kitchen was quiet. All the servants had disappeared. The only movement was the flickering flames in the fireplace and abandoned dough rising on the table beside them. And the rise and fall of their chests as they both breathed in and out. Hers was rapid. His was slow and deliberate. She watched as his broad chest expanded and then fell as air exhaled through his lips. Was it a calming meditation? Or was he inhaling the mint fragrance he released as he continued to gently play with her hair?

The slight movement of his hand turned out to have purpose and consequences. Her hasty bun was loosened. Little by little, he freed her hair from its confinement until it tumbled down over her shoulders. She watched him as the waves came free. His eyes darkened. His lids lowered. And she still kept herself still beneath his touch. Even when he slowly threaded his fingers into the loosened waves to cup the side of her head, she didn't move beyond her shaky breaths and her trembling body.

"You ask for more than it's in my power to give you. I can't control the alpha wolf. I can't call him to fight by your side. I can only hold Bronwal. Do you understand? This place and all its people. Their ultimate fate is my responsibility," Romanov said. But his hand tightened so that he held her even as he spoke of holding his people's cursed universe on his shoulders, alone.

"Then I have to hope the alpha wolf will choose to help me of his own accord. Without your call. Without your permission. Lev wanted to tear me apart for disturbing the baby's room. But Soren ran for help. He could have looked away. He could have left me to die. He didn't. There's a champion deep inside of him still. I have to believe the alpha wolf will be the same," Elena said.

"The alpha hasn't been a champion in a very long time. He's nothing but an abandoned savage. I'm afraid he'll turn his savagery on the world if he's called. And, unlike Lev, there's no one stronger to remind him of what he used to be," Romanov said.

Elena's spine stiffened. She drew her body back from the man who heated her bones and chilled her heart. Surprisingly, in spite of his tension and his powerful grip, he eased his fingers to let her go. She left the stool to step back from the table and from Romanov's heat. Her leg hurt. Her body was exhausted from lack of sleep and from her battle with the elements. But she wasn't weak. She never had been. Not even in her nightmares when she was reduced to frantic, fluttering wings.

"I'm small, but I'm stronger than you know. *I* will remind him," Elena said.

Romanov's hand had fallen to his side. He flexed his fingers open and closed as if he couldn't quite believe he'd let her go.

"The alpha could easily crush you with only one bite," Romanov said. "He's an enchanted monster driven nearly mad by a relentless curse." He stepped after her suddenly, and she was too startled to back away. He reached for her again before she could widen the gap between them. His body was only inches away. His hands clasped her shoulders and pulled her even closer, until their bodies touched in a full-length press that shocked every cell from her head to her toes. "You fear being captured by the witchblood prince, but you should fear death."

"You endure a fate worse than death. And yet it isn't the Ether that you fear. It's the materialization. What new loss will each one bring? Loved ones? Your own faculties? The idea that the Dark *Volkhvy* will claim what you've defended all this time. I don't fear the alpha wolf's teeth because my future with Grigori will eat away at me little by little. I prefer death to that."

Romanov's chin rose as if he'd been slapped by her words. But he didn't let her go. If anything, his hands tightened on her shoulders. Her breathing was shallow and quick, yet his scent enveloped her along with his heat. He'd been in the kitchen long enough that the scent of fresh baked bread clung to his skin, but it was the scent of the mountain that rose from his hair. It was a wild and snowy scent with the slightest hint of evergreen.

"You're wrong. It's the freedom of oblivion that I most fear. Because its call is more seductive than any I've ever experienced," he said. "Until now."

She wasn't prepared for his hands to slide from her shoulders to her back. Instinctively, she raised her hands to brace against his chest, but somehow she ended up with fistfuls of his faded linen shirt in her hands. Its lacings hung loosened and open at the neck, and when he pulled her closer she ended up staring at the pulse that throbbed at the base of his throat.

The heat of the fire was nothing compared to the heat that radiated from his body to hers. His hands burned on the small of her back and when he spread his fingers to actually hold her waist, the burn traveled to all her intimate places. Suddenly, Grigori was the last thing on her mind. Her nightmares were replaced by fantasies.

If she kissed the pulse of his jugular, it would be a mistake, but it would be one she chose to make.

The thought was all she needed to urge her forward. She went up on her toes. She leaned. She captured his hot, salty skin between her lips. She meant the taste to be a slight indulgence, an exercise in free will. But his fierce groan, the jerk of his entire body in response and the sudden desperate clasp of his hands caused her to open her mouth to taste him more fully and bathe his pounding pulse with a flick of her tongue.

"My God, Elena," Romanov said. His hands rose from her waist to her face, but he didn't push her away. He pressed her closer, groaning as she responded with a nip of her teeth and suction. His skin was so hot. His pulse so strong. His passionate sounds rumbled deep in his chest and vibrated against her breasts. He was wild winter wilderness, but he melted for her. He stood alone, but she held him and pleasured him and he wasn't alone anymore.

"You don't want to die. You want to live," Elena murmured against his throat.

"I crave respite," Romanov countered. His hands stopped her kisses, but he didn't push her far away. With the slightest pressure of his palms on each side of her head, he only made enough distance between them so that he could look down at her face. She opened her eyes. Her body was languid with desire. It pulsed in time with the heartbeat she'd tasted.

"That's not what you crave," Elena said. "You don't want to disappear into the Ether. You want to feel again. You want to connect."

"How can I resist? You awaken me. You refuse to keep the door locked against me," Romanov said.

"I won't be caged. I'd rather face my fears than hide from them," she replied.

"Then you admit you fear me?" he asked. His whole body stilled as if he braced for her answer.

"I think you want me to fear you. If I'm afraid, if I run away, then you can be as numb as you have to be to stay standing," Elena said. "But it isn't only my kisses that wake you. It's my cause."

"I have all the cause I'll ever need to stay standing, Elena Pavlova. I stand for my family. Not the Light *Volkhvy*. I don't stand against the Dark. I stand against the Ether that has eaten everyone I've ever loved," Romanov said. It was a hoarse confession. One that burned her eyes. "I'm not a champion. I'm a survivor. And there's a hungry wolf at my door. I fear him. As should you."

She drew in a startled breath when he swooped to claim her mouth, but her breath wasn't deep or long enough to keep her from going light-headed when his lips pressed against hers. This time he chose to kiss her. Not to relieve the torture but to intensify it. He groaned as his tongue found hers and the vibration traveled with velvet licks to the V between her legs.

Elena let go of his shirt and slid her arms up, way up, and around his neck. She appreciated his height and breadth even as she held on for dear life. Her head was light. Her knees soft. But his body was solid and hard against her. There was no interruption this time. He explored the depths of her mouth fully with practiced ease that nevertheless caused his body to shudder against hers with the pleasure he found.

His lips were gentle and sensual even though they were firm, moving hungrily to devour her every gasp. His tongue was flavored with honey and wine. The stubble on his cheek and jaw was pleasantly rough against her skin.

He held her face in place for his kiss for a long time, but when he dropped his hands to lift her shirt and find her skin she cried out into his mouth at the heightened sensation of his warrior's calloused fingers on her bare midriff.

Her cries caused him to pause, but only for a second, as if he caught himself waiting for her permission or denial, and then pressed on. She whimpered when his fingers dipped into the waistband of her pants and this time he didn't slow or stop. He jerked her forward and she found herself straddling his bent knee. He pressed her against his leg and she whimpered again because the pleasurable pressure and friction took her by surprise.

She rocked her hips to increase it and he groaned, but he also helped her move with his powerful hands cupped around her bottom. The thrusting of his tongue matched the rhythm of her hips and she felt the rise of his erection beneath his leather pants against her right thigh.

He called out her name when she reached for him to press and measure and pet the hard length of him through the leather. His heat and size and obvious pleasure caused her to rock harder against the leg she rode, and suddenly his head fell back and their lips parted. She looked down at his face and realized he had lifted her up and braced his hips against the table until she was above him.

Romanov's eyes were slits. His lips were swollen. His hair was a wild tumble around his face and shoulders. He looked passionate, disheveled and very touched. She continued to rub his hard shaft and move her hips and he watched her face as the ultimate pleasure finally claimed her. She cried out as she came. Her legs clenched around his muscular thigh. And his hands tightened on her, pulling her as close as she could get against him as she pulsed with the orgasm achieved while they were both still clothed and standing in the kitchen.

She collapsed against his broad chest and he held her there, not speaking, as time passed. The fire crackled. The dough hardened, neglected and forgotten. Distant sounds finally penetrated her consciousness once more.

"A long time ago I feared losing dance because it was all I had. I didn't know what else I would do once I couldn't dance anymore. But now I only fear Grigori. Because I'll find my way given the chance. My purpose is in me. I only have to remain free to find it," Elena said softly. While she spoke, she thought about the resolve in the woman's face on the tapestry. Her expression echoed an untapped feeling in Elena's heart. Something called to her. The discipline and dedication she'd learned in service to dance had only been preparation. There was something beckoning to her on the horizon that nearly overshadowed the dread of Grigori that permeated her past.

"Where is the sapphire sword and how do you protect it when it's not with you?" she asked. She also wondered what had become of the ruby and emerald swords, but she didn't want to talk about the loved ones he'd lost.

Romanov straightened and placed her limp body on the stool nearby. Even with the fire, she felt chilled as he moved away. This had been another mistake she would make all over again if she had the chance. But she was fairly certain Romanov wouldn't. His brow was furrowed and his fists had clenched as soon as he'd placed her to the side.

"If you call the black wolf, you'll face something darker and hungrier than your witchblood prince." Romanov stood several feet away from her. He ignored her question about the sapphire sword. He looked tall and powerful even in a simple linen shirt that had come partially undone and scuffed leather pants. He wore no armor or furs now. He wasn't armed. His strength was all in his honed muscles and large frame. Still, the determined set to his jaw and the planted placement of his riding boots would cause his stance to be intimidating to any adversary. Yet as he spoke of the wolf, his eyes were haunted, shadowed by real trepidation.

His concern was contagious. Elena's heartbeat quickened and her post-orgasm languor fled. Her body stiffened and she rose from the stool to face him.

"I'm not afraid of the dark," she said.

It was true. She wasn't afraid of darkness. Only of being trapped. Only of having her free will taken away.

But she wasn't blind. She could see that Romanov was genuinely afraid for her, and that knowledge caused gooseflesh to rise on her skin.

"Is there no chance, then, that the alpha wolf will choose to help me rather than hurt me?" she asked.

"He may have no choice. Like Lev, he may have been driven mad by his time in the Ether. He might no longer be a rational creature. He was always a beast that was almost impossible to control," Romanov said. She watched his fists clench and unclench as he spoke. With his mussed hair and fire-lit eyes, he looked nearly mad himself.

But his lips were still swollen from her kisses and her mouth still tingled pleasantly with remembered sensation of the passion they'd shared.

"You don't want me to summon the black wolf, but there are other reasons you want me to stay in the tower," Elena said. She stepped lightly toward him. He didn't back away. Because there was nowhere to go or because he secretly wanted her closer? Liked her closer? Would take her as close as possible if her quest for the wolf wasn't standing in their way?

"Every day you spend in Bronwal is potentially deadly. You court disaster every time you leave the tower," Romanov said.

"Do I court disaster by leaving the tower or by searching for the alpha wolf and finding you instead?" Elena said. She knew the answer. They had kissed. She'd experienced an earth-shattering orgasm. And yet there was so much more that could happen between them. It would be a disaster to allow the attraction between them to take them where it wanted to go. But she would choose to follow it if she could because it would be a glorious disaster she had chosen for herself after years of following a course set by others.

She'd narrowed the gap between them. He could have turned away to leave the room. He hadn't. He had watched and waited as she approached. His eyes were bright and his wild hair made her fingers twitch. But he was also simmering with a rising emotion that tasted like anger in the air. There were clouds darkening his expression, and his body appeared so tense and tight that his tendons might snap if he deigned to move an inch.

Elena, the deceptively delicate swan who was made of mercilessly trained muscle and bone rather than feathers, continued bravely until her toes stopped inches from his. She tilted her chin to meet his thunderous gaze.

"I'm lost. I can't be found," Romanov said. "You think you have found me instead of the wolf you seek, but you've found nothing. No one. A castle full of ghosts."

"It wasn't a ghost that pleasured my body moments ago," Elena said. She didn't reach for him. She wouldn't force herself on him. But there was more to his resistance than fear for her safety. He protected Bronwal, but he also protected himself. He'd lost too much to care again.

Her body trembled at his nearness. She vibrated with need. His body must do the same. That's why he held himself so still and tight. Because the pull between them was elemental and fierce.

"We're snowed in. Trapped together. But the *Volkhvy* Gathering comes closer every day," Romanov said.

"I will find the alpha wolf before the Gathering," Elena warned him. "And I will either be devoured or I will gain his trust."

"Trust moldered to dust in this place many years ago," Romanov replied. "Lev and Soren guard the last blade. They will sound the alarm if Dark *Volkhvy* appear. The other blades disappeared into the Ether and never returned. It's best you forget they ever existed. In time, the sapphire blade will disappear, as well."

Romanov finally broke away from the invisible magnetism that seemed to hold them together. He walked around her to the counter, picked up the remainder of a loaf of bread, then strode out the door without another word. Elena more slowly and thoughtfully followed suit. The bread was cooled, but still delicious, and she needed to keep herself fueled.

Imaging the sapphire blade winking out of existence caused her insides to hollow in spite of the bread she consumed. She wasn't sure why. But she had an instinct that the blade must remain in Bronwal in order for Romanov to survive. The blade was a part of the puzzle here. One she was determined to solve. One she was compelled to solve the same way she'd been compelled by the legends from the time she'd first heard her grandmother's tales.

Maybe the blade could help her against Grigori whether or not she was able to summon the alpha wolf.

Lev and Soren guard the last blade.

The last bite of bread she chewed was hard to swallow past the sudden lump of fear that closed her throat. She would have to face the red wolf…and the white in order to approach the sapphire sword again. And she wouldn't be able to stay away. Suddenly, she was certain that all her questions would be answered if she could hold the sapphire sword one more time.

For the few seconds she'd held the blade in her hands, she'd felt something in the cool wash of adrenaline that had flooded her veins. She'd heard something in her pounding heart. Then she'd fallen backward and the blade had slipped from her fingers and the feeling was gone.

But the memory of it remained.

And she'd seen the echo of it in the eyes of the woman on the tapestry in the baby's room.

* * *

He had failed to resist their connection. In fact, he'd done the opposite. He'd gloried in her passion. He'd soaked up every noise, every reaction—from the salty perspiration on her upper lip to the powerful thrust of her petite hips. He'd helped her achieve a shuddering climax, and the surprisingly supple bottom he'd kneaded while she clenched and came had almost sent him over the edge himself. Not to mention the heat of her against his leg and the curiosity of her fingers as she'd measured him through his pants.

It had been heaven and hell.

Heaven because her taste and touch had enflamed him faster and hotter than anyone before. Hell because he'd wanted to tear off her clothes and taste more than her lips. He'd wanted to feel her heat intimately with nothing in the way. He still did. His imagination had been given more fuel to work with and it had already been torturing him, day and night.

He was hard and ready. His mind filled with images of her spread beneath him. She would open. She would be slick with passion. She'd already shown him her hunger. He wanted to stoke her pleasure higher than he'd been able to with only the pressure of his thigh. He wanted to play her with his hand. He wanted to lick and tease until she begged him to join with her.

He'd watched her orgasm, but he'd never seen her bare breasts.

With her blond hair, blue eyes and porcelain skin, he could picture rosy nipples to match her rosy lips. He ached to see and suckle them. He was in a frenzy to explore for other rosy treasures, as well.

He went for the practice field. There was nothing else he could do.

Nothing short of a full-on shift would scare her in the face of her determination, but how could he loose the wolf when what he wanted most was to be a man in her arms? How could he purposefully frighten a woman who was obviously drawn to the sapphire blade?

Because, in the end, he would have no choice. She had to leave for the good of Bronwal and for her own good. He couldn't allow her to bond with the blade. He'd have to risk a shift to scare her away. She thought she wanted to find the black wolf, but once she saw him she would change her mind.

The enchanted monster inside of his soul howled with glee at the idea of freedom. He hadn't run beneath the light of the moon on four massive paws in decades. Since long before he'd seen the last glimpse of Soren's human face. His desire for Elena wasn't helping. It only made him feel more desperate to make her leave before he lost control. If she didn't want him in return, he could more easily ignore his need to claim her. But her obvious hunger for his touch shook him to the core.

Only he could guarantee that she made the right decision. She couldn't be allowed near the sword again. Of that, he was certain. Beyond that, if marauding *Volkhvy* and Lev weren't enough to force her away, he would have to take matters into his own hands.

Elena had come to Bronwal to seek help from the alpha wolf. But it was the alpha howling inside of his chest that had to frighten her away.

Chapter 8

Elena knew it was crazy. She should make sure to stay as far away from Lev as possible. It was madness to go looking for the red and white wolves in order to find the sapphire sword. The power in the gem wasn't hers to tap. It would probably be no more useful than an ordinary blade against Grigori. But even though logic told her it was silly to seek out the sword, her heart told her otherwise. When she'd been in the courtyard with the blade, she'd felt as if she'd found everything she'd been looking for, even though the black wolf hadn't been there.

She still hoped to find the alpha wolf. She hoped he would become her champion against the Dark *Volkhvy* who stalked her. But she couldn't stop thinking about the woman in the tapestry. She'd held the ruby sword as if she needed no other champion but herself.

It was only an hour before sunset. The castle was darkening by the second. She wasn't sure where Romanov had gone after their time in the kitchen. She had let him walk away. His resistance made her passionate capitulation more embarrassing. She had held nothing back in her response to his touch. She had been decadent in the way she had ridden his powerful thigh to take her pleasure.

What was worse, she still wanted more.

The idea of his bare, hot skin between her naked legs caused her breath to hitch and her sensual abandon to seem like a permanent result of her time here in Bronwal. God, he was so powerful and he maintained such control. Even while she was crying out with release, he was watching and holding and helping her reach the peak. He had denied himself surcease. And it had tortured her because she wanted him to give in to the pleasure she could give him, as well.

Her imagination could well envision his powerful body completely naked and shuddering beneath her touch. She had tasted the skin of his neck. She wanted to taste more. She wanted to trace every inch of him with her tongue and watch as he lost all control.

For her.

But what frightened her most was that part of her desire was hinged on the idea of waking him and bringing him back to life. He so obviously didn't want to wake. He was determined to resist the attraction between them and she was bound for disappointment.

She'd gone back to her room for the daggers she'd taken from the practice field. They were tucked in the back pockets of her jeans. She couldn't imagine using them, but she would if she had to. Against the white wolf or against one of the shuffling souls in the dark hallways of the castle, if either tried to harm her. She would defend herself. Elena reached to reassure herself that the hilts were within easy reach again and again. The daggers reassured her, but they didn't call to her in the same way that the sapphire blade called.

More than her fight against Grigori had brought her here. Hadn't she always been fascinated with the Romanov legend? She'd begged for the stories again and again. She'd been obsessed with the book long before she'd known she was in danger.

The key to the tower room hung around the chain on her neck. There was a hideaway available to her. She could duck her head in the sand. She could lock herself away. But that would solve nothing. It would be a temporary redoubt. Nothing more. She had to move. She had to strive for answers.

She couldn't ignore the sword. It called to her with a subtle song. One of enchantment, but also one of discipline and determination. She came to the main hall where Romanov had first carried her. This time the massive fireplace was lit. Shadows danced on the walls cast by the leaping flames.

The woman in the tapestry had been a warrior, but Elena had recognized the expression on her face and the passion in her eyes. She'd had the face of a prima ballerina. Her own face carried that look. She'd seen it reflected in the other dancers in her troupe. What were they if not warriors? They were graceful, but hardened. They faced a battle against fatigue and weakness and age every day. They fought against every soft, human failing and mercilessly trained it away.

The white wolf rose to his feet when she came into the room. His movement drew her eyes from the shadows on the wall. The red wolf was there, as well. He was already standing. Beside him, the sapphire blade rested across the arms of a throne. A larger throne stood beside it. They were carved from some massive, dark wood streaked even darker with generations of soot. She hadn't noticed the thrones when the hall had been unlit by firelight before. They were in a raised, recessed alcove that had been black as midnight the evening she'd arrived. Now, the firelight revealed the sword and the thrones and painted them all with shifting darkness that highlighted rather than concealed.

The thrones were as empty as the rest of the castle. And yet they weren't abandoned. The wolves stood watch, and as Elena stepped cautiously forward the details carved into the wood of the thrones became clear: wolves. There were wolf heads carved on the arms of the larger chair and on the back of the smaller one. Three wolf carvings in all. Their mouths were open wide, and each tooth had been painstakingly crafted, along with each strand of hair in the pelts on their heads.

The red wolf and the white wolf watched her approach.

The sword was on the smaller throne. The wolf head carved on its back was the largest of the three. The alpha wolf watched over the smaller throne and the sword. Elena didn't know what that meant. The head wasn't carved as a lifeless trophy. It was snarling and vital. Ready to defend and protect?

"In wood the alpha wolf helps you protect the sword. Where is he in life? Surely he hasn't faded away," Elena said.

The red wolf moved when she spoke. The white wolf stood planted in place, but his haunches trembled. Soren paced in front of Lev. He put his body in between his white companion and Elena.

The problem was that both wolves were in between her and the Romanov blade.

Now that she'd seen it, she was even more certain

that it had called her here. It wasn't the wolves that made her heart pound and a thrill like anticipation suffuse her skin. But she needed to hold the sapphire blade again to be sure. She needed to claim it. The tableau of empty thrones and waiting sword and protective wolves wasn't in her book of legends. Her grandmother had never mentioned the swords. Or the thrones. Yet Elena took another step forward. And then another.

This was a part of the legend she felt rather than remembered.

Somehow this was her part, even though she was a modern woman visiting a castle kept separate from the passage of time. She was no mere visitor. She'd been called. And the call had begun many years ago when she was a young girl listening to stories on her grandmother's knee.

"I'm here because I'm meant to be," she said. Her voice was soft but firm. It echoed in the cavernous room, but it wasn't swallowed or weakened. It was magnified. Lev whined and Soren blinked. Neither moved out of her way.

The daggers in her back pockets were there should she need them. She was pretty sure they wouldn't faze the giant wolves that protected the thrones. Even if she knew how to wield them.

"I came here for help, but I'm beginning to think that you're the ones who need my help instead. You're losing this battle. You've almost lost him. He's more than ready to fade away. It seems as if the alpha wolf is already gone," Elena said. "Let me have the sword. I won't take it away from Bronwal. I'll use it against Grigori. I'll use it to help you stand."

Soren listened to her every word. She was sure of it. He met her eyes. He blinked. And then he pressed back against the white wolf's trembling body. Lev allowed himself to be pushed out of the way. He stepped back, pace after measured pace, until she had a clear path to the sapphire blade.

"It isn't my imagination, is it? I need the sword. And you need me to have it," Elena said. "I've been distracted by my search for the black wolf. This is what I was meant to find all along."

She moved carefully closer to the thrones. She made no sudden gestures. She placed her feet softly on the floor. She kept her eyes on the sapphire. It winked darkly in the shadows of flames. Lev whined when she passed, but Soren stood, stalwart, in his white companion's way. Elena was terrified, but she didn't pause. It shouldn't be easy to claim the blade. This was a test for her to pass in order to prove she was worthy of wielding the enchanted sword.

She should have known that *Volkhvy* enchantments were more complicated than a human could understand. Slavic peasants had practiced simple hearth magic for centuries. But royal craftsman had carved the thrones for the Light *Volkhvy*'s champions, and Vasilisa herself had conjured the blades and enchanted the stones.

Elena might have felt the call of the sapphire blade since she was a child, but only the alpha wolf could approve or disapprove of her quest.

The rumble began in the soles of her shoes. It radiated upward through muscle and bone. It vibrated her chest until it rose to her ears and she finally heard the audible sound that had begun as a resonate, deep-chested hum.

The growl caused all the blood to flow from her face and arms, leaving them numb. It seemed every drop of life-giving fluid settled in her stomach, where a heavy knot formed as the first growl rolled into another without ceasing.

The light from the giant fireplace and the leaping flames were no longer the only shadows. A hulking darkness fell over her and the wolves. It climbed up and up to paint the entire wall. The darkness coalesced into a shape that engulfed the entire throne alcove.

As she tried to remember how to breathe, the shape became the black-as-midnight shadow of a wolf. The alpha wolf. Materialized out of the Ether to eat her alive. Or so it seemed in those seconds that she tried to remember why Grigori had seemed like any sort of threat at all.

Soren and Lev tucked their tails and retreated behind the thrones. Elena shook and shivered and tried to straighten out the signals from her brain that were alternately telling her to run, faint and stand as still as stone. When she saw the previously ferocious muzzles of the red and white wolves show up beneath the thrones, she was finally able to move.

She turned to face the black wolf.

He wasn't her alpha. She wouldn't cower and quake. If she died, she would die with daggers in her hands. They were there, suddenly, even though she had no memory of drawing them from her pockets. And they were steady in her palms. Her tremble was gone.

If Soren and Lev were as large as ponies, the alpha was as big as a draft horse. The doorway into the hall was an arched one, double and grand, and the powerful shoulders of his black body filled it. He stood with paws planted and his teeth showing sharp and white against the black snarl of his muzzle. Had she caused him to materialize from the Ether because she'd come for the sword? Perhaps his instinct to champion had left him, but his protective instincts were more powerful.

"I came for you, but I found the sword. You don't have to help me against the witchblood prince, but I must wield one of the Romanov blades. I feel the sapphire's call. Surely, as its protector, you recognize that?" Elena reasoned. "The woman in the tapestry wielded the ruby blade. I'm not trying to steal this sword or take it away. I'll use it against Grigori, but it will also be in defense of Bronwal. I promise."

She didn't cry. She didn't run away. She reasoned with a monster. And he listened to every word. Like Soren, he was more aware than an ordinary beast. Hope flared in her breast. The knot in her stomach eased. The daggers in her hands dipped down, and she almost sheathed them back in her hip pockets.

Except, unlike the red wolf, the black wolf's teeth were still bared against her. He stepped forward, not from animal instinct and rage, but for clearheaded, rational reasons she couldn't understand. Who could interpret a beast's reasons for determining enemy or friend? She'd tried. He might understand her words, but he refused to bow to the sapphire's call.

Her knees softened as fear reclaimed her.

Romanov had warned her that the black wolf was deadly. Her hope might have sealed her fate. But there was still one last chance she could grab— The sapphire stone had flared. She'd seen it from the corner of her eye. Even the black wolf had turned his face toward the vivid blue flash. It hadn't been firelight. The flame's glow was completely shadowed by the alpha wolf's body. *The stone had lit from within, in the same moment that she'd promised to defend the castle.*

The flash hadn't soothed the black wolf. In fact, it seemed to be the sudden light in the sapphire stone that had set his paws in stalking motion. He paced toward her and one of the wolves under the thrones whined. Soren or Lev? In sympathy or in anticipation?

"You won't kill a woman the sword has chosen," Elena said. But she had no idea if her supposition was correct. How long had the alpha been hidden in the Ether? And what did he care about an enchanted sword's preferences?

There was nowhere to run. Nowhere to hide. Even if she'd wanted to flee to the tower, the black wolf's powerful legs would catch her before she made it out of the room. From the corner of her eye, she saw the red wolf wiggle out from under the chair. He stood staring at her and the alpha wolf as if he wasn't certain what he should do. But when Lev also came out of hiding and aggressively tried to move her way as if he would stalk her too, Soren stopped him. The red wolf knocked the white wolf to the floor and placed one paw on his neck to keep him supine.

She'd been distracted. When she turned her full attention back to the black wolf, he was only a few feet away. She started, but she didn't back away. She stood her ground, a tiny, ineffectual dagger in each hand. The alpha wolf stepped closer and closer until his nose was above her head and between the small blades she clenched in her fists. She could do damage with them if he decided to attack. She could hurt him before she died. But the daggers wouldn't defeat him. At best, they would buy her seconds of time. As she tilted her chin to look into his emerald eyes, her hands were stilled by what she saw there. Intensity burned bright in the gem-like gleam of his irises.

It was an intensity she'd seen before.

"Romanov?" she whispered. Her fingers went limp and the daggers clattered to the floor. The black wolf flinched for all his size and strength. But he didn't lash out. He didn't growl or bite.

Ivan Romanov wasn't the master. He was the wolf. Her search had been over as soon as he'd materialized in front of her on the snowy mountain pass. Answers to so many of her questions suddenly crystalized in her mind.

"You've been in front of me all along. What haven't you told me?" Elena asked. In spite of the deadly teeth, she reached to touch the bottom of his jaw. She cupped his monstrous face in the palm of her hand. Her book of legends had shown her the Romanovs and their wolves. She hadn't understood. *The Romanov brothers are the Romanov wolves.* The russet, the white and the black.

The alpha wolf was stiff with emotion. He didn't relax into her hand. How could he? She had woken him. She had disturbed him from the deep sleep in which Ivan Romanov had buried him in order to maintain his stand as the last Romanov. His brothers were gone, but not permanently into the Ether as she'd supposed. They had shifted and either they had chosen to stay in their wolf forms…or they had been trapped in them unable to return as men.

Soren whined again and Elena looked toward the red wolf. Suddenly, she understood Bell better than she had before. The other woman longed to see Soren's *human* face. The clothes in the trunk and the hat Bell always wore…had they been Soren's long ago? He still had more understanding than an animal would have. He still remembered the man. Lev had forgotten. Would Soren forget eventually too? And now that Romanov had shifted to let the alpha wolf free, would he lose himself too?

"What have I done?" Elena said.

More pieces of the puzzle came together in a painful picture in her mind. Lev, the white wolf, had also been a man. The tragedy she'd stumbled upon in the baby's room became clear. Romanov had said he wasn't a pet. He'd never been a pet. But the family who'd lived in the room had been *his*.

Hot tears filled Elena's eyes.

"Why didn't you tell me?" she asked.

She looked back at Romanov, the alpha wolf, and found him staring beyond her head. Not at his brothers. His focus was on the thrones. She followed his gaze to find that it fell on the gleam of the sapphire stone.

"Lev's wife wielded the ruby Romanov blade," Elena whispered.

Romanov had shifted to keep her from the stone.

Sympathy had hollowed her gut, but pain caused it to tighten as if she'd been stabbed. Cold ache suddenly burned away and in its place came a sharp stabbing heat. He was here to protect the blade from her. He didn't think she was worthy of it.

She lowered her hand and clenched her fist. It took every ounce of her strength not to use it to strike him. To share the pain that tore her apart.

"You don't have to want me. Or accept the blade's decision. But I won't be frightened away. Don't you know that by now? The blade knows. I'm a warrior. Whether you fight by my side or not," Elena said.

Before any of the wolves could react to her decision, Elena pirouetted. She used her good leg to hold her weight and it spun her as it always had, tried and true. Then she ran and leaped for the dais, even though there were no strong arms there to catch her. She landed gracefully in spite of the pain in her injured knee. And she reached for the blade. None of the wolves tried to stop her. In part because Soren still stood on Lev's neck, holding him down.

Her hand closed around the hilt of the Romanov blade

and the sapphire flared once more. A vision of another woman filled her mind. She recognized Romanov's mother from the portrait in the hall. Vladimir Romanov hadn't only betrayed the Light *Volkhvy* queen. He'd betrayed the memory of a woman who had pledged to protect Bronwal by his side when he'd betrayed her queen. Elena clenched her teeth as she felt a glimmer of what the other woman must have felt. Maybe it was better to be rejected before you fell in love, not after.

She turned with the blade in both hands. She'd never been trained, but it seemed more comfortable in her grasp than it should, as if it had been made for her. She would learn how to wield it even if Romanov didn't approve.

The alpha wolf stood in front of her. Raised on the dais, she was able to meet his eyes. From her better position, she could see the midnight shine of his wild black fur and the epic proportions of his shoulders. There was no doubt that he was Ivan Romanov. The tale had finally pieced together in her mind from the legend and everything she'd learned since she'd come to Bronwal.

Her spine tingled with the impossibility of a man being able to become a beast, but she couldn't unsee what she'd seen in the black wolf's eyes. She'd climbed a mountain to find a legendary castle and this wolf. She thought she'd found his master, but he'd been here, hidden before her very eyes, all along. She held the sword up between them, but she could have easily been pledging her loyalty to him and his cause rather than taking a defensive posture. Her heart pulled her in both directions.

As she'd told Soren, the Romanovs needed her. The sword had somehow known it. It had called her across time and great distance. Now that it was in her hands, she wouldn't let it go. Not only because she felt safer than she'd ever felt, more ready to take on her evil magical stalker, but also because the pale blue glow of the sword's gem seemed to illuminate a path she'd been looking for.

"I've always longed to be more than a dancer. That's why the book of legends called to me even before I heard the sword. Let me help you. The sword has spoken. See how it fits in my hands? Help me to learn how to use it. Let's stand together against Grigori and the Dark *Volkhvy.* After the Gathering, I'll leave. I'll walk away. I'll let you and the sword vanish back into the Ether without me if that's what you want. But, for now, teach me how to fight," Elena said.

Soren whined again. Lev had gone limp. He panted on the floor beneath his brother's paw from his exertions to get free. Did the red wolf think he would have to rescue her from the alpha too? It would be pointless for him to try to intercede. If the black wolf decided to attack her, his much smaller brother wouldn't be able to prevent it.

But the eyes she gazed into weren't an animal's eyes. Ivan Romanov had risked the shift, but his beast hadn't swallowed him whole yet. There was a man's reasoning and a man's soul in the black wolf's giant body. Elena faced him and waited for him to decide if he would flee or teach her to fight. Because that was his choice. He could give up and let the black wolf's savage nature take over, or he could accept her as the warrior called to carry the sapphire blade.

She refused to believe that Romanov, even in his black wolf form, would attack her and try to drive her away if he was still in control. So she stood. She waited. She held tightly to the hilt of a blade she hadn't been trained to use. And she prayed she wouldn't have to try to kill the man she'd kissed only hours before.

Chapter 9

The standoff seemed to last for hours. Elena's arms protested the weight of the blade. For all her fitness, the particular muscles needed to brandish a sword hadn't been developed. Sweat dampened the waves of hair on her forehead, and her lower back screamed. Finally, because she had to, she made a decision. If he attacked, she would die before she had to admit she'd been wrong.

Elena lowered the sword. She released it with one hand and used the other to deliberately place its point on the floor beside her. The black wolf trembled in reaction to her movement. His entire body was stiff with tension, but he vibrated with energy as if one wrong move would cause him to leap. She lifted her free hand anyway. She placed it on the side of Romanov's great wolf head.

She wasn't sure if it was her shivering or the alpha wolf's she felt.

"You won't attack me. Not as long as you're in control," Elena said. The black wolf blinked, but he continued to shudder beneath her hands. Was that Romanov seeking to maintain control? Or was it Romanov trying to let go? Standing her ground and reaching out to the alpha wolf was the bravest thing she'd done. It was also the most dangerous. She'd seen the fatigue in Romanov's spirit. She'd seen all of his loss and pain. She had to trust that he would continue to stand and fight even though she had seen so much evidence that he should choose the contrary.

The black wolf rumbled low in his chest. Her body jerked in response and the tip of her sword came off the ground. But it wasn't a growl. It was vocalized pain. The great beast backed away from her touch. The rumble built and built until once again she felt it in the soles of her feet, but when the alpha wolf threw back his mighty head and released the sound in his massive chest as a ululating howl, it was that devastating call that shuddered her bones.

She had magnified Romanov's pain.

She couldn't undo it. She couldn't drop the sword or retreat back down the mountain. Not without giving up her freedom and the newfound sense that her purpose was here. As a dancer, she'd had to learn to press through the pain, to push past it. Romanov had been nearly consumed by it for too long. Maybe it was time for him to face it down.

"Come back to us, Ivan Romanov," Elena urged as the howl trailed off to nothing. The black wolf's nose came back down and he looked at her from where he'd retreated across the room. "Come back to us and help us fight."

Soren and Lev had howled along with the alpha. Their smaller voices had joined with him in expressing grief and frustration. Lev had leaped to his feet and Soren had allowed it, but the white wolf didn't attack her. He followed the example of his alpha wolf.

"I want to be ready when Grigori comes," Elena said. "I thought it was the wolf I sought, but I was wrong. It was the blade…and the man who can train me in how to use it."

The black wolf whirled around and ran away with powerful strides. Lev yelped and followed after. Soren stopped to look at her for several seconds before he followed his wilder brother.

She was left alone.

The Romanov blade easily took her weight when she leaned against it. Her legs suddenly felt insubstantial as if all her muscle had turned to smoke beneath her skin. She'd faced down an enchanted creature who might have eaten her in several gulps. Her head had told her to run, but her heart had told her to stand her ground.

She still wasn't certain which had been right.

She might have seen the last of the wolf and the man. They might disappear into the Ether and leave her to face Grigori alone.

As the legendary black wolf, Romanov ran through the snow. His great paws churned icy clouds into the air, and as they fell down all around him he was dusted with a fine coating of white. It glistened as the sun rose, dazzling his eyes. The airborne ice particles stung his nose and weighted his lashes.

Still, he ran.

Soren and Lev howled behind him. The hunt was on. There was a stag. Its blood pumped, warmed by the chase. It would have been natural to run the prey down. To take its life to fuel his own and that of his pack.

But something told him he'd better hold on to more of his humanity than that.

His hold was tenuous.

There was a powerful thrill in the idea of letting go to become a simple-minded animal driven by instinct. He wouldn't. He couldn't. But this time he wanted to more than ever before. No wonder Lev had escaped into the white wolf form when his family had disappeared into the Ether. Romanov understood that decision better than he ever had.

He crested a rise and looked down at the stag as it raced desperately across a clearing between patches of evergreen below. It was difficult, but he reined in his instincts and he let the animal reach the opposite side. It paused, as if startled by the possibility it could escape the giant, hungry wolf. Its head lifted, and white billows of respiration puffed from its flared nostrils. Its sides heaved and it stomped one of its front legs. It dared to try to warn him away?

That defiance was almost his undoing. The alpha wolf tried to wrest control from the shreds of his humanity. It almost succeeded. But then the stag must have scented his hunger on the cold breeze because it startled and turned to plunge into the woods.

He let it go.

Soren and Lev caught up with him. Even Lev respected his pause on the ridge top. His brothers didn't race around him as they once would have to nip submissively at his chin and heels. He hadn't been the alpha around them in a very long time. They were afraid. Both crouched at a distance. Watching and waiting to see what he would do.

Back at the castle, there was someone else waiting for him to choose, as if his choice hadn't been made the moment she'd materialized out of the snowstorm on the pass. The sword had known. For how long? How powerful was Vasilisa's magic? Could it really have found his intended mate across so many decades and miles? Or was this another cruel aspect of the punishment she'd leveled against the Romanov family?

Loss and love. Love and loss. The cycle seemed as endless as the Cycle of the curse.

He wouldn't accept the sword's decision. He wouldn't court the same devastation Lev had faced. He wouldn't ensnare Elena in the Romanov curse. But he would reclaim his human form. He would honor her decision to wield the blade. That much he could do without risk. He could help her learn to defend herself against Grigori now that the sword had chosen.

The Gathering approached, as did the Ether.

He didn't have much time to ensure that her stalker wouldn't enslave Elena before he and the sapphire blade disappeared. The risk wasn't in the blade, because he would die rather than bind her to the Romanov curse. The risk was entirely in the shift.

Because he would give in to the wolf rather than allow her to suffer for the witchblood prince's pleasure. He would save her from the Ether and from Grigori even if it meant all else was lost.

Chapter 10

Elena had to improvise a gym. She'd discovered in her standoff with the black wolf that her arms needed strengthening. Her searches throughout the castle hadn't led her to any modern amenities when it came to weight-lifting, but she remembered the training courtyard and the equipment there.

She might not have weights, but she knew how to use them, and there was a whole rack full of heavy training staffs carved from oak.

She'd go insane if she waited for Romanov to return even if she didn't fret over how he'd return, as man or wolf. He'd been gone an entire day and night. Instead of useless worrying, she swallowed her discomfort over pilfering for clothes appropriate for the training courtyard. She passed over numerous wardrobes full of dresses until she found a long-sleeve tunic to shield her from the cold mountain air. She paired serviceable fur-lined boots with her own jeggings. She did take a long red cloak from a trunk that she knew had been meant for a formal occasion. It was lined with black velvet and embroidered along the edges of its hood and hem with thorns and roses. It was a cold day and she didn't want to try to transport the equipment to an indoor location.

She thought it was a good decision when she stepped out into the sunshine, but once she'd chosen a hefty staff that seemed the appropriate weight to begin to build her strength, her exertion and repetitions didn't fill the courtyard as Romanov had filled it.

At one time this place had been filled with soldiers.

Elena looked around. Snow had covered much of the ground, but she could see the depressions in the dirt where Romanov and others had performed the repetitive movements necessary to build muscle and skill, dexterity and endurance.

She'd been backstage alone before. She'd been in empty halls with deserted dressing rooms. Practice studios were always a little echoing and haunted. But they filled again. Dancers and want-to-be dancers returned. Instructors and music would come. They always came. In a perpetual rhythm of practice and performance.

This was different.

The people who had trained here would never be back.

Even Romanov might be irrevocably lost.

The idea tightened her throat and dried her mouth. The area behind her eyes burned with unshed emotion. How could she care so much about a man she'd just met? The answer was in the legend. She'd always cared, but more than that…he mattered. His story mattered. His tragedy, his pain, his cause. Even if she accepted that she would never be more to him than what she was now, it mattered if the man was lost.

The heart that beat in his chest was Bronwal's heart. Even if it would never be hers.

"I return only to find Little Red Riding Hood in place of the swan," Romanov said.

Elena lowered the staff she'd been lifting like a hand weight with one outstretched arm. Its tip disappeared in the snow, but then it hit solid ground and it held, straight and tall. She gripped it with white knuckles, relieved that she had support to keep her from buckling in relief. Part of her had thought she'd never see him again. Another part had assumed the wolf would return rather than the man.

"I had to borrow some clothes. I packed too lightly. I'm not sure I really believed I'd find you here," she replied. She didn't tell him she'd had to have the cloak when she found it because it seemed fitting to have a red hood when surrounded by wolves. And then there had also been the thorns and roses, very like the ones on the tower door and its key. The cloak seemed to have been left for her, even though she knew that wasn't possible.

"You're welcome to it. And whatever else you need. No one will miss anything you take. They're past the point of caring," Romanov said.

He'd shifted from wolf form, but his hair was windblown and damp. His cheeks were flushed with cold and exertion. His clothes were much like the ones he'd worn when they'd first met. Leather pants. Tall riding boots. A long-sleeve linen shirt covered in a leather jerkin and topped with a fur-lined cloak. The fur cape on the cloak capped his shoulders and made him appear even larger than he was.

He was untouched by this century.

But even though he seemed a savage warrior she knew now that his touch was gentle and his kisses were seductively passionate, with a mix of hard and soft that she'd easily come to crave.

"We have two weeks before the *Volkhvy* begin to arrive. Both Dark and Light will come. Are you certain you want to wield the Romanov blade against them? If you do, they will try to kill you. You'll have more than Grigori as your enemy," Romanov said.

"From where I stand I see no difference between the Dark and the Light. They both torture. They both kill. I'll gladly stand. If you'll teach me how," Elena said.

"It isn't the standing I'll need to teach you. You stand on your own. I'll simply show you swordsmanship. I'll show you how to use the blade. I see that you're trying to strengthen your arms. You're already fit. We'll only enhance what's there," Romanov said.

"You're going to help me?" Elena asked.

"We'll help each other and then I'll be gone. Do you understand? The Ether will take me and the Romanov blade. No matter what damage we do to the *Volkhvy*. The curse cannot be broken. I will disappear," Romanov said. "Alone."

She gripped the staff tighter. He'd already rejected her. This was simply a reiteration. One that cut her, but she wouldn't allow the pain to consume her. There wasn't enough time.

"Agreed," Elena said softly. She braced her spine and jerked the staff up from the ground. She tossed it to him and turned to grab another. She would train, tirelessly. She would fight with all her heart because it wasn't wanted elsewhere. And once Grigori was defeated, she would leave this place stronger and wiser than she'd been before.

The sword had proclaimed her a warrior. If she had to let it disappear into the Ether, she would still be the person it had called. That knowledge gave her a purpose she'd never known before. The dance had always been something she did. It hadn't fit in her heart, only in her muscles and her mind. The sword seemed different. It fit with all of her, in and out. Where it led her after Bronwal would be up to her own feet and free will.

That she would never forget Ivan Romanov was a given. She would simply have to survive losing him the way she'd survived other losses.

The courtyard would never seem empty to her again. For an entire week, she and Romanov filled it with sweat and blood. Her tears, as usual, were stored up for nightmares that never came. When she finally collapsed at night, there was only the sleep of exhaustion.

It was more brutal than any training she'd endured. But her body responded like the fine-honed tool that it was. Oh, she had to resort to the neoprene sleeve to support her injured knee, but in every other particular she grew stronger. She was athletic and graceful. As a dancer, she was an expert in copying motion, in replicating genius. And her instructor in this was brilliant as only time and enchantment could make.

There was pain. In varying ways. Physical pain from overexertion and constant demand. Emotional pain from Romanov's touch and his constant nearness paired with his continued rejection.

He pressed close behind her to position her arms and legs and hips in the appropriate offensive stance. His wild wintry scent engulfed her. Heat radiated from their bodies to mingle in the cold air around them in an aura just shy of steam. She held her breath. He continued explaining what she should do to disarm an opponent as if there was no attraction vibrating between them.

It was torturous. But it was a sweet torture she grew to anticipate every morning.

Her cloak's hem grew stained. The muscles she used to dodge and parry and block grew harder and stronger. Her endurance increased from what had already been prodigious levels.

The training became a dance between them. His touch on her, professional and impersonal. Her response in perfect symmetry with his instruction. In spite of his large frame and solid build, he was incredibly graceful. The power in his muscles enabled him to easily move—to spin, to lift, to turn, to hold.

Oh, the holding.

Even as she became certain that she could stab the Romanov blade into Grigori's heart without hesitation, she soaked up the pleasure she felt from Romanov's touch. If she survived, the memory would have to last her for the rest of her life. She wouldn't be welcome back in ten years' time, and she wouldn't be able to handle it if she came back to find him forever gone.

"You aren't concentrating," he said. And he was right. At least in so far as he knew. She had allowed herself to become lost in sensation rather than follow-through on the expected deflection.

She would have been dead if he hadn't halted his own strike by dropping his sword on the ground. Instead of a strike, he jerked her forward with a ferocious hold on both of her wrists. They stood face-to-face with arms above their heads and their bodies pressed together.

They'd been breathing heavily from exertion. The friction of her breasts sliding against his chest caused her breath to catch. But holding her breath wasn't enough to stop the electricity that arched between them.

And, this time, Romanov didn't fool her.

He was affected too.

She tilted her chin and met his hooded eyes. He searched her gaze and his eyes widened when he noted her desire was barely held in check. The hands on her wrists eased. His attention fell to her lips as she moistened them with a dart of her tongue.

"It doesn't matter what our bodies want," Romanov said quietly. His voice vibrated against her, deep and low. "The Ether can't have you. I won't let it happen."

"You think if you kiss me, I'll be drawn into the curse? You've kissed me before. What harm is there in another?" Elena asked. She knew the harm for herself. That she'd become even more hopelessly addicted to a man she could never have.

"You're assuming I could stop with kisses," Romanov said. "That's no longer true. If I kiss you again, we'll go further than we can go and still maintain your freedom."

It was true in more ways than he understood. It would be hard, even now, for her to ever be free of his impact on her life. Having free will and being free from entanglements were not the same.

"And now you've ensured that I want your kiss more than before," Elena said.

He jerked. His whole body was tense and hot against her. But then he held more still than she thought possible. A hair couldn't have floated between them, but he held his position. Not coming closer or moving away. Then his eyes closed and he breathed in, long and deep. And she knew what he was doing because she'd been doing the same thing all week. He was soaking up the sensation of her body trembling in his arms. He was trying to feel all that he could allow himself to feel.

No more. But no less either.

She trembled because *this* with Romanov shook her

more than actual lovemaking had with another man. Perhaps it was best if they couldn't consummate their relationship. Standing with her arms held high and their bodies barely touching slayed her senses and her emotions. Especially when she watched him take what pleasure he could take in it. Actual intercourse with this man might destroy her.

A cacophony of angry barks sounded from inside the castle.

They'd been training with practice swords. The sapphire blade was in the throne room guarded by Lev and Soren.

"I hoped the burgeoning power in the stone might warn them away," Romanov said. He let go of her hands and turned toward the castle. He left the practice sword on the ground. Instead, he walked purposefully to the entryway and reached for a much sharper blade kept on a rack sheltered from the elements just inside the door.

Elena lowered her arms and followed. She still kept the daggers in her hip pockets, but she didn't pause for another weapon. The sapphire sword waited for her. She would use the very thing they sought to steal against the invaders who had infiltrated the throne room and disturbed the wolves.

Lev and Soren continued to bark, but now their alarmed noises were interspersed with sounds of fighting—snarls and growls and the occasional high-pitched yelp. At the sound of the first yelp, Romanov picked up speed and Elena followed suit.

They ran into the throne room, side by side, their movements already coordinated by their time spent training together.

There were two men and one woman in the throne room. They were wearing modern tactical gear, but they fought with their bare hands—the greenish glow of power emanating from their fingers seemed to be their only weapon. As the woman held Lev away from her throat, the green light flared and the white wolf fell back as if he'd been shocked by an electrical charge.

"The waking sapphire has called more powerful *Volkhvy*, Elena. Be careful," Romanov warned. He waded into the battle his red brother was waging against the two men. Soren still had cagey human intelligence at his disposal. He hadn't attacked blindly. He led the two male *Volkhvy* away from the thrones so Elena could get to the sword. But Lev was already back on his feet. Human intelligence or not, he was an enchanted wolf created by the Light *Volkhvy* queen to fight this enemy.

The female intruder cried out when the white wolf leaped on her back and drove her to the floor before she could steal her prize. Elena leaped over their writhing figures. She needed to claim the sword for herself before the *Volkhvy* managed to get to the blade. But as she leaped, her injured knee didn't bring the foot on that leg far enough up and away from the woman's glowing fingers. The Dark *Volkhvy* grabbed her ankle and pulled her down.

She barely managed to catch herself with outstretched arms before she landed hard. Breath was forced from her lungs as the marble ground suddenly compressed her abdomen. Yet it wasn't the struggle to breathe that kept her down. It was the arcs of painful power flaring from the woman's hand to her leg.

Her entire body quaked as every nerve fired and every muscle jerked out of control.

Grigori had never been able to touch her. The blood her mother had spilled fueled a protective hearth spell that kept him away. That this lesser *Volkhvy* physically harmed her now was evidence that the time her mother had bought her was waning. Fear of Grigori suddenly blossomed anew inside of her chest. He wasn't here. It didn't matter. She'd dreamed of what he would do to her when he could finally touch her. In a flash, she recalled every unwanted caress.

Lev helped her. He clamped down on the woman's forearm and she shrieked as she was forced to let Elena go. Her body stopped quaking as suddenly as it had started. Elena collapsed and eagerly gulped air as her lungs began to work once more. She wasn't sure if Lev's help was intentional or not. As she struggled to her feet, she was grateful all the same.

She moved much more slowly this time. All three intruders were occupied. Their curses filled the air. Their black blood mingled with red. Too much red, but she couldn't pause. She would be worthless without the sword. Elena limped up the stairs to the thrones. This time when she reached for it, she held the sword in an appropriate grip. Her training had been professionally absorbed and now implemented. She pivoted back around, strengthened by the power in her hands. The blue glow from the stone was pale, but unmistakably brighter in reaction to her touch.

All the Dark *Volkhvy* paused to look up at Elena on the dais.

"The sapphire blade is mine," she proclaimed. "I will defend it."

Her figure was petite. Her voice was firm, but quiet. The wolves and the man who also defended the blade should be much more intimidating, but the sapphire's glow spoke of the sword's opinion. She was the warrior the intruders should fear. Her touch bonded with the blade and called Vasilisa's power inherent in the gem to life.

And there was nothing Dark *Volkhvy* respected more than power.

"Go. Warn all your brethren, Dark and Light, that Bronwal is defended," Romanov ordered. He didn't support her claim on the sapphire sword. He wouldn't. But he didn't deny it either. Both of the men he fought had been injured badly. Their black blood stained his sword and curls of steam rose from its sharp edge. But Romanov bled, as well. She could see scarlet slashes on his face and chest.

And that's when she knew.

It was too late for her to choose to walk away. Not because of the blade, but because of the man. Anger rose like bile in her throat. Fury heated the blood that pumped through her heart. How dare they defile this already besieged man?

As Elena gathered her muscles beneath her to jump into the fray, the three Dark *Volkhvy* became hazy and indistinct in front of her eyes, then disappeared.

"Dominique wasn't capable of Ether manipulation. These three were definitely more powerful than the usual thieves. Powerful *Volkhvy* can disappear and reappear at will from place to place. Possibly from time to time," Romanov said. He cleaned his sword on the edge of his cloak, but it was a habit more than a necessity. The dark blood had already disappeared, as well as the witches it had come from.

"And they were afraid of me?" Elena said shakily. Knowing that magic was real and seeing it manifested in front of your eyes were two very different things.

"The power in the sapphire could kill them. There's

nothing a nearly immortal creature fears more than death," Romanov said.

"It's frightening for a mortal creature, as well," Elena said. Now that the adrenaline rush had fled her body, she was left shaking in reaction to her instinctive stand against the intruders. She might have been called to wield the sapphire blade, but that didn't mean becoming a warrior was easy. Her legs shook, and without thinking she sat on the nearest seat available.

The room grew quiet.

Lev and Soren stopped smoothing their ruffled fur and licking their injuries. They stared at her instead. And Romanov walked forward slowly one steady step at a time.

She was on the smaller throne. The one with the alpha wolf carved onto its back. The wolf carving was above her head. She didn't have to turn and look up at it to remember every tooth, every hair.

"You brought me here that first night. I couldn't see the thrones. There was no fire. The alcove was invisible in the darkness. You stood with me in your arms rather than set me down," Elena said.

"No one has sat on that throne since my mother died," Romanov said. His intense gaze was trained on her with some unwavering emotion she couldn't name.

"The larger one was your father's," Elena said. She looked beside her where the larger throne stood. "It's yours now."

"I'm the last Romanov. The throne is mine, but there's nothing to rule here. Bronwal is an abandoned place. We do nothing but linger and languish at Vasilisa's pleasure," Romanov said.

Elena placed the Romanov blade across her knees.

The sapphire had dimmed, but they'd all seen it glow. She settled more fully into the throne.

"Perhaps that's our problem. You're prisoner to Vasilisa's pleasure and I've been prisoner to Grigori's. We have existed to serve their needs instead of our own," Elena said.

"I won't allow my needs to place you at risk," Romanov said.

"And I'm not allowed to determine what I will risk for myself?" Elena asked.

Once again, she sacrificed much to open herself to rejection. He hadn't asked her to be his queen. He never would. To him, she was as much an invader as the ones they'd vanquished, no matter what the sword said. She'd destroyed what little peace he'd found in his lonely duties. She'd brought all his pain to light.

"You don't know what the Ether is like," Romanov said. But as he spoke he stepped up the stairs of the dais, one by one. Elena rose to meet his approach. She held the Romanov blade down by her side. He stopped at her sudden movement. He stood only a few feet away.

"I know what your kisses are like. I know how your body feels between my legs. How your shoulders feel in my hands," Elena said. "I know if Grigori captures me tomorrow I'd be happier to have the memories of your touch to sustain me through my imprisonment."

"To join with me is to court a curse more horrible than you can understand. Ask Lev if his wife was happy to lose her baby to the Ether once Vasilisa's judgment fell. We were her chosen champions, yet she showed no mercy. No one was spared, not even a newborn child. Madeline was a warrior who fought by Lev's side for Vasilisa. It didn't matter. She and her baby disappeared in the first Cycle," Romanov said. He stepped nearer as he spoke, as if proximity would convince her. He fisted his hands.

Down on the main floor of the hall, Lev slipped away into the dark hallway beyond. Soren whined and ran after his brother. Neither had wanted to hear the tale.

"How long did he last once she was gone?" Elena asked.

"I haven't seen Lev's human face since the first materialization that Madeline didn't appear. He shifted to search for her. *Volkhvy* use the Ether to travel the world. Lev thought Madeline and Trevor might have materialized somewhere else. In our wolf forms we're nearly tireless. For a century of Cycles he searched the world for her. Until he forgot how to be human again," Romanov said. "Until he seemed to forget his pain."

"He shifted for her," Elena whispered. "Not to run. Not to hide."

"He used his enchantment to try to save her," Romanov said. "But he failed."

Elena didn't shed tears for herself. But for Madeline and the great love Lev had felt for her and the baby, she cried. Her cheeks were scalded with hot, liquid emotion. She didn't call attention to them by wiping them away. Besides, Romanov's green eyes seemed brighter, as well.

"And you think it would have been better if they hadn't been together at all," Elena said.

"Soren lost much, but not as much as Lev," Romanov said.

"And you? You're so much better off because you're determined to stand alone?" Elena said. She refused to draw closer to him even though his pain beckoned.

"I won't share my burden with an innocent," Romanov said.

The curse was horrible, but much of Romanov's pain

was self-inflicted. He'd lost too much to risk new connections. He was determined to suffer alone. Yet she'd been called to this place. She'd found it when others had failed. She was here for a reason.

This time Elena wouldn't leave her sword in the throne room. She stepped forward to pass by Romanov, but she paused when she reached his side. Their hips were parallel. She didn't face him, but she did look up to meet his eyes.

"You sell me short. The blade has spoken and I believe it's spoken well," Elena said. "Because I wouldn't fade away."

She had some pride. She didn't completely bare her heart. She didn't tell him she would brave the curse for him as long as she knew he would be waiting on the other side when they materialized again. She'd only just acknowledged it for herself.

She hadn't gone for the sword in order to protect it from the Dark *Volkhvy* intruders. She'd gone for it in order to help Romanov and his brothers repel invaders. And not even magic had been able to stop her.

But her insides were in a tumult and her legs were numb, especially the one that had channeled the *Volkhvy* woman's power into her body. That leg was a reminder that Grigori would touch her soon if she didn't stop him.

As she paused to speak to Romanov, she swayed on her feet. His eyes widened and he reached for her. His large arm wound around her back and his warm hand braced her hip. The move placed his entire body against her side, not pressing, but supporting. Elena could have jerked away…if she wanted to prove her fortitude by falling on her face.

Something was wrong. The Dark power the *Volkhvy*

had used to hurt her was still jolting through her body making her muscles weak.

"You're hurt," Romanov said.

He didn't wait for her to confirm what he could see with his own eyes. Instead, he bent to scoop her up the way he had when she'd collapsed in the snow. She was flooded by thoughts of other times she'd been in his arms. The kisses they'd shared. The pleasure. The pain. She had a sword in one hand. She couldn't wrap her arms around him. She had to be content with one hooked around his neck and the other held down by her side to keep the edge away from his body.

Now that he'd made his feelings clear, she should keep her distance but she preferred not to faint. The power had found its way into her head and her vision had gone blurry. Her equilibrium was gone. The room spun around them as Romanov stepped down the stairs.

"She needs to rest. Fetch Patrice," Romanov ordered.

He seemed to speak to his brothers from a great distance. Down a long tunnel. One that spun in a kaleidoscope of shapes and colors. Elena closed her eyes against the dizzying whirl. His chest was the only solid thing besides the sword in her hand in a world gone mad. She leaned her face against it. Without intention, she found his heartbeat beneath her cheek. It thumped steadily while she hoped hers did too, in spite of her detachment to its feel and sound.

The Dark *Volkhvy* had used great force to break through the last of her mother's protective spell. Maybe such negative power coursing through her was more than her mortal body could take.

Elena held on to Romanov and the sword. They were all she knew as he carried her up to the tower room. She didn't note the passage of time as he hurried on the stairs or the change of light as he laid her on the bed and turned to throw open several windows. She didn't feel the cool rush of wintry air on her flushed skin or the soft blanket beneath her. She reeled when his hold disappeared, doubling the ferocity of her grip on the hilt of the Romanov blade. When he returned to her side, she cried out because he reached to move the sword and she thought he was trying to take it away.

"I only want to position the sapphire against you, Elena. It's glowing. I think Vasilisa's power might help you recover," Romanov said. His voice was nearly a growl.

She allowed him to move the sword. He pressed the cool stone against her chest. She grasped it with both hands then. She held the hilt between her breasts. Its long shaft lay on top of her, from her lower ribs to her knees.

At first she felt no improvement. Her head swam. She was afraid to open her eyes. But then almost imperceptibly the breeze tickled across her face. The numbness that had tried to claim her began to recede. Finally, she felt her heart beat inside of her chest. There was no noticeable electric current from the sword. Not like there had been from the Dark *Volkhvy*'s touch. Vasilisa's power was more of an emanation that her body soaked up. Like heat. Like the rays of the sun.

"I brought mulled wine. I thought it might fortify. Also cheese and bread," Patrice said.

Elena recognized the housekeeper's voice. She couldn't speak to thank the woman for responding to her distress. She couldn't thank Soren and Lev for obeying Romanov and going for help.

"This is my fault. The black wolf could have easily dispatched them," Romanov said. "They hurt her because I avoid the shift."

"Better *them* hurt her than *him*, I say. That black wolf can't be trusted. I've seen the Ether in his eyes," Patrice said. Elena wanted to protest. She wanted to say that the black wolf hadn't hurt her. That Romanov was in control. But her lips wouldn't open no matter how she willed herself to speak.

"I am the black wolf, Patrice. You know that," Romanov said.

"I'm not as Ether-addled as you think. I know who and what you are. And I know it would destroy you to hurt this one. Best not risk it. Best not risk it," Patrice replied. Her voice faded as she must have left the supplies she carried to wander back the way she'd come.

"You...wouldn't," Elena managed to utter. Sensation returned to her little by little. She could feel her body again. Her legs were no longer numb.

"You misplace your optimism," Romanov replied. Elena's lashes fluttered when she felt the slightest brush of calloused fingers on her cheek. He sat nearby. He must have pulled a chair closer to the bed. His caress was incongruous, a butterfly's wing from a man who could crush someone with his bare hands. But it continued. She wasn't mistaken. He outlined the whole of her face, softly, as if he memorized her repose or the color returning that signified she wasn't near death.

"Not...optimistic. An optimist hopes," Elena said. "I know." She swallowed and licked her lips. It felt a triumph especially when it was followed by the ability to slit open her eyes. He was only a blur leaning over her. But he was a welcome blur. One that encouraged her to blink and try to regain her focus.

She had been afraid of the black wolf. She had even entertained the possibility that Romanov would cede control to the beast and allow it to consume her. But his fear of the same caused her to fully believe it would never happen. He had enough doubt in himself for both of them. She was suddenly fully confident that he would never harm her, even if it meant sacrificing himself.

"I am the black wolf," Romanov said. "Its instinct and savagery are a part of me, and with every Cycle as we tire of holding on to our humanity the wolves take greater hold."

"A wolf would never harm its mate. I'm not afraid," Elena said. She closed her eyes again. Immediately regretting the claim. It was a groggy thing to say. Once the words were out of her mouth she wished her lips hadn't begun working again at all.

"No," Romanov whispered.

His voice was close. Very close. Warm lips pressed against the corner of her mouth. No, she wasn't his mate? Or no, he would never harm her? Her head went light again at the possibility of the latter promise and also because he slid his lips from the corner of her mouth to the center. She was awake. She was alive. All sensation had returned. His slightly open tasting of her lips proved it. As did the gasp he inspired when he boldly teased her with a flick of his tongue.

Elena released the hilt of the sword. She was able to lift her hands to cup the sides of his face. Thank God, because he might have pulled back if she hadn't stopped him. He might have moved away. She wasn't strong enough to hold him in place, but her touch caused him to pause long enough for her lips to open and her tongue to twine with his. He responded by sinking into her and the kiss as if her taste and touch saved him from a dark abyss. As if he was the one who had been near death, but her kiss had woken him from despair.

"You won't harm me," Elena murmured between

deep, tender delvings into the velvet recesses of his mouth. His only response was a groan of pleasure that may or may not have been conceding her argument and then the repositioning of his body on the bed beside her, which seemed like the truest concession.

The sword was between them, but it didn't keep them apart. They merely accepted the danger of its sharp edges, carefully, as part of their embrace, its unyielding presence nothing of a deterrent when compared with greater obstacles they still had to face.

He kissed her until she was light-headed again. This time from want of his touch, not dark magic. She allowed her fingers to wind their way into his wild hair. Heat rose from his scalp in spite of the open windows. Their twining tongues stoked flames hotter than the remnants of the fire behind the grate. A raven's hoarse cry reminded her of the birds that constantly swooped and soared around the tower, but their movements couldn't compete with the whirl of desire Romanov caused in the pit of her stomach.

He paused when she tried to press closer. The sword had finally become too much of an impediment. Their lips separated and Elena was afraid he would pull away. She forced her fingers to loosen in case he did, but instead of breaking away he only edged back far enough to take the sword from between them. He carefully moved the blade to the other side of her body and then he stilled.

Elena watched as his green gaze tracked over her rumpled hair and her flushed face. She licked her swollen lips and a slight smile curved one corner of his sensual mouth. His lips were swollen too. Paired with the untamed black waves of his hair and his pale skin, his passion-darkened mouth was more than enticing. She allowed one hand to slip from his hair down to his lips. She extended one finger and gently traced his full lower lip. By the time she'd traveled from one edge to the other, her finger trembled in reaction.

The masculine vulnerability of his well-kissed mouth sent a delicious curl of hunger to her stomach and lower. She melted as he allowed the caress. She pressed her thighs together to keep from spreading them and begging for his touch.

But she didn't have to.

He felt her movement. He let go of the sword to cup her hip with that hand. He gauged her tension and he kneaded her muscles to ease it. Of course the motion of his strong fingers so close to her need only made her tension worse.

"Romanov," she said. It was nearly a moan. He looked up from his hand to her eyes. What he saw there made his gleam with appreciation. His smile hadn't faded with her touch. It increased with her moan, tilting his lips beneath her trembling touch. "If you're going to leave this bed, do it now. If not, prepare to be kept here till morning," she warned.

"You need to rest and recover. If I stay, there'll be less resting," Romanov said. He was teasing her as if they weren't toying with a *Volkhvy* curse. What had changed? Why wasn't he leaving her here alone behind a safely locked door?

Her question must have shown in her eyes.

"I should leave. But I can't. You were gone. Before my very eyes. First, in the *Volkhvy*'s grip and then in reaction to it. And the only thing I could think was that I hadn't touched you when I could. I hadn't appreciated every inch of you while we were together," Romanov confessed. "I will leave this room only if you want me to leave. If not, we will steal this time together and you'll still be free. I will never make you my wife. I'll never chain you to my name or to the curse."

Elena understood he was making an honorable pledge, but her newfound connection to the sword made it particularly poignant to hear his determination to set her free. Freedom was what she'd wanted above all things, but she'd wanted the freedom to make her own choices. Now, it seemed as if Romanov prevented her from fully embracing the sword's call because he wanted to protect her. That, in addition to the idea of lying with him and then losing him, made her hands tighten on the nape of his neck.

She pulled his lips back to her so he could make no more horrible promises she didn't want him to keep. She would take this stolen time he offered to share with her. Later would be soon enough to regret it.

He took her move as an invitation to stay. His mouth met her open lips and their tongues danced and delved again with an eagerness neither of them tried to subdue. Her whole body welcomed him, softening, opening and melting against him. He was a big man. When he half leaned over her and nudged one of her legs to the side so that his warm thigh slid between hers, she gloried in his weight. His broad chest mashed against her sensitized breasts and she hooked her leg around his waist to encourage him even closer.

But he pulled back instead. He broke their kiss and dropped his lips to trail down the side of her jaw and then farther down still to the throbbing pulse at the base of her throat. His mouth was soft and firm. He kissed her skin as thoroughly as he'd kissed her lips and he teased her with occasional moist licks of his tongue.

"You're so deliciously delicate and yet so strong. I tremble at the thought of harming you in any way, yet you have proven time and again that you aren't afraid," he said. The whisper of his words against her neck caused a thrill to shiver down her spine.

"I'm only afraid I'll startle you with my hunger," Elena said. But she hesitated for only a moment before the press of his lips along her collarbone caused her hips to rise in response. She pressed her heat against his hard, muscular leg. The sensation was even stronger than it had been before, when he'd pleasured her in the kitchen, because this time she knew there would be more.

"I want your hunger," Romanov said.

He had continued to knead her hip, but now he lifted his hand to the neckline of her tunic. It was linen and crafted simply and loosely. It was gathered and threaded with a string that tied at the neck, and the knot had already loosened with her movements of the morning. His fingers easily flicked the tiny bow free and he slowly parted the material, which opened all the way down to the middle of her chest.

The lace of her bra and the swell of her breasts above the modern undergarment were exposed.

"Brace yourself," Elena breathed. "Because I'm very hungry." Her chest was rising and falling quickly with her respiration. Her hands gripped his shoulders. But even that steady anchor didn't stop her body from jerking when he trailed the warm pads of his calloused fingers along the top of the lace he'd uncovered. She followed his intent gaze down to his caress. Her nipples had swelled and hardened. They peaked rosy and pink, begging for his touch beneath the translucent white lace.

"I can see that," Romanov said.

In a move that made her gasp, he reached to twist her
bra free. The plastic fastener in the center of the lace
cups didn't slow him down. A flick of his strong fingers
caused the undergarment to part. And the elastic on either side pulled the lace off of the swell of each breast to
reveal her hardened nipples. Her pale skin was flushed
with pleasure as blood rushed to his touch, but that pink
flush couldn't compare to the darkening of her areolas
and nipples as his teasing fingers found them.

"Oh," she cried out as his large hand went from teasing to encompassing. His touch was hot as he weighed
and lifted the globe of one breast, but its heat didn't compare to the moist fire as he leaned to take the entire tip
of her breast in his mouth.

He suckled and her hips bucked. Her hands clenched
and pulled, ripping his tunic instead of bothering with his
ties. She didn't allow the sound of the rent to slow her. In
fact, the sudden give and tear spurred her on. She pulled
harder until the fabric came away from his torso in her
hand. She threw it to the side all while he caused her to
rock and toss her head back and forth with the suction of
his mouth and the velvety friction of his lathing tongue.

"Elena," he groaned, loudly, breaking his suction and
moving his lips down her body.

Now that his chest was bare, his skin burned against
her everywhere it brushed. He kissed and licked until
he came to fabric. She muttered a protest as he stopped,
but he only paused long enough to pull the tunic over
her head. She lifted her back and arms to help him. He
slid the straps of her bra off her shoulders as well, and
tossed both garments to the side. Then he looked down
at her. His eyes gleamed in appreciation.

She was suddenly reminded of the legend and the

wolf. He was a man in her arms but he was also every bit the wild alpha. She reached for him, afraid he might be too wild for her to keep in the bed long enough to mate.

To remove her shirt, he'd crouched between her legs. Her hands dropped to hold either side of his hips. His supple leather pants were tighter than they'd been before. She could see the bulge of his erection. She could see where the cock she'd explored before was long and thick and curved to the side. It barely missed showing over the top of his waistband. She could see where the damp head of it pulsed, waiting to be freed.

His stomach was lean and hard. He sucked in air as her fingers reached for the crisscrossed ties that held his pants in place. This time she slowly worked the leather lacings free. Allowing him the anticipation of her obvious intent. She made sure to brush against his erection again and again as she worked the lacings free.

"Your hunger is nothing compared to mine," Romanov said. Sure enough, his warning was a growl and his body trembled beneath her touch.

Elena was still half-reclined with her legs spread around his knees. When she had unfastened his pants and spread the leather, the white of his undergarment was loose and easy to pull down. His erection came free and jutted out toward her with a heavy bounce.

She needed him to fill her. She had gone to molten liquid, but she didn't want to rush their time to completion. Instead of falling back and begging him to rip off her jeggings, she reached for him. She held his erection in both of her hands. He cried out at her touch. He thrust into the tight grip she made with her fists end to end. But when she urged him closer and rose up enough to tease her tongue across the swollen head of his cock, he held perfectly still.

Was she too bold? Had her hunger finally been too much?

"Elena," Romanov moaned. She looked up to see his head thrown back. His knees had spread and braced on the bed on either side of her body. She moved one hand off his shaft to make more room for her mouth to engulf him. He wasn't still then. His hips jerked and she enjoyed the friction of her suction and his thrust.

His hands threaded into her hair as she worked his erection with her mouth. He was hot and salty and sweet. And so hard against her tongue she couldn't help but fantasize about how he would feel when he finally thrust inside of her. She throbbed between her legs. She was dewy with heat. But more than anything since he'd brought her to orgasm with nothing but his hard leg and a kiss, she'd wanted to pleasure him in return. Every thrust of his erection between her lips and every cry of her name gave her as much pleasure as he received until it was Romanov who stopped her.

His hands tightened. He gently pulled himself out of her mouth. She opened her eyes to protest, but he silenced her with a deep, hot kiss made even hotter by the taste of him they shared on her lips.

As he kissed her, his hands left her hair and fell to her jeggings. She was glad she wore the simplest stretchy denim. But he took her by surprise when he gripped her hips instead of pulling her pants down.

"I want you every way that a man can take a woman, but I don't want to hurt your knee. Help me gets this off without jarring your leg?" he requested.

And this was the man who had feared he would shift into a giant wolf and devour her?

Elena lifted her hips and worked the denim down her hips. He pulled her borrowed boots off her feet, first one and then the other. Then he helped her with her pants, slowly and gently.

She was left wearing nothing but a scant lace panty when they were finished. Romanov's eyes darkened when he saw the dampened, dark curls between her legs, but he leaned to kiss her scarred knee first. His touch as he held her leg for the gesture was softer than she could have imagined such a large man capable of. He killed with those hands. He'd defended Bronwal for centuries with them. For her, they were so careful. So considerate.

But then they scorched as both hands rose up the top of her leg without breaking contact with her skin. Elena watched his touch caress closer and closer to the juncture of her thighs. When he reached the lace that covered the curls that drew his attention so intensely, he was suddenly not slow at all. He grabbed the elastic of her bikini briefs and slid them down to her midthigh. Not slow, but still considerate of her knee. The move allowed him access to her while still keeping her from spreading her legs.

He touched her then.

Large, calloused fingers dipped into her curls and she cried out when he found the sensitive flesh he sought. She tried to spread her knees, but the lace caught and held her in place. She could only burn for more while he teased. His hooded gaze watched her frustration as it warred with enjoyment. His exploration wound her tighter and tighter. Her hips moved as he began to gently and softly thrust along her moist crevice.

"Please, please," she begged. She'd never needed release as badly as he caused her to crave it. But it wasn't only an orgasm she wanted. She wanted to mate with this man. She wanted him joined with her. She wanted him as close as she could possibly take him.

Instead, he gave her the teasing thrust of his middle finger, thick enough to make her cry out and jerk her hips up to meet it. She grabbed his arm and he allowed it. He allowed her to encourage a harder and deeper thrust of his hand.

"What do you want, love? I'm afraid to hurt you. You'll have to show me," Romanov said. He sounded as if he was teasing, but he wasn't. He was still afraid he would hurt her even now when she bucked under his touch, crazed with desire.

She came then around his thick finger with soft, jerking sighs.

"Elena," he breathed as her inner muscles fluttered against his touch.

But there was still hunger and his mere touch wasn't enough.

Elena pushed his arm back and he allowed her to move him. He patiently waited for her to direct their actions even though his erection was massive. As he watched, she pulled the lace from her legs and threw it on the floor. Then she boldly pushed the legendary warrior back until he lay supine on the bed.

She wanted him in every way a woman could take a man. She wanted to show him that her knee wouldn't prevent their joining. But she had also wanted to take him for days and she wasn't about to let the chance pass without taking full advantage of his offer.

He was incredible. She paused to appreciate the tableau. His wild hair was spread darkly over the white linen on her pillows and his muscular body was intimidating even in repose. His erection lay curved to the side across one of his hard thighs. He was obviously more than ready. In such flagrant excitement, his control of his body was beguiling.

She'd been bewitched by Ivan Romanov long after she had been stalked and he had been bespelled by another.

"I'm not a virgin. I've been with others. But never with anyone who was so strong. Your control is a siren call to my body. I want to make you lose it," Elena said.

"You test my control beyond measure," Romanov said. "But my control is yours. I give it to you because I can give nothing more."

A poignant tug on her heartstrings seasoned the moment. He gave her this because he couldn't give her his name.

Elena mounted her hot warrior. His skin burned between her thighs, but she was slick with expectation and her previous orgasm. He helped her spread her legs and position his shaft. With his hand, he teased the head of his cock against her opening. But she'd had enough teasing. She was throbbing and ready once more.

She lowered her weight onto his erection. Her body stretched to take him inside. Deep inside. She rocked to heighten their mutual pleasure and also to work her folds to open wider and wider to accept his full girth and length.

Her knee did twinge. But she did it to herself with her frenzied movements as she rode him and she didn't care. Not when his head fell back and his eyes rolled. Not when his hips jerked up to meet hers in a fury of thrusts that bounced her breasts. His skin glistened with sweat. She tasted salt drops on her upper lip when she licked them. His hands slipped on her hips.

And still she took him deeper.

Her inner recesses pulsed around his steely member.

She raised her arms high above her head and even without wings she flew.

He pulled out as he pulsed with his orgasm and even

that was proof that he cared. About her. About a possible child. Even as he lost control for her, he kept it, as well.

She would never fear the alpha wolf again.

Losing Ivan Romanov was her only concern.

Chapter 11

He navigated the Ether with ease, as did many of his kind. He loved the chill of it against his skin and the vacuum of its hunger as it tried to take his soul. Many said his family was addicted to its constant pull. After all, his ancestral home had been built on the very edge of the world where the veil was most thin, and, even when they weren't traveling, the hunger of the void was a constant thrill they all experienced from infancy.

Grigori never stayed long away from the rush. He had been the witchblood prince of the Dark *Volkhvy* since his conception, but he'd been free to come and go as he pleased. He pleased often. Living on the edge of the Ether was nothing compared to traveling through it from place to place all over the globe.

As the son of the Dark *Volkhvy* king, it was fitting that he rose to prominence as the darkest, most Ether-influenced of all who had come before him. He was too busy taking to worry about the weaker witches who warned him to be careful. He had gloried in every depravity his power would allow until a Russian peasant woman had stood him down.

She'd used love as power. And none of his travels had prepared him for the strength of the shield she bought for her daughter with her blood. Every moment since had felt diminished.

Except the time he'd spent delivering his special promises in Elena Pavlova's nightmares. More thrilling than challenging the Ether's inexorable pull, his time with his swan soothed him. The visualization and manifestation of what he wanted to do to her when she was finally in his power had eased his impatience.

She'd taken that away from him.

Grigori paced the length of his quarters. His rooms had been built on the top floor of a complex that almost seemed to be a part of the cliff from which it jutted, an architectural masterpiece of steel and glass and stone. One entire wall of his loft-like space had been made of glass. It faced toward a canyon abyss that no human could have traversed. No human could have seen the shimmer of Ether either, though Grigori stared at it often. It bisected the canyon in a sheet of nearly imperceptible power. At times, when the light and weather provided the exact conditions, the Ether wavered like the northern lights before his rapt attention.

The Ether's vacuum was the greatest when it was most visible. He'd often been brought to his knees by the pleasure of its hunger. There were times when he'd imagined its hunger had somehow transferred itself to him.

His hunger for Elena was as powerful as the Ether itself. He'd had no way to ease it for weeks. The connection that he'd established to her through her dreams had been severed.

Only now had he discovered why.

Grigori was tall and lean. His muscles wrapped around his bones in corded perfection. The dark power that continually coursed through him burned away all but what was necessary. He had to keep it at a fever pitch to fight the Ether's pull, especially when he was at home. He looked like a devoted athlete. One addicted to Pilates and the ketosis craze.

And right now his spare frame shook with fury.

The witch who had brought him the message from Ivan Romanov was on his knees. His blood poured onto the polished marble floor, black puddles on white. Steam rose all around him. It proclaimed his weakness. If Grigori's blood had spilled, it would have ignited into blue-tinged flames.

Two Dark *Volkhvy* servants held Dominique by the arms. It wasn't necessary. He had nowhere to go and no power left to take him there. But it was more convenient to Grigori to have him lifted and displayed rather than wilted on the ground. The better to lash out at him again and again. Dominique had failed the witchblood prince. He wouldn't do so again.

"She is protected," he whimpered. "She doesn't stand alone."

He had repeated the same phrase even after Grigori had reacted with slicing jolts of power that flayed the skin from his back and chest.

Elena had taken a few lovers before. Grigori hadn't cared. She'd still been his, night after night. His claim had been unchallenged by momentary pleasure taken with mortal men.

But the Light *Volkhvy*'s dishonored champion was no mortal man.

The name of Romanov was still spoken in hushed tones of anger and fear among the Dark *Volkhvy*. There was no creature capable of threatening a powerful witch…except the Romanov alpha wolf and his brothers. The rising of the Dark had occurred in direct correlation to the fall of the Romanov family. And Vasilisa, the Light *Volkhvy* queen, was too wrapped up in her vengeful punishment to care.

"He still stands. Bronwal is defended. And Elena has sought shelter there to seek his help against you," Dominique said.

Grigori didn't wait for his servants to act. He leaped forward and grabbed the bleeding witch. He used Dominique's slashed and bloody body to push open the glass doors that led onto the platform outside. The observation deck had been built to take in the spectacular view. Its edges and its flooring were more glass than steel. Dominique began to scream long before Grigori easily hoisted his body over the rail. His rapidly falling form was soon a tiny speck, but the witchblood prince watched until it hit the Ether and winked out of sight.

Eaten by Ether was too good for the worthless witch.

But at least now Grigori knew.

He'd been to the Bronwal Gathering often as a young man. The power expended to fuel the curse was an incredible lure even for *Volkhvy* who had power to spare. The Dark and the Light were drawn to the mountain every ten years for a decadent ball. What wasn't to love? He'd even enjoyed the dangerous element of being close to the one being who could kill him. They all did. They bated the wolf, knowing full well the wolf was almost gone.

He stands.

Did he though? Did he stand with Elena? Or was he a broken creature barely holding out against the Ether's pull?

Grigori's fury eased. His servants had backed away from him with their heads down and their hands grasped behind their backs. He might have thrown them to the Ether as well, but he didn't. He now knew where to go to collect Elena Pavlova once the power of her mother's blood ran out.

Chapter 12

She bathed by firelight. The water was pleasantly warm against her sensitive skin. This time, rose petals floated around her. Romanov had closed the windows before he went to fetch the bath. He hadn't reappeared, but servants carrying the tub and the pitchers and buckets had. They didn't seem to mind the extra work she'd added to their nonroutine. In fact, more of them seemed to meet her eyes and speak to her and each other as they worked. Maybe their faculties improved the longer they were materialized. Maybe it helped to have something ordinary to do.

Bell made an appearance. She brought rose water in one of Patrice's vials. It sloshed fragrantly into the tub when she opened it and filled the room with its light scent.

"Where is Patrice?" Elena asked. She had wrapped herself in a 1950s-style smoking jacket she'd found in the wardrobe. It was crafted of thick, quilted ebony velvet and it served very well as a modest bathrobe while servants came and went. She was no longer surprised by the evidence of the passage of time she found each time she opened a cabinet or drawer.

"She's around. Don't worry. She isn't going anywhere as long as she's needed," Bell said. "And we make sure she's needed, don't we?" Her hazel eyes flashed from the shadows of her ever-present cap. Elena had reached out to touch Bell's arm and the other woman had responded by hugging her, as if the contact had startled but pleased her.

"Some of us hold on. Some of us don't. It gets harder every time," Bell said into her hair. And then she ran out the door and down the stairs.

Now, Elena bathed and tried to imagine what it was like to fight the Ether the rest of your days. The Ether must be like Grigori. Hungry. Always lurking. Eager to pull you away from the world and everyone you loved. She'd been startled by Bell's sudden hug, but the other girl must crave human interaction from a person who wasn't addled by Ether.

Romanov had resisted its pull for a long time. Even after all his loved ones had succumbed. What chance did she have to convince him to allow her to resist by his side? Regardless of what he'd said when she first arrived, he was still a champion, and champions weren't used to needing help with their battles. Even ones as amorphous as this. The sword had called her, but its call was useless if Romanov didn't accept its decision.

Her body was tender and replete from their lovemaking. She stretched her legs and arms, and, though the cooling water soothed, it also caused gooseflesh to rise on her skin. She had to rise. She had to seek out the man who was still determined to send her away. He'd given her this bath rather than pillow talk because he didn't know what to say. She'd been wrong when she'd thought he didn't think she was worthy of the sword. His rejection was all about protecting her. She was certain he had feelings for her.

If he cared less, he might have let her stay.

Ivan had a responsibility he couldn't shirk. The fact that his Audience with Vasilisa happened to coincide with his need to avoid Elena was fortuitous, not planned. It was both torturous to leave her after their lovemaking and absolutely necessary. Impossible pledges had risen from the depths of thawed places he hadn't even known still existed in his heart, and he'd had to get away.

He couldn't even fool himself into believing that he'd never touch her again.

As long as he was materialized as a man, he would be drawn to her. The cold Ether in all of its infinite power, he could resist. Elena's humanity, he could not. Her warmth and hunger were irresistible; her warrior's spirit completely beguiling.

He should have been bracing himself for his mandatory time with Vasilisa. She required a meeting every materialization. She was ancient. She was powerful. And she was still angry with his family after all these years. She needed to see them suffer. At first, they'd thought it was a mercy that she didn't annihilate them following Vladimir's betrayal. They'd tried to carry on as her loyal subjects during the materializations. But it wasn't long before they realized that death might have been preferable to an eternal purgatory of punishment. She would never relent.

Ivan had borne the brunt of her attention once he'd taken command. He had to face her every Cycle. If he refused to give her an Audience, she might decide to further punish his people in some horrible way. But he'd long since given up hope of seeing her anger fade or her forgiveness earned.

He strode through Bronwal to the Audience Chamber with no plan or preparation. His thoughts were consumed with Elena. So when he arrived to find his brothers already stationed outside the door, he was startled. He was usually the first to appear.

"I'm not late. You're early," he said to Lev and Soren. Soren was the only one who reacted with a cocked head. Lev only stared straight ahead. He was almost like the statue of himself in the gallery. "Want to come inside?" He held the door open, but neither wolf responded to his invitation. He didn't blame them. Vasilisa's manner of appearing had always been difficult to witness.

The Audience Chamber had once been a chapel; its high arched windows were constructed of intricate stained glass depicting religious scenes and saints. They were beautiful and nearly forgotten, larger-than-life obscure figures that muted the light from outside. All other chapel accoutrements had been removed. There were no kneeling benches or crosses. There was no altar. In the entire vaulted room, there was only a huge Baroque mirror, elaborately crafted of gold-leafed metal in the design of roses and thorns, and a single, tall candelabrum that provided enough artificial light to see.

The candles had been burning for a while. The room was filled with the scent of melted wax, and a fresh molten flow had joined centuries of dried and hardened wax that had flowed before.

Ivan approached the mirror until he was close enough to see his shadowy reflection in its antique, rippled glass, but he left plenty of room for what was to come.

The candlelight flickered while he waited. He didn't wait long. No matter how many times he saw the glass begin to bow outward in the shape of a woman he was always bothered by the silvery mirror flowing across Vasilisa's face and form. It ran like water sluiced off of a sea creature that rose from the depths, first liquid and then foaming around her moving body. She stepped out of the mirror, which was, in fact, an enchanted portal she'd crafted so she could come and go from their lives at will. She'd used it to visit their father after their mother's death.

What had been crafted for love had been warped for revenge.

She used it now to subjugate the last Romanov. Ivan didn't kneel. He didn't have to. He had no other liege. No one else held sway over the *Volkhvy* power that ran in his veins. It was her power. He'd had a mortal mother, but Vasilisa had also been his creator. She had made him the black wolf.

"Queen Vasilisa, I am still here," Romanov said. He'd greeted her with the same words every materialization for a century. It had never been intended as a pledge of loyalty. It had always been defiance. And the savvy ruler knew it. She had allowed him the luxury up until now. He always wondered, every time he uttered the words, if it would be the last time.

"So I see," Vasilisa replied.

She was older than the castle itself, but she appeared to him as a handsome middle-aged woman. He never knew what fashion from what century she would choose to wear for these meetings. This time she was dressed in an elaborate gown with a nipped waist and an oddly pronounced bottom. It was intricately crafted of brocade silk in jewel tones of violet and amber. Her snow-white hair was piled high on top of her head in coiled curls held in place with gold pins. Her hair had always been white. He remembered the shock of it when he'd been a young boy. Her white hair and unlined face. As Vasilisa came from the glass, the pins in her hair sparkled and Romanov saw the perpetual roses and thorns in their design.

"I never know if it will be the black wolf waiting for me. Have you never thought of it? The black wolf could devour its maker as easily as it has devoured countless Dark *Volkhvy*," Vasilisa said.

"And then what would happen to my people?" Ivan asked. "They wouldn't be freed from the curse."

"No. They wouldn't. That would have been a self-destructive spell for me to weave. Casting my own downfall as their means of release?" Vasilisa walked slowly around the room. Her shoes were anachronistic compared to the rest of her dress. They were high-heeled boots of a more modern design. They flashed as she lifted her skirts daintily over puddles of molten wax on the floor.

"I would have let the black wolf take you many years ago to save my family," Ivan confessed. She already knew it. Saying it aloud only gave him comfort. He distressed her not at all. This was their usual conversation. Vasilisa seemed to need to air her grievances again and again. And he couldn't resist the urge to join her. It was a repetitive battle they waged with familiar accusations and false civility in place of actual blows.

Death by a thousand forced conversations with a being who radiated hatred of the blood she'd made.

"Your mother died at the hands of a Dark *Volkhvy* king. She died for me. And now her son threatens me with teeth that I allowed him to have," Vasilisa said. This was why she came every Cycle without fail. To condemn him and his family over and over again.

"My mother died for you. She died trying to defend your prince consort when they were attacked by the Dark *Volkhvy.* And you cursed her family. It only seems fair that I would end the curse if I could," he said.

"You know nothing of what your father did to deserve this curse. I respected your mother. She was a fine warrior to carry the sapphire blade. Your father was a savage. He didn't deserve the power he was given. I'm not surprised he was the first to fade," Vasilisa said. As usual, his defense angered her and yet she seemed eager for the emotional release of their verbal thrusts and parries.

"My father betrayed you. You punished him. I won't fault you for that. My mother wielded the blade long after their love failed. When she died, there was no one else to balance out his greed. I was too young. My brothers were even younger."

"You are Romanovs," Vasilisa said. She raised her voice. Her body stiffened. There was the anger he'd always known. It wasn't quick and hot and gone. It simmered, low and forever. As long as he appeared, with every Cycle, she would arrive to rehash the events that had led to their long, arduous demise.

"My father did what he chose to do with the power he'd been given," Ivan said. "The power you gave him. We've only tried to survive the aftermath of his bad choices."

"He betrayed your mother and my consort long before he betrayed me," Vasilisa said.

"Yes. He did. Before she died, he had mistresses. You weren't his first bad decision, but you were the worst," Ivan said. "I'm just glad he didn't pursue you until my mother was gone. She was loyal to you. She believed in the Light."

"Naomi was my warrior. I never would have betrayed

her. I never would have betrayed my prince. Vladimir knew that. He waited until they were dead," Vasilisa said softly. "Or he ensured that they would die."

"How would she have felt about what you've done to us?" Ivan asked. He ignored her new accusation. What did it matter if his father was an even worse traitor than he'd realized? But he was genuinely curious about the mother he'd only known when he was a child. He was surprised when Vasilisa's face visibly flinched. Her eyes widened. Her teeth clicked shut. In all the meetings he'd been forced to attend with her, through all the Cycles he'd endured, he'd never seen her betray any emotion other than anger.

Had he gone too far?

"Were you going to tell me about the sword?" Vasilisa suddenly asked. Her reaction hadn't been in response to his words. She'd been responding to a slight sound outside the door. Lev had growled. Now, he whined, a much softer, pained sound. And Ivan stiffened when a familiar voice warned the white wolf to stand down. This meeting was about to take a turn nearly endless repetitions hadn't prepared him for.

"It called her here, but I'm not going to let her stay," Ivan said.

"Do you honestly think who stays and who goes is your decision?" Vasilisa asked, so sweetly that shivers tickled down his spine.

Her connection with the sapphire had grown stronger. After her bath, she pulled on fresh underwear and jeans. She shrugged into her black long-sleeve T-shirt and tall leather boots. She wasn't sure who had washed the clothes she'd worn, but she was grateful. The energy in the gem on the hilt of the Romanov blade hummed beneath her skin. She wound her damp hair up into a messy bun and belted the sheath she'd found for the blade around her waist. It had taken her a while to find a sheath that was still in good condition. She'd tried and discarded several whose leather was pitted and cracked before she'd found one that had survived the neglect.

She'd found the belt and the boots in the same place. They were sitting together in a dark hallway, as if the person who'd worn them had simply vanished.

The sword belt hadn't been made for the sapphire blade, but it worked. She slid the sword home with a firm hand, and it wedged into a loose iron ring lined with a leather loop. The tip of the blade ended up all the way down by her injured knee, but there was enough give in the construction of the belt to allow her to manipulate the blade out of her way as she walked.

By the time she walked out the door and down the stairs, she felt more like a swashbuckler or a musketeer than a warrior. Or perhaps a tiny dancer playing a swash-buckler? She had yet to prove herself or put the sword's choice to the test, but she had to believe she could and would use it when the time came to defend Bronwal and herself.

And Romanov.

Before Vladimir's betrayal, the Light *Volkhvy* queen had created the swords and the wolves. If she'd intended the swords to choose worthy mates for her wolves, she must have done it for a reason.

Even enchanted champions were stronger when they weren't alone.

She'd climbed the mountain to find a legendary wolf to save her, but the hum of power the sapphire caused beneath her skin suggested that she might be able to contribute to the salvation of them all.

Chapter 13

When Elena found the wolves outside of the door she had been drawn to, almost like a human magnet, she was certain she'd found Romanov. The hum of power beneath her skin made her heart flutter and her skin tingle almost as bad as it had when she'd been "electrocuted" by the Dark *Volkhvy* woman, but it seemed as if her body was adjusting to *Volkhvy* power. Either that or the sapphire channeled it in a way that her mortal form could withstand.

The white wolf snapped out of his nearly frozen stance. He'd been staring straight ahead. When she stepped closer, he became limber once more. He dropped his head. He planted his front paws. He growled. The sound skittered along her spine. It was a clear warning. Soren whined. But he didn't leave his post on the opposite side of the door.

"Romanov is in there, isn't he? I'm going in. If I have to go through you, Lev, so be it," Elena said.

The sword slid easily out of the hilt she'd found. There was barely a scrape of its blade against leather and then a slight vibration along the shaft like a soft metallic song.

She hadn't been training long, but she'd been training all her life. One dance wasn't so very unlike another. Her body easily assumed the stance she'd been taught. And it wasn't a defensive one. She moved forward. Soren whined again. This time his concerned sound was paired with movement. It was the red wolf, not the white wolf, that stepped to block her way in front of the door.

Elena paused. Without thinking, she switched the placement of her feet and her arms to a defensive stance. She wouldn't attack Soren. Not unless she absolutely had no other choice. The red wolf's eyes were still intelligent. They sparkled like warm copper pennies as their gazes connected. He had saved her from Lev when she'd disturbed the baby's room. How could she hurt him now?

"Where is your sword, Soren? Where is the warrior that would fight by your side?" she asked softly. The red wolf only blinked at her. His brown eyes were intelligent but enigmatic.

This time it was Lev who whined. Elena looked at the white wolf. His tail had fallen and he'd tucked it between his legs. His knees had loosened and he'd dropped his belly to the floor. Did he understand her question or had something else scared him?

Her answer came from behind the wolves. The large oaken door opened inward. The overwhelming scent of candles wafted out along with the stronger scent of roses. She'd bathed in rose water, but this scent was more lush and wild. It didn't come from her skin.

"Welcome to Bronwal, dearling. I'm afraid you'll have to come inside to meet me. I'm only allowed in the Audience Chamber before the Gathering," a woman's voice echoed in singsong tones from the candlelit room beyond the door. There was an odd jewel-tone quality to the light that Elena didn't understand until she stepped forward. The wolves parted, one on each side. Soren's hackles had gone high. Lev's belly was now on the ground. He didn't growl when she passed. Before she crossed the threshold, she saw a glimpse of stained-glass windows that explained the quality of the light.

"Elena, no. Walk away. The Audience will be over soon. She'll be drawn back to where she came from until the Gathering," Romanov said.

But Elena wouldn't leave him alone in the room with that threatening voice.

She came forward with her sword still drawn. The hum of power beneath her skin was nearly unbearable. She bore it. She clamped her teeth against the vibration and the pain it caused in her knee.

She didn't expect to see a petite Victorian lady in the middle of the room near a mirror. The mirror's glass swirled like a whirlpool of silvery liquid. The swirl reflected the stained glass causing a kaleidoscope effect on the vaulted ceiling above them.

She knew the identity of the woman she faced before anyone spoke another word. The reaction of the wolves and Romanov's desperate tone gave her clues, as did his use of the term "audience." Only the queen who had made him could require Ivan Romanov to attend her.

Vasilisa wore the colors of twilight paired with the color of the sun.

There was more purple than gold in her dress, as if the gold was fading away.

"Oh, this is such a surprise," the Light *Volkhvy* queen said. She was between Romanov and the mirror. She had obviously been walking around the big warrior who stood almost at attention. He hadn't rushed toward the door to try to stop Elena from entering. She was fairly certain his verbal warning had been a superhuman effort on his part. This audience was an enchanted one. He had no choice but to be here and be teased and tormented by the queen who had cursed his family.

Elena's hand tightened on the sword. The sapphire nearly burned her hand with its power. But its power had come from Vasilisa. She was almost certain she wouldn't be able to use the Romanov blade against the queen who had made it.

"Where did you come from, dearling?" Vasilisa asked. "I'm impressed that you've woken the blade after so long. The last woman to wield it was a great favorite of mine. She killed many Dark *Volkhvy* to defend the Light."

"I've come from Saint Petersburg," Elena answered. The information came too easily to her tongue. She looked from the violet-clad witch to Romanov. His hands were clenched, but he hadn't turned to face her. Was he compelled to stand there at the queen's pleasure as she'd been compelled to answer the queen's question?

"Don't look surprised. He is mine. And now that you've claimed the Romanov blade, you are mine, as well," Vasilisa said. She came closer to Elena but she stopped well before they came face-to-face. Elena looked down at the floor. The queen had stopped inside the circle of light radiating from the mirror's swirling face.

Vasilisa was tied to the mirror.

"*No.* I'm not going to marry her. I'm going to send her away," Romanov said.

Vasilisa turned to stare at Ivan Romanov. He was vulnerable standing there unable to move, but he was also impressive. Because even frozen in place by the Light *Volkhvy*'s power, he was still taking a stand.

"My enchantments aren't affected by silly mortal ceremonies. The blade has called her and she has claimed it. All that's left is for you to claim her. I suspect that's already occurred, whether you'll admit it or not," she said.

Elena's face burned.

The queen turned back to her and laughed as if she'd sensed her emotion.

"My enchantments also aren't affected by carnal actions. Can you imagine how complicated that would have been with Vladimir Romanov claiming every skirt that walked by? I'm talking about connection and emotion. Mortals might say heart and soul. What say you, Ivan Romanov? Does this warrior claim your soul?" Vasilisa said.

"I stand alone," Romanov replied. Too easily for it to be a lie.

Elena didn't drop the sword. She couldn't. Her hand went cold as the constant vibration of power she'd experienced since she'd picked up the blade disappeared. The sapphire flickered as if it tried to fight Romanov's decision, but then its glow faded away.

"And now I can see another claim on this woman," Vasilisa said. Her arms had fallen at her side and her figure moved backward toward the mirror without any obvious steps. The silvery whirlpool left the frame to reach out toward the approaching queen. "She is claimed by the witchblood prince. His mark is upon her. It rides her shoulders like a shadow she can't escape. The sapphire's power hid her for a while, but now she's exposed." The liquid mirror began to engulf the queen's face and figure. It flowed around her. It ran into her eyes and nose and mouth. Elena couldn't breathe as she watched in horror. "Only the black wolf can stop Grigori. And the black wolf doesn't dare to show itself at the Gathering.

I couldn't protect it from all the Dark and Light that will come to the ball, even if I cared to try."

Her last words were gurgled rather than expressed. Elena gagged as the queen disappeared into the glass. Her body had been completely absorbed.

"It's only a portal. She's fine. I doubt if she even breathes air. It's probably vengeance that pumps through her lungs," Romanov said. The tension in his broad back had eased. He turned to her and she saw that his green eyes were his own. His rejection hadn't been a trick of the queen.

She forced her numbed fingers to let go of the sword. It fell with a ringing clank on the flagstones of the floor. Elena looked up at the saints in the windows. They were vivid in their pain, each martyred for one cause or another. Ivan Romanov belonged up there with them. Memorialized in stained glass.

"I told you I wouldn't bind you to the Ether," he said.

"Instead, you would allow Grigori to find me," she said.

"He has to come to the Gathering in order for me to kill him," Romanov said.

"I should be the one to defeat him with the Romanov blade. He is my monster. My nightmare. You can't kill him with your bare hands as you kill the lesser witches," Elena said.

"I will do whatever I have to do to stop him," Romanov said.

"You heard the queen. The black wolf can't take on a whole Gathering alone. They've been baiting you all along. That's why they come Cycle after Cycle. Each one hopes to be the one who can deliver the last Romanov's head to the Light *Volkhvy* queen or the Dark *Volkhvy* king. She created you, and now she will stand back and allow you to be killed if you shift during the Gathering to protect me," Elena said.

"I will do whatever I have to do to stop him," he repeated.

She was left alone in the chapel when he walked away.

"Except give me your heart," she said. The stained-glass saints died as martyrs all around her and they gave her no reply.

Chapter 14

The absence of the sword's hum was a keen ache in her bones. The ache she also felt over Romanov's rejection was overshadowed by concern. He had stood for Bronwal and his lost family for so long. She hadn't realized what risks she would be asking the legendary warrior and his black wolf to face when she'd first climbed the mountain in the snow. Escaping Grigori had dominated her mind.

If she escaped him now at the price of Romanov's life, she would be tortured in a completely different way.

She didn't leave the sword where it had fallen in the chapel. Romanov had walked out without picking it up. He'd left it dull and silent at her feet. She had leaned over and picked it up herself. She'd resheathed it, and it was back at her side. She wouldn't meekly accept his decision. The sword had chosen, and she had accepted its call.

Romanov had rejected her, but what if he decided to shift to save her? What would that say about his true feelings for her? Would the sapphire sing to life in time for her to prevent his sacrifice?

She had to hope the sapphire understood Romanov's heart better than she could.

But hope wasn't enough. She only had one more week before the Gathering, and in that space of time she had to make Ivan Romanov change his mind. The sword had to be brought to life again before Grigori arrived. Somehow she had to get Romanov to accept her as the wielder of the sword and his mate, in spite of his desire to protect her. She had to risk her pride and her heart for a legendary warrior who might simply be fulfilling his duty. They'd had a fiery connection from the start. The chemistry between them was unmistakable. But the sword required a pledge of the heart, and Romanov might have lost his ability to love long before they met.

Elena in the chapel with Vasilisa had been almost more than he could bear. He'd always hated the Audience. The mirror was a horror. The Light queen had the power to destroy all he had left with the flick of her hand. Even when he'd been treated as a treasured pet as a young boy, he understood she wasn't human and feared her. Her feelings were more volatile and changeable than a mere mortal's could be. When his father had betrayed her and the curse had come down on Bronwal and all connected to it, his fears had been confirmed.

He'd walked a fine line with her ever since.

The Audience was required. He was compelled to attend and held in a paralyzed state while it occurred to ensure that the queen had safe passage. All of that had been a trial and tribulation he endured for his people time and time again.

But up until Elena walked over the threshold of the chapel's door, he hadn't known true terror.

If Vasilisa even suspected he cared for the petite ballerina, she would be lost. Hadn't the Light *Volkhvy* queen taken everyone he'd ever loved away from him? The sword had almost given him away. The sapphire had almost refused to lose its glow. He'd had to let the black wolf totally claim his heart in order to fool Elena and the queen. Once Elena believed him, the sword finally let her go.

He'd felt the sapphire die. He'd felt the cold numbness claim the woman he could have loved. And the black wolf had howled long and loud in the deep recesses of his body. Its savagery had helped him fool Elena, but even the wolf didn't want to let her go.

All the while, he'd stood facing the mirror, unable to turn around. He hadn't seen Elena's face. Worst of all, he hadn't been able to go to her when Vasilisa saw the mark of Grigori upon her. The black wolf did more than howl when the Light queen said that the witchblood prince had claimed Elena. It had clawed and chewed and shredded his soul with its vicious teeth trying to get out.

He had exposed Elena. To protect her from the queen, he'd betrayed her to Grigori. And the only way he could put it right was to loose the alpha wolf to prowl, even if that allowed Bronwal to fall.

Grigori knew where she was.

The afternoon faded into evening, and every second seemed to tick away like a bomb she was powerless to defuse. Her connection with the sword had hidden her from Grigori. Now that the connection was gone she felt exposed. It wouldn't matter if she tried not to sleep. She'd tried that before. She'd used coffee and caffeine pills. More and more until her hands shook and her heart raced. And still she had always eventually slept. He hadn't been able to physically touch her, but he was always there as soon as her eyes closed. One blink too languorous at 3:00 a.m. and suddenly she was gone into a nightmare world she couldn't escape.

And that was when she'd been protected by her mother's spell.

The Dark *Volkhvy* woman had touched her.

Elena remembered the shock of the power flowing through her and the knowledge that her mother's protection was almost gone.

Elena trained for hours all alone in the courtyard with a sword that didn't sing. But once the sun went down, she retreated to the tower room. The key to the lock was still around her neck. She'd recognized the roses and thorns on the mirror in the chapel. It wasn't odd that the Light queen's motif was worked into the construction of Bronwal. It had been built for her champions.

There was no use in locking the door. She did it anyway. Grigori wasn't welcome. She wanted to make that perfectly clear even if her will didn't matter to him at all. He might not need her permission, but it still felt empowering not to give it. Eventually, after hours of waiting as wakefully as she could in a chair, she moved to the bed she'd shared only the night before with Romanov. The sheets had been changed. Patrice or Bell had come and gone. She didn't even have the comfort of his scent on the pillows.

She placed the Romanov blade beside her. It was a cool comfort, but a comfort nonetheless. Even powerless, it reminded her of whom she had chosen to be. She wouldn't allow Grigori to take that from her even if he hurt her in her dreams. The fear that he might be able to physically touch her now caused her stomach to clench.

But then she heard toenails on the stairs.

First Lev and then Soren appeared at the door. She saw their great white and red heads position themselves on either side like sentries. They weren't as big or as powerful as Ivan, but they were here. Perhaps their presence would keep Grigori away.

He found Lev and Soren where he'd ordered them to stand. They were wide-awake and alert even though it was well past midnight. He quietly approached and looked in the door. He didn't try the handle. He needed to believe it was locked against him. One glimpse of Elena asleep on the bed they'd shared made him want to join her there and pull her into his arms.

He didn't.

Instead, he turned and placed his back against the door. He crossed his arms over his chest.

Her whereabouts might be visible to Grigori once more, but if he tried to appear he would face all three of the Romanov wolves.

Chapter 15

She had wings again. They were large and white and beautiful in the moonlight…until they were covered in her own blood. The cage was too small. Smaller than it had ever been. It constricted her movements including her ability to draw breath into her plump, feathered breast. Elena frantically beat against the bars of the cage. It was useless. She didn't care. After weeks of freedom, the confinement was worse. Much worse.

Because Grigori was there.

He wasn't with her in the nightmare as he usually was. He was with her body where it slept in the tower.

"Your wolves won't save you," he said. His voice was sultry and low and so close to her that she realized he was bending close to her ear in real life. She felt his heated breath against *skin*, not feathers. In this nightmare, she was a swan in a cage. In real life, she had fallen asleep and Grigori had found her. He was there. Leaning over her helpless, sleeping form. "I'm only here to remind you that you're mine. You can't escape me. Your wolves are an inconvenience. No more. No less. And no matter what he's done to you, it hasn't erased my mark."

She stilled in her cage. Her tiny swan heart fluttered in distress. She needed to take to the sky. She needed to flee. But she was helpless. When the press of his hot lips came against her cheek, she could only react as the swan. She erupted in a furious, frantic explosion of bloody feathers. She flapped her wings even though they caught against the bars of the cage. She struggled even as she bled. She fought. She screamed as a swan with wordless cackles and cries. And Grigori laughed. He enjoyed her anger and her pain.

But it wasn't his laugh that woke her from the nightmare.

Romanov called her name as Grigori's soft and silky touch began to slide along her helpless arms. Romanov's familiar voice rang out and delivered her from her sleep paralysis.

She sat up. She struggled against a tangle of sheets.

Thud.

The scent of ozone filled the air, but it was dissipating through an open casement window. She had checked all the latches before she got in bed. It was pitch-black outside.

Thud.

Once she was free of the sheets, she ran to the window to latch it again, but that's when she saw the shadowy form of a large raven distinct against the grayer black of the night sky. It circled around the tower, calling and calling.

Thud.

Its call sounded like Grigori's laughter. It hadn't been

a dream. The witchblood prince had been in her room. He had touched her. Only Romanov had stopped him from continuing to molest her as she slept, trapped in a nightmare she couldn't escape from by waking.

"Elena!"

The tower room door splintered in a loud crash as Romanov came into the room. He'd used his shoulder against it. She'd heard the thuds, but hadn't processed what was happening. She'd only heard her name.

"He was here. Physically here. He kissed my cheek," Elena said. "He touched my arm." Her insides were hollow. Her heart barely seemed to beat. "He was never able to do that before. My mother's protection has faded away."

It was like losing her mother all over again. The shield had been powered by blood, but it had been love that had strengthened it and made it hold against Grigori. Her mother was gone.

Romanov came to her. He reached for the sword in her hand that she hadn't even realized she'd carried with her to the window. Its stone responded to his touch when his hand closed over hers. The pale blue light rose up and illuminated his face.

Elena stepped forward to press against him. She needed his solidity and his strength.

The stone's glow increased. But Romanov didn't pull away. His hand tightened over hers on the sword's hilt, and his other arm came up to wrap around her back. He held her. He pressed her against his chest. Only then did she feel the trembling that racked her body. It wasn't fear. It was anger. Pure fury that Grigori had dared to touch her. He'd done much worse in her nightmares for years. She'd experienced every depravity he could think of in her dreams. But nothing was worse than the actual violation of his lips on her skin.

"I will kill him. I'll spill every drop of his black blood," Elena swore.

Romanov didn't argue. He held her while his brothers paced around the room. The large wolves were obviously shaken by the invading presence they could sense had been there.

"I was just outside the door. We thought you were safe. Until you cried out in your sleep. The window should have made a noise. Lev and Soren should have smelled him," Romanov said into her hair.

"They're used to the scent of ravens. And Ether. I've smelled it in the hallways. It's like ozone after a storm. Grigori had never been able to get close enough to me for me to smell it before," Elena said. "But he reeked of it." Suddenly, she buried her face against Romanov's chest. Long locks of his hair hung down. She snuggled into them, breathing deeply of his wintry, masculine scent. His scent drove Grigori's away.

The glow of the stone responded to his reaction to her nuzzling. It grew brighter, bathing both of them in its light. The entire room was lit by the softest haze of blue now. It couldn't be ignored.

"The stone knows what you try to deny," Elena said softly. She pulled back to look up at his face. His eyes held hers in the low light; they seemed a darker green in the shadows.

"I'm not ruled by Vasilisa's blade," Romanov said.

"You'll die if I can't wield the sword," Elena said.

"You'll die if Vasilisa thinks that I care for you," Romanov replied.

He leaned down to kiss her and her lips opened eagerly beneath his. The kiss wasn't tender. It was bruising and angry and all the more sweet because he lost control for a few seconds before he regained it and pulled away.

Elena looked over his shoulder at the crushed tower door. It had come halfway off its iron hinges. The latch hung busted to the side. More evidence of the powerful feelings he wouldn't share.

"This was never a refuge, but it's even less of one now that Grigori has tainted it. I can't sleep here again," she said. She reached for the key around her neck with her free hand. She lifted its chain from around her neck. The key dangled from the silver chain, more useless than it had ever been. She'd never been willing to use it against Romanov. While he watched, she dropped it on the floor at their feet. There would never be bars between them again.

"You can't be alone. This happened even with me and my brothers outside the door," Romanov said. He held her too tightly but she didn't pull away. If his ferocious grip was all he could offer, she wouldn't push him away. "Come with me. The sword will light our way."

He didn't let go of the hand that held the sword. It ended up gripped between them by both of their hands as they walked down the stairs. The faint blue glow spilled over the steps in front of them and they followed it away from the ravens, the key, and the wrought-iron bars made of thorns and roses.

Chapter 16

They didn't stop on any of the main floors. Staircase after staircase wound down through the center of the castle. Romanov had said they would follow the sword, but it was actually his steps that led them, illuminated softly by the gem's light. He paused to enter the door of a large chamber beneath the kitchens. Elena waited outside. It was a room she hadn't explored, and through the narrow opening he'd left, she could see walls lined with books and the foot of a massive bed. She assumed it was his room. The air held the scent of paper, old ink, leather and the slight hint of ash from a fireplace she couldn't see.

When he carried some bedding out of the room, he brought the scent with him. It was pleasant and sensual in a homey way. She hadn't imagined him sleeping or reading or warming himself by a fire. Apparently, legends needed the comforts of hearth and home even when they tried to deny it.

The stone had faded greatly by the time he returned to her side, but once he'd shifted the bedding to one side and clasped her hand, the stone brightened again. It was like a mood ring for their relationship. He refused to acknowledge their connection, but his silence didn't fool the stone.

Several more flights of stairs took them lower and lower until they were below the keep. The polished flagstone roughened into coarser stone until the last stairway was nothing but steps that had been roughly carved out of the mountain itself. They had descended beneath man-made levels into a natural cavern that opened up into a cathedral-like space beneath the castle.

The sapphire gem in the hilt of her sword suddenly flared and Elena paused on the stair. Romanov allowed himself to be pulled to a halt by her stop.

"It's beautiful," she said. The light from the stone filled the cavern with its soft blue glow. Natural mica in the cavern's limestone twinkled like stardust above and around them.

"And cold when you don't have a wolf's coat. That's why I brought the blankets," Romanov said. His breath fogged in the air. "Welcome to the black wolf's lair. It's the one place I could think of where even a witchblood prince would be afraid to follow. I haven't been here myself in some time."

Elena shivered, but not because of the cold. She could imagine the alpha wolf in this place. It was a fitting lair for an enchanted wolf.

"Even Lev and Soren don't come here," Romanov said. He tugged on her hand and she followed him the rest of the way down the stairs. The walls narrowed and curved so that the cavern became a tunnel. The air was slightly warmer. Their breath no longer showed. The tunnel was large enough to accommodate the black wolf, but small enough to be cozier than the cavern. And, when the tunnel curved to end in an irregularly shaped oval room with a depression on its floor, she knew they'd reached their destination.

Romanov spread the bedding out on the smooth stone floor.

Once again, the stone's glow began to fade. The room darkened around them. The stardust on the walls twinkled when she moved closer to Romanov. He'd brought several blankets, furs and a heavy quilt. The nest looked appealing, not the least because the man himself had settled to his knees on the bedding once it was laid.

"Vasilisa isn't here," Elena said as she sank to her knees beside him. She placed the sword within reach on the edge of the depression. When she released the hilt, the gem faded more still. They were in darkness but it was a slightly bluish dark that sparkled around the edges of her vision.

"No, she isn't. We're alone," Romanov said. "Except for the blade."

"The blade already knows," Elena said. She flaunted his denials. She dared him to continue to reject her.

But her bold words turned to a gasp when he reached for her face in the dark. She could barely see him. His expression was shadowed. But she recognized the intensity there. She saw his intention. His strong calloused fingers cupped her face on either side. He tilted her chin and he held her firmly in place. Her breath caught as he slowly lowered his lips to her upturned mouth.

When their lips touched, the sapphire pulsed in time with the throbbing beat of her heart. The strobe effect combined with the mica on the walls caused her head to swirl. She closed her eyes and realized it wasn't the light or sparkle that made her dizzy. It was Romanov's tongue teasing in and out of her lips in time with the beat of her heart. She reached for him and found the heat of his skin through his linen shirt where his leather jerkin had ridden up at the waist. He moaned against her tongue as she tasted his lips and caressed the heated skin she could feel through his shirt.

"Elena," Romanov breathed against her mouth when they paused for air. "I won't let Grigori or the Ether have you. When this is done, you'll be free."

"I thought I wanted freedom, but now I crave something more. I want to fight by your side. Forever or as long as the fight goes on. I won't accept anything less from you, Ivan Romanov," Elena vowed. "You've brought me to your lair. Now let me into your heart."

"She would destroy you to punish me. I'm the last Romanov and she won't rest until I've been completely subdued," he said.

He raised his head away from her lips and his warm hands slid from her face. She held him, but he seemed prepared to pull away. His body had gone stiff beneath her hands. His spine was ramrod straight as they faced each other, knees to knees.

Elena twined her arms around his neck. She didn't grasp him. She only held him. She only pressed the length of her torso against his. She was rewarded by an intake of air and the tilt of his chin as he closed his eyes at the sensation of her full breasts against him.

"Then she'll never rest," Elena said. "The Ether will never take us. Not when we have this to look forward to with every materialization."

She pressed into him harder and he didn't resist when her weight urged him back on the quilts. She straddled him once he was stretched out beneath her. She reminded him of what they'd shared before with a gentle rocking of her hips. And she was rewarded with a sudden hardening beneath her bottom. It seemed as if all they'd ever have was stolen time, but she'd decided she could live as a swashbuckler after all if Romanov was her reward.

"It isn't only the Ether I'm afraid of for you, Elena." Romanov reached up to cup her face again. His move stilled her hips. She held herself still with her hands on his broad chest. He pulled her down so he could look into her eyes in the soft blue light. "My mother died at the hands of the Dark *Volkhvy* king. She was holding the sword when she fell. It didn't save her. My father didn't save her. Warriors fall even when they have the full protection of the Light. I can't lose you to the Ether *or to the fight*."

Elena couldn't breathe. She could see the darkness in his emerald eyes. The shadows she'd thought were only Ether taint. He'd been hurt long before the curse by his mother's death. He'd been trying to save Bronwal far longer than she'd imagined. His mother had been killed battling the Dark *Volkhvy*, and he'd had to continue to fight for the deadly queen who had demanded his mother's sacrifice. Suddenly, Elena knew… Vasilisa had cursed the Romanovs by choosing them as champions and enchanting their blood. Ivan saw the sword and the shift as a curse.

Even before the Ether began to devour the castle ten years at a time.

The legend that had enchanted her since she was a child wasn't a legend to Ivan. It was a nightmare from which he could never awake. He cared for her. She was certain. But she was more certain than ever that he wouldn't allow the sword to claim her.

* * *

He'd always loved the galaxies that shimmered here beneath the earth. He'd claimed this place a century ago because of the mica in the walls. Now as he saw them sparkle above Elena's head he was glad that he'd found the cavern one wild hunt long ago. He'd been in his wolf form back before there was any danger in it. He and his brothers had been chasing a large hare more for sport than for food. It had darted down a hole close to a crevice that led into the cavern. He'd sought refuge here after that. He would shift and lie beneath his own private stars while his parents fought and his mother cried.

After she died, he would come here to retreat from Vasilisa when she came to see his father. Everyone suspected they had become lovers. The queen's prince consort had died in the same Dark *Volkhvy* attack as his mother. Ivan hadn't cared about his father's assignations with the queen. But he couldn't forgive the "Light" queen for being the cause of his mother's death. She'd been strong and brave and honorable.

And then she'd been gone.

He'd been left with nothing but the demands of his brothers and the harshness of his father. Then he'd been left with nothing but the entire Romanov enclave and everyone in it. Vasilisa hadn't even blinked when she'd condemned her young wolf shifters to hell. He'd endured it alone.

Until Elena Pavlova came.

She couldn't have any idea how tempted he was by what she offered. A mate. A partner. Stalwart support in the face of the endless vacuum that sought to annihilate him. He'd felt its pull long before the curse. After his mother's death, he would stay too long in his wolf form and have to force his way out.

But this time was different.

"I had no say in my mother's sacrifice, but I can prevent yours," he said.

"She died for a cause she believed in. The sword wouldn't have chosen her if she didn't willingly pick it up," Elena said. "Vasilisa is wrong in many ways, but she's right to fight the Dark *Volkhvy*. I've seen the witch-blood prince's dreams and desires. He has to be stopped. Not only from tormenting me. Stopped altogether."

"You're a dancer. Not a warrior," Ivan said. He lifted one of her arms from his chest and trailed his fingers along its graceful curve. Her muscles were harder though. He could feel the bulge of her bicep beneath his thumb. They silently proclaimed his words a falsehood.

"I am both. I've always been both," Elena said.

He pulled her closer and silenced her with his lips. She resisted for only a moment before she allowed her body to melt against his. He plumbed her mouth with his tongue, exploring the different textures of silk and velvet while his fingers threaded into the blond waves of her hair. The glow from the sapphire had given the flaxen strands a blue halo. He closed his eyes against a truth he tried to deny. She couldn't be the sapphire's warrior.

He wouldn't allow it.

A faint scent of roses came from her skin, but it combined with her unique energy to create a lighter, fresher scent than the heavier scent of Vasilisa. The *Volkhvy* queen's perfume brought to mind lush, blood-red roses in such profuse bloom that they approached decay. Elena's skin reminded him of spring and potent pink buds just beginning to open.

He'd grown up with the queen's motif, a claim and a poignant reminder, throughout the castle. But Elena had somehow taken it and changed it. There was beauty and hope in the buds and strength with resilience in the thorns when she touched them.

"You're trying to distract me," Elena protested. They'd parted only enough for air. Her words were a soft whisper of breath against his lips. He was already rampantly erect. He throbbed against the heat she'd settled firmly against him. He ran his hands from her hair, down the delicate curve of her back to cup the firm mounds of her bottom. He pressed and she hmmmmed an approval. The sound vibrated against him.

"You need to forget what happened earlier tonight. We both do. What better way than this?" he asked. He lifted his hips to rub his shaft against the hot V between her legs, and she moaned in response. Her eyes rolled back and she slid her hands up from his shoulders to his face. She cupped his jaw and met his eyes. It was dark. There were shadows that hid thoughts of what might come between them. It was a stolen respite. A chance to focus on the intense physical connection they'd found without the battle of where it might lead them.

He would protect her. He would pleasure her. Until the Ether claimed him.

And he would gladly be swallowed by Ether for eternity to keep her safe.

When he gently flipped her off his hips and onto the quilts that padded the rock beneath them, Elena didn't have time to protest. When he stood to shrug out of his shirt and leather jerkin, she didn't want to protest. The view was too spectacular. Not only the broad expanse of his masculine chest, but the backdrop of a thousand stars behind him. The sapphire's glow caused the mica to sparkle. It also highlighted the dark waves of his wild hair and bathed every inch of him in pale blue light.

He was tall and broad and his erection swelled out his pants between his muscled thighs. He stood above her as if he appreciated the look of her spread beneath him. His attention tracked over her body from her head to her feet and back again. Her nipples hardened beneath his gaze. The heat of her flush was obvious against the cool air.

"I've never shared this cavern with anyone else before," he said quietly. He stepped closer and dropped to his knees between her slightly parted legs. She smiled and opened to make room for him. He accepted the unspoken invitation to settle warmly against her, and the heat of her flush was nothing compared to the heat they generated when his naked chest was so close to her.

Elena was suddenly very happy that he'd shared his refuge with her.

Ivan touched the soft corner of her smile as if he wanted to catch the elusive expression before it faded from her face. She wanted to tell him her smile wasn't going anywhere while they were together. Instead, she reached to twine one long silky lock of his hair around her finger, and then she caught hold and used it to pull his mouth to her lips. He pressed closer and more intimately between her legs as they kissed and his weight was glorious. He'd worried about her knee before and she'd enjoyed riding him, but the length and breadth of his large body on top of her was a different sort of thrill all together.

"It's cold here. You might want to stay dressed," Romanov said. His hand held behind her good knee as she'd lifted that leg to allow his hips better access to her heat.

"I'm not cold. I'm never cold with you. In the middle of a snowy courtyard, you make me steam," Elena said. It was true. He had. And not only from exertion. While they had trained, she'd been on fire in much more intimate ways. He chuckled low and deep. Then he grew suddenly still and serious. His hand on her leg tightened.

"You know I noticed. Every tremble. Every sigh," he said.

She claimed his confession by licking the edge of his slightly parted lips with a teasing tongue.

"As I noticed your response to our closeness. Your tension. Your heat," Elena replied. "There's no chance I'll be cold when we're lying together, skin on skin."

She helped him, then, to pull off her tunic and slide her leggings down her hips. Her underthings came away easily, as well. The air was cool. Her nipples pebbled and gooseflesh rose on her skin. He stood to pull off his boots and pants and he paused only a moment to throw all their clothes to the side, but that pause made her mindless of the chill.

Because he was beautiful in the soft blue light. He was as perfectly formed as a statue, except he was warm and real and hers…if only for a little while. His erection jutted from a nest of black curls and the sight of his eagerness caused her to flood with need.

He might be a tormented legend, but he was naked and hers to soothe for the rest of the night.

He came to her then and gifted her with the skin-to-skin she'd craved almost since they'd first met, and definitely since they'd practiced side by side in the courtyard. They had ostensibly been training and not engaged in foreplay with swords, but her body and his had known that every glance and every brush of their fingers was leading to this.

"I'm not cold at all," Elena said. She wrapped her arms around his back and placed her hands on the sensual curve above his bottom. She spread her fingers, but she thought it was the embrace of her open legs that made him moan. She pulled him close, and he rewarded her with the hot and heavy press of his erection against her moist, throbbing folds.

He undulated his hips to stroke his shaft teasingly against her, and she lifted her hips to meet his strokes in a rhythmic welcome. The slide and friction was almost more than she could bear. Her body was hungry for a complete connection. She murmured pleading suggestions of where she needed him, and he complied.

The sapphire's glow seemed to bless their union when he found her opening with the head of his shaft. He reached to position himself and she held on to his back as he worked his hips to fit fully inside of her. She was wet and ready. He'd melted her from the start, but his naked body on top of her caused an even slicker reaction. He was well-endowed, long and thick with excitement, but her body eagerly stretched to accept every inch. In fact, she was the one who increased the speed of their thrusting and only then did he throw caution aside to match her frenzied writhing.

"We've reclaimed this night," Elena promised into his hair as he buried his face into her neck. "All else is forgotten." His hands had come up to cup the heavy globes of her breasts and he held one to suckle as he thrust and thrust, completely lost to claiming what she offered. She cried out from the heat of his mouth and her body tightened around his shaft as she came. He might refuse to claim her with his words, and her heart may have been wounded, but her body knew his rejection was a lie. Her body knew the truth. They were a team.

He was her mate.

His body knew the truth, as well. He rose up, bracing himself with his hands on the floor on either side of her shoulders. His hair spilled down all around her, creating a wild tent that tickled as he moved. In the blue light, she could see the intensity tightening his face even before he opened his eyes. But when their gazes met and held, she saw the truth shining even in the shadows.

She looked into his eyes as his body jerked and tensed. He didn't close them against her as he buried himself all the way to her womb. He came with quaking spasms and a harsh cry that was nearly a howl. Only then did he close his eyes and throw back his head. The heat of his seed sent her over the edge again and her body quivered around him as her soft cries of pleasure joined his.

While Romanov slept, Elena walked around the edges of their sanctuary. She'd wrapped one of the quilts around her shoulders when she rose from the makeshift bed after she'd pulled on her discarded boots. The quilt trailed behind her as her fingers trailed along the walls. The mica seemed magical even though it was only caused by nature. She tried to memorize every silvery speck of dust.

She would never forget Romanov's touch or that he'd allowed her to come to this place that seemed a physical representation of the magic in his heart. He wouldn't allow himself to love her, but he had opened up and given her all he could while still trying to keep her safe.

She wished she could convince him that he needed her by his side. His safety was important too. Together, they could defeat Grigori and face the Ether.

Elena looked down at her hand. Some of the mica from the walls had transferred itself to her fingers. She closed them into a fist to hold the sparkle in her palm. She willed it to be actual power. The sword had dimmed. It glowed softly near Romanov's sleeping form, but with every second she stood apart, its glow faded. As Vasilisa had told them, making love didn't complete their connection.

Romanov had to accept her as his mate. If he didn't, he would fight Grigori alone. If he fought the witch-blood prince and he didn't shift, he would lose. If he did shift, the entire assemblage of witches would be after his head. Never mind that he might lose himself to the beast. If she could wield the sword, it might make the difference between whether Ivan Romanov lived or died or faded away.

Elena opened her hand. She dusted the loose mica away from her fingers. Sparkling dust wouldn't save him. She had to work with what she had. If Romanov didn't choose to make her his mate so she could wield the powerful sapphire sword by his side, she would agree to leave with Grigori.

Her heartbeat slowed, thick and sluggish, in her chest, but the hollow she'd had since she'd lost the dance was gone. It had been filled with burning purpose. She was a warrior. She'd fight for Romanov.

She might not have the sword's power, but she had the power to become the swan.

It would be her choice, not Grigori's. She could endure the cage and the bloody feathers if Romanov lived on. The legend she loved couldn't be allowed to fall.

Chapter 17

There was no denying it. The girl had shaken her. Vasilisa the Luminous, the Light *Volkhvy* queen, wasn't used to surprises. The few she'd experienced in her extraordinarily long life had not been well-received. One of those, the betrayal of her champion and lover, Vladimir Romanov, had resulted in the longest and most enduring rage she'd ever experienced.

Her home was the royal seat of the Light *Volkhvy*. It was one of hundreds of islands that formed an archipelago that surrounded Scotland. To the outside world, it was stark and barren. Even the birds that made their home on most of the other islands shied away, repelled by a force they could neither see nor touch. Vasilisa's ability to manipulate the Ether kept the true enchanted nature of the island hidden from man and beast, as well as provided an artificial atmosphere protected from the extremes of climate that the other islands in the Outer

Hebrides experienced. As she walked through the rose garden that formed the innermost sanctum of her private retreat, she tried to slow her heartbeat and ease her jangled nerves.

She'd been so angry she hadn't felt Elena Pavlova respond to the sword's call.

The petite dancer claimed to have been called from a young age. If that was so, Vasilisa had been blind for two decades while her enchantments ran on without oversight or tending. That wasn't the behavior of a queen. The wild tangle of her rose garden only served to illustrate the same irresponsibility. She'd been furious. And not only because she'd experienced real pain when Vladimir betrayed her.

She'd loved him.

He'd been her gray wolf for years, loyal and true. Or so she'd thought. She'd plucked him from the royal Romanov family. He'd been an obscure cousin who was eager to prove himself once he was given the chance. At first, he'd seemed the perfect choice. He'd taken to the shift amazingly well. He'd recruited and developed an army of followers to fight by his side. Then he'd sired three strong sons and pledged them to her service, as well.

She'd given him Bronwal as a reward. She'd given him the sapphire sword for his wife and then later the ruby sword for the wife chosen by one of his sons.

Madeline.

Poor Madeline and her tiny babe.

The women had been even more precious to her than the wolves because they had chosen to serve her and the Light *Volkhvy*. She honored their service. Which was why she'd never approached Vladimir until his wife and her prince consort had died. She hadn't loved her prince.

Their marriage had been one required by her followers to cement her rule. But she had been faithful to him until he was gone.

She should have stayed away. It was wrong even then to go to Vladimir. She'd dishonored the memory of her sapphire warrior and her prince consort with her lust, and she deserved the horrible price the universe had exacted from her.

She had only worn purple for centuries. No one had ever wondered why. Her grief was her own, abiding and deep.

In the center of the rose garden, on a rough marble dais, a glass enclosure seemed to rise up out of the stone itself. Its edges were obscured and crystallized where rock met glass, but in the center of the oblong container, the glass was clear enough to see the two sleeping forms held and protected inside.

Even in her rage, her love of the women who wielded her swords had won out. She couldn't abandon Madeline and her newborn son to the Ether. Instead, she'd allowed the Ether to put them into a deep sleep, nearly as deep as death, and she'd brought them here. She didn't visit the center of her garden often. She couldn't bear to see the peacefully sleeping baby. Not when her own baby had been murdered by Vladimir Romanov. Today, as she looked down on the innocent faces so soft in repose, she knew her pain didn't excuse what she'd done. Vladimir had been the one who killed her daughter, Anna.

Her revenge against the other Romanovs was wrong.

It had taken the ferocity of Ivan's swan to ease her rage and open her eyes.

Elena had claimed the sapphire sword. And she'd done it even knowing that Vasilisa was a flawed leader.

Her warrior women were more honorable than their queen.

The Gathering approached on swift, ruthless wings. She'd turned a rage-blinded eye toward the *Volkhvy* who attended every year to torment her wolves. She'd even participated, encouraging the decadent ball in order to hurt the last Romanov when she'd known the Romanov who'd actually hurt her had been taken by the Ether almost from the start.

Vladimir hadn't been strong. He'd been weak. If his betrayal hadn't proven that to her, his disappearance had. But the curse had also been the making of the new alpha. Ivan Romanov had become everything she'd hoped her champion would be. Her rage and grief over her daughter's death had blinded her to that.

It had taken Elena Pavlova to open her eyes.

The girl and her connection to the sapphire sword had been entirely unexpected. Vasilisa's wolves inherited their abilities. Her magic had manipulated their father's genes to create the powerfully enhanced champions she needed against the Dark. She had ordered the swords to be made so that the wolves would have companions in battle. Her magic had infused each gem with Light.

But the women who were called to the swords picked them up of their own accord. They, of all her followers, chose to fight for the Light. They hadn't been born to it. They hadn't been made. And yet they were the strongest of all. Mortal women who chose to take up the fight.

Vasilisa pressed a kiss against the glass and backed away. Neither of the container's occupants stirred. Madeline cradled the baby in her arms, but neither of them seemed to breathe and neither had aged or changed. Beside their bodies, the ruby sword lay, dark and dull.

Could she abandon her newest warrior to the Dark or to the Ether?

As always, the sleeping baby reminded her of her own lost child. Her rage hadn't faded. She hadn't loved her prince, but she *had* loved. As only a mother can love. It shook her now and caused her hand to close too tightly around a rose. Its ruthless barb pricked her finger. The blood welled blackish scarlet against her pale skin, but she didn't lift it to her lips. She stared, transfixed, as it swelled. The blood ran down her finger and fell to the ground, unstopped, where it disappeared into the soil.

Vladimir had betrayed her in a more horrific way than most people knew.

Her deepest pain had been a secret expressed only by the ruthlessness of the curse and her mourning garb. Anna was gone. She'd been dead for centuries. Vasilisa had hidden her child from Vladimir with innocent villagers. In his gray wolf form, Vladimir had attacked the village of Sovkra. And from the first she'd heard of Anna's murder Vasilisa held her name close to her heart unable to bear the sound of it on anyone else's lips.

But Vladimir was also gone. He'd been gone a long time and perhaps it was time to forgive his sons.

She was the Light *Volkhvy* queen and it might not be possible to stop what she'd set into motion. The witch-blood prince had laid a powerful mark on Elena. If the black wolf didn't accept her as his mate, the sapphire sword's power was nullified. She could try to stand in Grigori's way. She could buy Ivan Romanov time to claim the warrior's heart that Elena had offered him.

But her pain stood in her way. She couldn't forgive. She would never forget. The Romanovs suffered for what their father had done because she suffered. Her grief was as fresh today as it had been centuries ago.

Even if Romanov claimed Elena, Vasilisa could only lift the curse if she wholeheartedly blessed her wolves and their warriors once more.

Her blessing would have to be given freely and fully at the exact time when it was needed, but could she cleanse the taint in her heart left by Vladimir Romanov?

The prick on her finger tingled. She was the queen, but she was vulnerable. It had always been so. Power attracted those hungry to claim it and never more so than in the *Volkhvy* culture where power mattered most.

She closed her eyes against the sight of her blood seeping into the ground. Had Vladimir torn tiny innocent flesh with the vicious teeth she had given him? Tears flowed freely to join with her blood in the shadow of her roses.

Chapter 18

Only freeing the wolf had allowed him to deny her.

Ivan Romanov stood on the ramparts of the castle.
The sun rose above the horizon to bathe the neighboring
mountain peaks with golden light, and the wind whipped
Ivan's hair wildly around his head. He played a dangerous
balancing game. He was still in control. He still walked
on two legs. But he'd allowed the wolf the greater part
of his heart since last night. He'd discovered the ability
when Vasilisa had asked him about Elena and the sword.
The black wolf allowed him to deny his feelings for her
because the wolf had been tamped down for so long that
now all it wanted was the hunt and the feast, the run and
the fight. He'd allowed those feelings to overwhelm his
feelings for Elena during those moments with Vasilisa.

He'd immediately caged the wolf after that, but he'd
had to loose it again last night. When he'd taken Elena
into the hidden cavern to shield her from Grigori's touch,

he'd opened himself too much to their connection. He'd shown her his secret sanctuary and she'd shown him her heart. She didn't simply offer to wield the sword or to fight by his side. She offered to care for him. The sapphire had lit the cave in a way he'd never seen. It had almost seemed as if his lover was responsible for the starlike glitter on the walls.

He closed his eyes against the strands of his hair that lashed against his face. But then he held them away with two hands fisted at his temples instead. When he closed his eyes, he saw Elena with her head thrown back and her hips thrusting up to meet him. She'd been bathed in the soft blue light of the sapphire blade and he'd known she was meant to bring it to life.

He'd allowed the wolf to rise because that knowledge almost led him to doom her with a pledge he could never allow himself to make.

Was this how his brother Lev had begun to degenerate? Had the white wolf claimed his brother's heart before it had completely claimed his form? The black wolf howled with his every heartbeat. He could hardly see the glow of the sun because what he wanted to see was the blood of his enemies. The alpha had been too long denied. It was thirsty for *Volkhvy* blood. Dark, Light, it made no difference. The wolf wanted them all to fall before him.

When the time came, it would be easy to shift and allow the black wolf to devour Grigori. He could almost anticipate the perfect vengeance of showing how he felt about Elena by destroying the creature that had tormented her mercilessly for years. It would be the only way he could express what he felt without exposing her to the Ether. The only thing that marred his anticipation was the knowledge that in saving her he would also lose her forever.

The black wolf howled inside the heart it controlled as it waited impatiently for the shift it knew was coming. It was only a matter of time before the wolf devoured him, heart and soul.

Choosing to fully loose the wolf would be his last conscious act as a man.

Elena wasn't sure what had gone wrong. Ivan had been opening to her. She'd sensed his emotion. He hadn't brought her to the cavern simply to hide her from Grigori. He'd wanted to show her the refuge he'd sought when he was younger. He'd shown her his secret place and he'd shared the vulnerabilities he'd felt as a child.

But as their connection had seemed to burgeon, he'd given himself completely over to passion. She hadn't complained. She'd joined him in physical release, again and again. Even when she'd lost all hope of him declaring his love.

It was enough for her that he declared it with his refusal to claim her as his mate. He was protecting her, and for a champion that was the greatest declaration of all. Unfortunately, it wasn't enough for the sword.

Her only pain came in wondering how he was able to keep silent about the feelings she couldn't deny. Just as the mica sparkled on the walls of his cavern, her love for him seemed to radiate from every cell in her body, as they lay naked together.

But, again, it wasn't enough.

The sword had gone dark.

She'd been awake when the stone dulled. By its dying light, she had traced the face of the man who refused to love her. With trembling fingers, she'd lightly brushed over his forehead, the full sweep of his dark lashes, the hollow of his cheek and his square jaw as if she could memorize his features. His lips had been soft and full in repose. The thick sweep of his hair, for once, had been swept back and out of his face by his position. She hadn't fallen in love with his appearance, but it was beloved to her all the same. The cavern's walls had retreated into shadows as all the artificial starlight had died. Tears had filled her eyes when she could no longer see his face. Romanov had slept through it while she cried. No one had seen her, but if they had she wouldn't have been able to stop. She was strong in all things but this.

He was determined to save her even if it meant losing himself.

She would try to stop him.

She would give herself to Grigori if she had to.

But she was afraid. Because if he loved her as she loved him, her sacrifice might make him seek out the oblivion of the wolf even if he didn't need to shift to fight Grigori.

Chapter 19

She and Romanov moved around the entire castle, each avoiding the other but fully aware of every step taken. It was an elaborate dance as the sun tracked across the sky. The sword had come between them even as it was supposed to bind them together. She saw the awakened sapphire as proof that she could stand against Grigori. Ivan saw its glow as proof that the Ether would take her and torment her the way it had all the loved ones he'd ever cared about. It was a standoff and a stalemate. One she didn't know how to break.

It wasn't until late in the afternoon that Elena realized her black wolf had disappeared.

Romanov was no longer in the castle. She didn't know how her body recognized that he was gone. There was only a vacuum she couldn't explain. She wasted no time going for her ski suit and snow boots, although she was terrified it would be too late to find him.

What if he had decided to end his fight and disappear into the Ether in order to be certain that their connection wouldn't overcome his "honorable" intentions?

What if she had ended his long-enforced isolation in a way she hadn't intended when she'd tried to claim the sword?

The snowstorm had ended days ago. The sky was clear and the sun beamed brightly in the sky, but it was still hard on her knee to trudge out beyond the castle walls into the deep snow. She did it anyway.

If she found the wolf or the man, it would be worth the hike to ease her mind.

Of course, Lev could also be outside the walls. It was a risk she had to take. She'd strapped the sapphire sword around her waist. It was still a sword even if it didn't glow. Romanov had taught her how to use it. Lev would be practically invisible against the blinding white of the sunlit snow. Unlike her. She wore the bright red cloak over her snowsuit to add another layer against the mountain cold. But if Lev attacked she would defend herself. Until then, she'd look for Ivan Romanov. Her cloak might make her more visible to Lev, but it would also help Romanov to see her. She'd bring him home. It had been wrong to avoid him all morning. She should have pushed her pain and pride aside to make sure he wasn't contemplating a desperate act to try to save her.

She followed a trail that had been broken in the deep snow. It led to a thick evergreen wood on the west side of the wall. *Evergreen.* Romanov's scent was her only clue besides the beaten pathway. Once she stepped into the forest's shadows, she was able to walk with less effort. The ground had been protected from most of the snow. It was barely dusted with white. Frozen pine needles crunched under her boots, and above her a heavy, frozen canopy of white blocked out the sun.

Would she find the wolf or the man or nothing at all? Or would the white wolf find her first?

Elena heard something besides her own footsteps. She paused and the forest fell quiet. She drew the sword from the sheath at her side. The sound of metal rasping against leather was loud in the silent wood. Had it been her imagination or a breeze around the trees? No birds sang. No rodents stirred. For long, breathless seconds it seemed she was alone.

Wolves were predators and the shadows were deep. Lev could very easily creep up behind her and she'd never know until he pounced. Elena spun around, betraying her fear with her sudden movement. But there was no one there.

"Romanov," she shouted. It came out quieter than she would have liked. Fear compressed her lungs. She couldn't draw enough air to propel the call from her tight chest. She wouldn't go back without him. If he hadn't disappeared into the Ether, she would find him. She would face the black wolf or the man.

A sound much farther in the distance disturbed the silence. She barely heard it over the pounding of her heart, but it sounded like animals fighting. She heard growls, barks, then the sharp yelp of a canine in pain. The noise was too far away to be the noise she'd heard moments before, but that was explained as Soren melted into sight from the evergreen shadows.

He came to her side showing no fear of her drawn sword. Like her, his ears pricked at the sounds of fighting. He looked up at her and then toward the distant melee.

"Did you follow me outside the walls or did you follow your brother?" Elena asked.

Soren simply blinked before he bolted deeper into the woods. Elena followed. She had told Romanov that she was a warrior. She had yet to prove it to him or to herself. Soren howled and picked up speed when more yelps rang out. Elena followed as fast as she could run on the uneven ground. She was glad that she didn't have to run through the snow. She would never have kept up. As it was, she relied on the sounds of the fight to guide her whenever Soren slipped out of sight. And yet he was always waiting for her when she came around a rise or a bend. He would take off again only when he was sure she saw and followed.

He was purposefully leading her to the fight.

They burst out of the woods into a sudden dazzling glare of sunlight. But Soren halted at the edge of the clearing they found, and her forward momentum was stopped by his giant body. He stood sideways, barring her passage. The pause gave her eyes time to adjust and her mind to comprehend what they'd found.

A huge pack of natural wolves had Lev surrounded. They'd bloodied him until his fur was splattered with scarlet. The snow was trampled and pink around him. He was an enchanted shifter, twice their size and preternaturally ferocious, but there were dozens of wolves trying to kill him. Elena's hands tightened on the hilt of her sword.

They would have succeeded already if Lev hadn't received reinforcement. Romanov was the cause of the yelps they'd heard. He hadn't shifted. He was still a man, but he wasn't an ordinary man. He wore his fur-capped cloak and brandished a sword. He cut down every wolf that leaped for his throat, one after another.

While he slashed, he yelled curses at the white wolf

and the red. The white wolf for seeking annihilation. The red for endangering *her* life by leading her here.

Romanov was the one surrounded by a vicious pack of hungry wolves trying to kill him and his brother. But he worried about her joining the fray. Elena quietly spoke to the red wolf that stood in her way.

"I am his partner. Whether he has accepted that yet or not. The sword has chosen. And I have chosen. Now get out of my way," she said.

She didn't have magic to help her. She only had muscles and determination. They were all she'd ever needed. She ran into the clearing easily, glad that the fight had already flattened the snow. If she died, she would die by her lover's side, by her own choice and because of her own actions whether Romanov liked it or not.

Soren ran with her. He didn't try to stop her again. He outpaced her in a flash and leaped over the fallen wolf bodies to land beside Lev. There were fewer wolves than Lev had had to face alone. Soren made fewer wolves still with his wicked teeth and claws.

Elena went to Romanov. He was an incredible sight. All fury and fight and righteous anger over her and Soren's disobedience to his will. She ignored his rage and did what she had to do. Slashing and stabbing until the wolves in between her and Romanov began to give way.

Then she saw Romanov's eyes. They blazed nearly black even in the sun. His curses were more like howls and his fighting wasn't smooth. His wolf was close to the surface. As close as it could be without the shift. She was certain of it. In spite of her desperation to keep the wolves from her own throat, she spoke to Romanov.

"Shift if you must, but not because of me. I don't need the black wolf anymore. I need you."

Suddenly, more wolves came from the forest. One,

two, a dozen more ran to join the fight. The movement called her attention to the edge of the wood. There were half a dozen men standing there. They stared at the clearing where the fight raged on. She'd been wrong. The wolves weren't behaving as natural wolves would behave. These were multiple packs joined together by enchantment.

"Is this Vasilisa's work? Are those her men?" Elena shouted. She had made it to Romanov's side, and now they turned to press their backs together as he'd taught her to do when they'd practiced in the courtyard together. She was small, but she used his size and strength to her advantage, bracing off him to shoulder the attacks against her.

"This is the work of the Dark *Volkhvy*. Several have banded together to attack us. They lured Lev into the woods. If I hadn't been keeping an eye on him, he would have gone down. He didn't even begin to fight until I arrived," Romanov shouted. His voice vibrated against her. "And you've brought them the sword they seek."

"They may pry it out of my cold, dead hands," Elena said. Adrenaline caused the words to come out as a laugh from deep in her frozen middle. The wolves had shredded the edges of her scarlet cape as they continued to attack, but so far she had managed to keep their teeth away from her skin. The edges of the cape fluttered in the winter wind.

"The shift isn't pretty to witness. Do not turn around," Romanov ordered. This time Elena obeyed. Not because she was squeamish about his abilities. She couldn't divide her attention from the wolves that attacked to see what he intended to do.

She already knew.

He'd risked the shift to try to frighten her away from the sword.

Now he would risk the shift to protect her and his brothers against the *Volkhvy*.

She'd been a fool to think he would escape into the Ether and leave them to face the Gathering alone. He would stand as long as he could. It would be the shift or the *Volkhvy* that would take him in the end. He would never give up.

She would bet her life that the black wolf would continue to stand as Bronwal's champion even when every ounce of his humanity was gone.

His shift happened behind her back. She could only feel the trembling earth beneath her feet, and then her body was shaken with the force of the black wolf's howl. The lesser *Volkhvy*'s enchantment of the pack couldn't stand against the alpha wolf's presence. Dozens of wolves had piled onto Romanov's form as he'd fallen to the ground during his transformation. Elena whirled in time to see the pile explode away from the black wolf in all directions as he rose to his feet.

The wolves and the *Volkhvy* who controlled them ran at the sudden appearance of the powerful black wolf. Elena couldn't blame them. Her knees went weak and she had to tighten her fingers around the hilt of her sword. She took in the aftermath as she ordered her own feet to stay planted right where they were, no running away allowed.

Lev was down. His white coat was covered in blood. But Soren had protected him. The red wolf stood over the white wolf. Soren's sides heaved and he, too, was speckled with damp splotches of blood.

Elena could only spare the two wolves a glance before her gaze was drawn back to the black wolf. He ap-

proached her. She stood her ground. She lowered the
sapphire sword. He was still Romanov and he wasn't her
enemy. He stopped in front of her and without a pause
she lifted one hand up to cup his mighty jaw. He blinked
at her, but he didn't jerk away. He allowed her touch. He
even briefly rested his muzzle in her palm.

And then he spun away and called to his brothers with
an ear-splitting howl. Only Soren could obey. Lev wasn't
able to get to his feet. The black wolf ran toward the spot
where the Dark *Volkhvy* had thought to watch their bewitched pack kill the weakest of the Romanov brothers.
They hadn't counted on Soren, Ivan and Elena showing
up to defend Lev. The witches had disappeared into the
trees, but Elena had no doubt the black wolf would hunt
them down.

She turned to make her way over to Lev's side. He
was alert and breathing. He whined as she approached,
but he didn't get to his feet.

"Did you really take on that pack alone? Contemplating suicide, are you? As if Romanov would ever let you
go. He's determined to save us all. Even if it kills him,"
Elena said. She stabbed her sword into the ground and
began to rip the scarlet cloak into bandages to bind the
worst of the white wolf's wounds. He was enchanted.
Surely he would heal. He growled once or twice but she
ignored it. Her heart was full of a warm sense of sister-
hood. Lev had been the mate of the woman who had
wielded the ruby sword. Helping him was the least she
could do. Even if he threatened to bite off her hands.

Soren returned with a team of servants to carry Lev
back into the castle. They came prepared with a wooden
sled pulled by Soren himself. His power was evident
in the way he effortlessly brought the heavy sled, even

through the forest where the pine needles formed the only track for its curved treads.

Elena didn't ask about Romanov. She would find out soon enough if he was lost to the wolf. For now, she could only trudge back to the castle behind the sled. She refused to add to its weight. She had made it through the entire fight without a single injury. Her silk cloak was shredded and her snowsuit's downy insulation spilled from several tears that would have been gruesome if the thick material hadn't protected her skin.

But she was unscathed.

Except for the shaking. She allowed one of the servants who had returned with Soren and the sled to place a blanket around her shoulders. Shock was settling in as adrenaline faded away. She was shaken by the violence and Lev's injuries and by the evidence of Ivan Romanov's abilities. She'd seen him as the black wolf. She'd seen his intelligence shine from the black wolf's eyes. But this was the first time she'd seen the black wolf shine from his even before he shifted.

It was the first time she'd felt the power of his shift. It seemed as if the quaking of the earth was still with her.

And it was another first, as well. She loved him, wolf and all. Not in spite of his ferocity, but because of it. Perhaps she was still looking for the black wolf after all.

Ivan tended his wounds alone. The shift had taken care of many of his injuries, and he would heal quickly from those that didn't entirely disappear. Even though he had shifted back to his human form, he could still feel the tentative touch of Elena's hand. She hadn't cringed away from him. She had been afraid, but she'd still extended her fingers. He'd been eager to hunt down the Dark witches, but he'd paused for her touch. He'd taken that moment to make sure she wasn't hurt. Remarkably, she hadn't suffered a single bite. She faced down a pack of cursed wild wolves and she'd done it with the Romanov blade gripped perfectly in her hand.

It hadn't glowed. Even as they'd fought together, the stone had stayed cold and dark.

He should be happy about that. He'd succeeded. He'd rejected their connection even though it was the most powerful force he'd ever felt. Why did he feel as if it was a mistake? If Elena stayed free of the Ether, then he would have saved her from a torment he could barely withstand. Others were more easily consumed.

Yet he'd seen her face so much, time and time again, with incredible strength and fortitude. It would be a lie to say that he still believed the Ether would take her easily. She would stand. He was certain of it.

If he chose to continue to stand against the Ether alone, it wasn't to protect Elena from a trial she couldn't face, but, rather, a trial she shouldn't have to face.

This was a Romanov burden. One he would continue to shoulder alone. He would stay away from Elena. From a distance, he'd seen her follow the group of servants he'd sent to fetch Lev. She was fine. He didn't need to hold her to prove it. He didn't need to kiss her to celebrate their victory.

The black wolf had taken care of the Dark witches with Soren's help. That had been the only celebration he needed.

But the wolf in his heart disagreed. It urged him with a primal need to hold his mate close after battle.

Elena saw Lev settled with Bell and several others attending him. Soren was close by if his brother became unruly. For now, the white wolf accepted the ministrations of his people.

"His wounds will heal quickly. It takes a lot to bring him down, and he's never down for long," Bell said. She straightened from the bandages she had knotted carefully around one of Lev's hind legs. She met Elena's eyes. "This isn't the first time he's tried."

They both knew Bell was talking about Lev's flirtation with death. Apparently, losing himself to the wolf wasn't enough for him. Maybe even fading into the Ether wouldn't stop his deep-seated grief. He must have loved his family very much to feel the pain of their loss so keenly even when he was no longer the man he'd been. He'd risked a bloody, painful death to end it.

"Thank you for helping to save him," Bell said. She glanced from Elena to the red wolf who stood a silent vigil in the far corner of the great room. The fire blazed and a makeshift bed had been made for Lev near enough to the hearth for warmth and light, but not near enough to overheat him as he healed. The direction of her attention quickly shifted back to Lev, but Elena still understood. Bell was grateful that Elena had helped Soren in order to prevent his sacrificing himself for Lev.

"When I heeded the sapphire sword's call, I chose to defend Bronwal and everyone in it," Elena said. The sword was back in its sheath at her side. She'd cleansed its blade in the snow with an edge of her ruined cloak. Suddenly, she was very aware of her own aches and pains, as well as the wolf blood that had dried on her clothes.

Always observant, Bell noticed her discomfort.

"Go up to your room. I'll send up some hot water," she said.

Elena wanted to refuse the extra trouble, but she didn't have the will. Cleaning up would settle her shakes and get her away from the stares of the servants who had come to help with Lev. Besides, Romanov hadn't made an appearance yet, but he was bound to check on his brother. She couldn't face him yet. Not with trembling fingers and wobbly knees.

The tower was dark and quiet even though the sun was still high outside. The fight had been over much sooner than it had seemed. There were still many hours left in the day before she had to worry about the sun going down and the possibility that Grigori might return.

Elena unfastened the cloak and allowed the ruined red silk to fall to the ground. She kicked it to the side. She unbuckled her belt and laid the sword on the foot of her bed. She hadn't been injured, but it took a close look to see the blood on her clothes wasn't hers. Maybe that's why the servants stared when they carried several buckets of water to the tub that stood by the fireplace.

While Elena waited to remove the rest of her clothes, Patrice arrived with a small bar of soap and a large linen cloth. She placed them on the edge of the wooden tub and then she leaned over to stir and wake the coals in the fireplace. She added two oak logs to the embers.

Elena was surprised to see her. The older servant had seemed to be becoming more and more addled as the Cycle wore on. But Lev's injuries must have woken her from the walking dream she seemed to have retreated into.

"Bell said that you saved the boys. She said Romanov wouldn't have shifted except to protect you," Patrice said.

"Bell is wrong. Romanov will always protect his brothers and everyone in this castle. However he must," Elena said.

Patrice murmured in response, but Elena couldn't make out her words. After a moment of clarity, it seemed as if the older woman was back to her dream. She walked out of the tower room without saying goodbye.

And Elena was finally alone with a steaming tub.

She pulled off her ruined clothes and threw them on the pile with the scarlet cloak. The logs Patrice had placed on the fire had caught. They crackled and burned and the room's chill was softened, but not so much that the water didn't beckon. She stepped into the water and sank down into its welcoming heat.

The bar of soap Patrice had brought was lightly scented with evergreen. Elena breathed deeply as she lathered it up in her hands. It reminded her of the wintry wood, but also of Romanov's skin. Her after-battle shakes were fading away.

"I completely destroyed this door," Romanov said from the threshold. It was an understatement. The bars were twisted and the door sagged to the side. He'd practically ripped it from its hinges to help her the night before.

Elena had thought he would check on his brother. She should have known he would check on them all. He stood at the door and he held the edges of its frame with a white-knuckled grip as if he'd hoped to find it locked against him even though the lock was ruined.

Instead of a lock, he had to depend on his own strength to keep him outside.

She hoped his strength would fail.

"A lock wouldn't protect me from Grigori," Elena said.

She was covered in the frothy lather Patrice's soap had created in her hands. Her skin only showed in several wet flashes against the white bubbles, pink from the water's heat. But she noticed the direction of Romanov's eyes and how they widened when the lather began to slip away from her breasts. First the hardened nipple of one breast was revealed and then the other.

He didn't look away.

The last of Elena's shock was gone. She'd needed to see him on two legs. But there was also no room for shock when her body was reacting to his presence. Her stomach grew heavy and heated as her nipples peaked beneath his gaze. He still held the door's frame. He still refused to step inside. But one of his legs had bent at the knee as if it would carry him forward without his permission. And his knuckles were whiter as if he used every bit of his strength to keep himself from answering her body's silent invitation.

It was a sudden decision that caused her to stand. Water and bubbles sluiced off her body.

"Elena," Romanov said. Was it in protest or appreciation? She thought the latter. His color was high. His chest rose and fell as if he'd grown winded while merely standing at the door. He also leaned slightly inward and his bent knee extended to place one booted foot inside the door.

Another sudden decision had her reaching for one of the small buckets that a servant had left by the tub. She dipped it in the water at her feet while Romanov stared, riveted by her actions and all the pink skin her movements revealed. She watched him as she lifted the bucket high. His chest was no longer rising and falling. He held his breath. When she upended the warm water over her shoulders and washed most of the lather away, he released a long exhalation.

In the firelight, her wet skin glistened.

And Romanov let go of the door.

It was her turn to hold her breath as he stepped inside. He came to the tub with no further hesitation. Her body shivered now from cold and anticipation. The battle was far from her mind. She trembled when he stopped at the edge of the tub. He towered over her. Would she ever grow accustomed to his size and strength? She was used to leaner, more graceful men. Romanov's muscles were intended for battles like the one they'd just fought. He needed to swing a sword and plant his feet. He was so solid, she couldn't imagine him ever giving way to an attacking foe. Not a pack of enchanted wolves or a troop of Dark *Volkhvy*.

The idea that something as amorphous as time and Ether might fell him caused her to reach out her hand and place it on his downturned face. He looked at her as if he would memorize her features in the firelight. She looked up at him to do the same. He'd received several deep scratches. They joined the white scars of previous battles on his handsome face.

"I watched you return to the castle from the ramparts, but that wasn't enough," Romanov said. He reached to touch a tendril of her hair that had escaped the messy bun at the top of her head. And then he moved more decisively to burrow into the mass of waves to remove the pins she'd used to hold it up and out of the way. The battle had already loosened it. His strong fingers quickly caused it to fall down around her shoulders as the pins flew.

Elena was fascinated by the play of emotions over his face—concern, frustration and desire. She gasped when he finished with her hair because he immediately pulled her to him with a warm calloused hand on the nape of her neck.

His lips descended to crush against hers. She wound her damp arms around his neck to hold on and to press her naked body against him. He was fully clothed. The contrast was thrilling. But it was also poignant. She laid everything bare while he remained a mystery.

She held nothing back. Her mouth opened eagerly for his plunging tongue. He held her head for his crushing kiss and she gloried in his complete loss of control. He wasn't holding back now. For the first time, he gave in to the connection between them. Even more so than he had the night before.

But the firelight was suddenly overwhelmed by the flash of blue light from the sapphire behind them. It blazed and the entire room was bathed in blue. Romanov ripped his lips from hers and jerked away. He whirled away from her arms. They fell at her side, but only for a moment before she wrapped them around her aching middle.

Now, she shivered from the cold. The water at her feet had chilled. The fire had already burned low. The sapphire faded as Romanov moved away.

"We killed them all. Every last one. The black wolf was eager to fight," he said. "You don't need the sword to fight Grigori. You have me."

He left the room before she could reply. She watched him leave and he didn't even glance back over his shoulder. The sapphire was cold and dull again before his footsteps had faded away.

"But I don't have you," Elena said. She stepped from the tub and wrapped a sheet around her cold skin.

Chapter 20

The black wolf had interfered. Grigori had been touching his swan for the first time. His hands still tingled from the forbidden contact with her skin. The protection her mother had bought from the universe with her blood was almost gone. She'd been softer than silk beneath his hand.

And she'd been so very afraid.

Her fear was an aphrodisiac because it fueled his power like a battery that he could constantly recharge with the mere application of his dark desires. The memory of her trembling and vulnerable beneath his touch was better than any trembling he'd inspired with dreams. Who knows what he might have been able to do to her if the Romanov wolves hadn't interrupted?

Her mother's knowledge of hearth magic had taken him by surprise, but it was Elena who had shocked him. He hadn't been prepared for his little swan to take flight.

He'd never imagined she would seek help from the one being who might be able to stand in his way. He'd been so certain she would be his when the power of the blood ran out. He'd never suspected that she might know *Volkhvy* secrets. The Light queen of the *Volkhvy* had been practically sleepwalking for centuries. Her anger at her Romanov champions had caused most of the old protections against the Dark to fade away. The old legends were dead. Or so he thought. No one spoke of them anymore. Cell phones and social media had taken the place of books and campfire stories that had armed generations against his kind.

Except one old woman who had taught her daughter and granddaughter the old tales and the old ways.

She'd been too canny and wise for him to kill. He'd had to wait for nature to take her in its own sweet time. But he'd never imagined she'd passed on the legend of the Romanovs to her granddaughter or that a woman born in this time of lattes and laptops would take the legends to heart.

It wasn't her belief that truly shocked him. It was her determination to travel a thousand miles and climb a mountain in the snow to find a cursed castle and a mythical champion to fight him.

That…and the sapphire sword.

The delicate swan he craved was not a warrior woman. He would put her back in her place…in his cage, under his power, forever at his mercy. The sword would be lost to the Ether and entirely out of her reach. She would be delicate and vulnerable once more. Even if he had to clip her wings and her uninjured leg to ensure that she accepted her true nature.

He preened as he thought, literally soothing his ruffled feathers. They were as black as obsidian, but they weren't a raven's wings. They were much larger and more powerful than that. When he shifted, he was larger than a natural bird, just as the Romanov wolves were larger than natural wolves. And just as Elena was a womanly swan with some of her human features intact. She would have feathers on her breast, but they would be full, lush womanly breasts. Her wings would stretch from her perfect, delicately boned shoulders.

His Ether-fueled powers gave him infinite possibilities for his pleasure. Currently, he was a large cob swan anticipating making Elena his mate. He was capable of being fully formed as a bird, but he could also keep his human arms…and other attributes…if he chose.

He would choose with Elena.

And they would mate for life…or as long as her life lasted.

His pets never lasted long once he had full power over them. His appetites always got the best of him once they had free rein.

In order for all of his plans to proceed to fruition, he would need to destroy the black wolf first. The creature had been created by the Light *Volkhvy* queen to fight his kind, but, in truth, the queen had never fully understood what his kind was capable of becoming. The Dark *Volkhvy* themselves didn't know of the power they could channel from the Ether if they were brave enough to seek it. No one had absorbed as much power as he had—not even his father, the king.

Elena hadn't been his only obsession for the last decade.

It was almost time to solidify the Dark *Volkhvy* behind a new leader, one who knew how dark they could be.

He would settle for no less than the black wolf's head, his vulnerable swan slave and the throne.

* * *

The servants who were left in the castle made no preparations for the Gathering. There was nothing like the usual hustle and bustle of a big event about to take place. If anything, the hallways were more deserted than ever as Elena sought out the one person who might be living in the present enough to help her.

There was very little time left to make Ivan see reason. She was down to hoping she could convince him on the night of the ball before Grigori arrived to make his claim. And if she weren't able to convince Romanov, then her last chance before she chose to leave with Grigori would be the Light *Volkhvy* queen.

Elena had been a performer her entire life. She knew one didn't inspire a queen's intervention in rags or jeans.

"I need help to get ready for the Gathering," she said when she finally found Bell. The young woman greeted her with a big grin. Her determined good humor was a welcome relief from the hopelessness Elena found in everyone else. "I need a dress fit for a warrior, a wife and a swan. My main accessory will be the sapphire sword."

Bell was wearing a maid's gown paired with more modern combat boots and her usual boy's hat. Her smile tilted slowly with a hint of mischievousness.

"Maybe you'll be worth all the water I've had to carry after all," she said. "I'd survive the Ether one more Cycle if it means you'll give those witches hell. This castle needs a new mistress."

"Romanov doesn't want me here. And I might not be able to stay. But I'm going to do all I can to change his mind *and* Vasilisa's before I go away," Elena promised.

At the mention of the Light queen's name, Bell stopped smiling. Her face tightened and her eyes grew grim. Under the shadow of her oversize cap, her big hazel eyes tracked over Elena's face as if to ascertain if she meant what she said. Elena thought Bell would warn against trying to influence the queen, but she should have known better. Once the young woman seemed to determine that Elena was earnest, a small smile returned to her lips.

"We've got our work cut out for us if that's what you're trying to accomplish," she said. "We'd better get going."

Bell was a survivor. You didn't survive by giving up without a fight.

Elena stopped her friend with a firm hand on her shoulder.

"Anywhere but the baby's room, you understand? I promised Lev I wouldn't disturb that room again," she said.

Bell nodded. Her eyes softened.

"Trevor was a fine lad. And he was loved by all. You're kind to care," she said. She continued pragmatically, "Madeline's dresses would never fit you. She was tall. Almost as tall as Lev. Well, as tall as he used to be, God rest his soul."

Bell's pragmatism warred with all the losses she'd suffered. Elena reminded her of all the people Bronwal had lost, but she also offered a course of action. Staying busy seemed to be something the young woman relied on.

"This place has been reduced to mourning for too long," Bell said. Elena squeezed the small shoulder beneath her hand. Bell was too young to have to shoulder all the work, responsibility and worry that she must have had to take on since Patrice lost her mind. And yet, more often than not, the young woman smiled.

"I came here for help, but I found a place that needed *my* help. But I can't do this alone," Elena said.

"I can find you a dress," Bell replied. "The castle is

full of clothes that people have left behind." The other woman walked around Elena slowly. She narrowed her eyes and seemed to be gauging her shape and size. "I always forget how small you are. You seem bigger somehow when you leave a room than when you first come in."

"There's more to me than meets the eye," Elena said. "I've felt from the start that the same could be said about you."

Bell's eyes widened. Maybe the young orphan wasn't used to people noticing anything about her. She looked up to meet Elena's gaze, and her smile grew slightly bigger.

"The first night you arrived I recognized something in your eyes—a feeling I've often had. When times are dark, but you know you can put one foot in front of the other as long as it takes," Bell said. "I haven't had the easiest time of it since the curse. In the beginning, there were plenty of sane people to keep the first ones who fell apart from harming anyone in their madness. But with every Cycle, fewer and fewer returned. Until one day I was pretty much on my own. Since then, I've had to take care of myself."

"You couldn't ask Romanov for help?" Elena asked. Bell stood next to her, shoulder to shoulder. They seemed to be close to the same size with only slight differences in the width of their shoulders and hips. Bell was curvier with an hourglass figure. It had been some time since Elena could take to the stage, but her body had been honed by too many years of discipline to soften now.

"He's been busy the last few Cycles. He has to keep up with his brothers now that they're in their wolf forms full-time," Bell said softly. She bit her lip and Elena regretted delving into subjects that made her sad.

"Soren can still look out for himself," Elena said, trying to lighten the mood.

"The red wolf tries to look out for all of us. But he's kept busy with Lev," Bell said. She sounded wistful. Her eyes had gone glassy, as if she was no longer seeing Elena's measurements, but rather something that made her pensive.

"Lev is a challenge. He's very dangerous," Elena said.

"I'm afraid he won't last much longer. Once he disappears into the Ether for good, Soren… I'm not sure how he'll survive it. They were born only seconds apart. They've been inseparable ever since," Bell said. The young woman stilled, and suddenly Elena saw behind her smile and her busy behavior. She was a survivor, but how much longer could she survive once the red wolf was gone?

"I'm going to try to prevent that from happening," Elena promised.

Elena was glad to have Bell's help. The young girl knew the castle like the back of her hand. There was no corner she didn't know how to reach, and many could only be reached through back passages and secret doorways that Elena would never understand.

"The Ether changes everything. Including the layout of the castle. It never comes back the exact same way twice. But there are clues to watch for. Landmarks, if you will. A tip-tilted lantern or a mark I've left on the wall," Bell instructed. She pointed at a white mark painted on the wall ahead of them. It almost looked like a flower. "That's me. It's supposed to be a bellflower," Bell explained. Then she continued, "It must be hard for you to imagine what Bronwal was like before the curse. Before it deteriorated. It was enchanting, specially blessed by the Light *Volkhvy* queen herself. I was the little orphan child who had woken in a storybook."

"It's hard to grow up with legends," Elena said.

Bell had stopped in front of a door. To Elena it looked like every other door they'd passed, but Bell pointed to a swirl in the oak that looked like a leaping frog.

Elena hesitated on the threshold when Bell opened the door to step inside.

"Don't worry. You aren't disturbing anyone here. This room was the dressmaker's workplace. She had a team of seamstresses and they sewed night and day to keep us all clothed—from Soren's mother, Naomi, and Madeline, all the way down to me. And the men, as well," Bell said.

Elena followed her into the room. Bell ran her hand along a table and it came away covered in dust. But for the neglect, the room looked as if all the seamstresses had simply stood and walked away from their work for a coffee break. There were unfinished pieces on each station. Scissors and thread, needles and material left where they had fallen when the women faded away.

Bell dusted her hands together and smiled a rueful smile.

"Believe me, I regret not showing my appreciation more for them when they were here. I'm horrible with sewing. I can't manage one straight stitch," she said.

"I've never tried," Elena said. Her time had been all for the dance. There hadn't been any left over.

"The work they completed is stored in these wardrobes and trunks back here," Bell said. She turned and motioned toward a long line of mahogany wardrobes that lined one entire wall. Stacked around the wardrobes were trunks like the one Elena had helped Bell lug up to her aviary.

"Most of the dresses should have been protected from

dust, and the wardrobes were lined with cedar to try to keep the moths away. Not so in most of the living quarters. We used up most of the more practical clothes long ago. That's why so many servants you see are in rags," Bell said. "It takes a lot of effort to maintain any semblance of normalcy, but it's also horrible to not even try."

She smoothed her skirts as she said it. Elena realized her unconventional appearance was as much necessity as personality. Bell made do with what she could gather and scrounge.

Elena reached to tip Bell's hat up. The crown often threatened to cover her pretty hazel eyes, although the shadows it caused on her features did tend to make her smile shine.

"I wondered what the hat was about. I guess it's what you could find," she said.

But the other woman grabbed for her hat as if Elena was trying to take it. She pulled the rim tight against her brown hair.

"I'm keeping this safe for someone else. When he comes back, I'm going to give it to him," Bell said.

"I'm sorry. I didn't know," Elena replied. She allowed her hand to drop to Bell's shoulder and she gave it a squeeze. The wide panicked eyes and somber mouth that had claimed Bell's face seemed like a glimpse into her true self, as if the forceful cheer she usually conveyed was a persona she used to survive.

"Most of us are waiting for someone or lots of someones. When you lose hope, the Ether takes you," Bell whispered. Elena understood. If she hadn't had hope, she thought Grigori might have been able to take her long before now.

"But, look, there'll be lots of formal dresses here to choose from. The practical things have been picked over, but the most elaborate gowns haven't been disturbed in ages. The *Volkhvy* are the only ones who dress for the Gathering. It's become the grandest occasion for them. They all try to outdo each other," Bell said.

"That's why this is important. I want to show the queen that the Romanovs haven't given up the fight. And I want to show Grigori that his swan is armed and not in a cage. Most important, I want Ivan to give me his heart and the sword. I want to finally claim it fully, empowered with our connection."

"I want to help you," Bell said. "The Romanovs have been too disconnected for too long."

She flung open one of the wardrobes, and a swarm of fluttering moths flew out surrounded by a cloud of fabric dust.

"Oh, well. I was wrong about that one. Let's try the next," Bell said sheepishly.

They went down the row of wardrobes checking one after another until they finally found several that hadn't been invaded by gnawing insects. And in the dresses they found, Elena finally got a glimpse of the scope of Bronwal's previous splendor.

"I told you...an orphan among legends," Bell said. But she said it with a smile because Elena's wonder was contagious.

She buried her hands in the textures of damask and brocade. She feasted her eyes on the sheen of silks and satins. She laughed out loud at the airy lightness of chiffon and organza.

"This reminds me of home. Although these kind of skirts would only get in the way," Elena said. She lifted one of the full ball gowns out for a closer inspection. It was far too heavy and cumbersome for her needs, but she twirled around in it anyway.

"You were a dancer before you came here," Bell said.

"I'm a dancer still. Once a dancer, always a dancer. Once you've been forged in the fire of the Saint Petersburg Ballet Company, it never goes away," Elena said. She placed the dress back in the wardrobe. She needed a dress that was light and airy around her legs, designed in such a way that it wouldn't impede her movements with the sword.

They rifled through trunks and drawers in companionable silence broken occasionally when a dress elicited appreciative or horrified sounds. Until Bell exclaimed, and Elena turned to see the other woman holding a green dress made of liquid silk. As Bell unfolded the dress from its tissue-lined drawer, its train spilled down and thousands of embroidered flowers showed on the backdrop of green.

"They're bellflowers," her friend said. There were tears in her voice, as if something poignant from the past had been taken from the drawer.

Elena went to her. Beside Bell's current patched and worn outfit—a pauper's clothes—the dress seemed meant for a princess. But, when Bell lifted her eyes up to meet Elena's, her eyes matched the green dress, not her servant's clothes. The sheen of the silk had turned her eyes from hazel to a forest green.

"That dress was made for you," Elena said.

"I never went to dances or parties. Some thought I should," Bell said softly. Elena immediately supposed that by "some" Bell referred to Soren Romanov.

"Of course you should have," Elena said. "He was right. Did he have this dress made for you before the curse fell?" she asked.

"I don't know," Bell said. "I'll never know."

She folded the dress back into the drawer. She covered it carefully with the tissue paper. Maybe it would have been too painful for her to try it on.

"Besides, we're looking for something for you to wear to the Gathering," Bell reminded Elena.

There was nothing she could do for her friend except respect her wishes to forget about the green dress. Elena turned back to the project at hand, but her mood had been tainted by yet another reminder of how cruel the curse had been to the people of Bronwal. She was silent for a long time, until a brush of feathers against her hand caused her to cry out and pull away.

"What is it?" Bell asked. She'd been lost in thought in front of the drawer she'd closed on the green dress, but she rushed back to Elena's side. She reached for the hand Elena was cradling to see what had caused her to emit the cry of distress.

"It's nothing. I'm fine. The feathers startled me, that's all," Elena said. She forced herself to reach into the wardrobe and bring out the dress that had frightened her. It was weightless in her hand, crafted almost entirely of layers of chiffon. The feathers decorated the bodice and the shoulders, and they'd been expertly applied. They would lie crisscrossed over the breasts in a smooth pattern exactly as they would lie on a bird's chest. The feathers on the shoulders were looser and accompanied by down so that they conveyed the idea of wings when they fluttered with the slightest air currents.

"This one, you'll have to try on," Bell said. She touched the soft down on the shoulders with one finger.

There were several screens in the room decorated with enameled nature scenes. Elena would have been perfectly comfortable changing out in the open, but she didn't want to startle the young woman who came from another time.

Maybe the Middle Ages had the equivalent of locker rooms or dressing rooms, but Elena couldn't be sure.

Besides, there was something of her nightmares and her shattered dreams in this dress, and she was too shy to face it in front of curious eyes. She'd worn feathers many times before. She'd been feathered in her nightmares many times before.

But she'd never donned them for a purpose that was completely her own.

The appropriate undergarments had also been in the wardrobe, but Elena chose to wear nothing with it but the panties she had on. She wasn't so curvy that she needed the support, and she wasn't inhibited enough to need the coverage. The dress would fit her perfectly with no help. It settled against her as if it had been made to ride her bare skin.

The feathers provided enough modesty so she didn't feel like an exhibitionist when she came from behind the screen. And her shyness had faded away. This wasn't a nightmare where she was trapped in a swan's body. This wasn't a reminder that she'd lost the dance of her dreams. If anything, it reminded her that she would always have the dance in her heart. Because she walked gracefully in the flowing layered skirts. They didn't impede her movements at all.

Bell sighed out loud when Elena came into view. She'd been looking at the other dresses, but she turned around and her eyes went wide again along with the sigh.

"You're no foundling," Bell said. "You would have fit in at Bronwal before the curse."

She slowly walked to Elena's side. In her hand, she carried a delicate cap of white. She set it on Elena's head and then placed her hands on Elena's upper arms to turn her around toward a large mirror. The cap was little more than a wisp of lace shaped like a tiara. It softly framed her forehead with delicate swirls of feathers on either side of her temples.

"This is it. There can be no better choice," she said.

It was true. Elena could face Grigori in this dress. She could make one last plea to Romanov about her place by his side. And she could face the Light *Volkhvy* queen.

Chapter 21

As night approached, Elena struggled. The sapphire in her sword didn't glow. Grigori would be able to find her. But the wolves had vanished and Romanov was nowhere to be seen. The windows in her tower were shut up tight, but they'd been tight the night before when Grigori had flown inside. Only the power of her mother's sacrifice had kept her inaccessible. With that protection almost completely faded, there wasn't a tower or a lock on earth that could keep her safe. She could feel her vulnerability all the way to her bones.

But Grigori wasn't her only concern.

If she went to the black wolf's lair for sanctuary, she would also be stepping into Romanov's arms. He had rejected her time and time again as the bearer of the sword. How could she indulge in his kisses and his touch when he was closed off to more?

She briefly considered Bell's aviary. In it, she wouldn't

be alone. She would have a friend by her side and one of the wolves at her feet. But, in spite of her fear, she couldn't bring herself to intrude. The orphan and the red wolf seemed to have some sort of special bond. It was obvious that Soren watched over the child his father had saved so long ago, even though she had become little more than a servant to the family. In turn, Bell seemed to watch over the red wolf. They were an odd pair but a pair nonetheless.

Besides, if Grigori followed her to the aviary, she would be placing Bell and Soren in grave danger. Neither of them could stand against the witchblood prince, and no matter her training or her determination, her sapphire sword might not be enough to stop him without its glow.

Frustration bubbled up in her chest and stole her breath. Romanov was too stubborn. He was so busy doing the right thing to protect her that he didn't stop to think how it placed everyone in greater danger. Herself included.

She had no choice but to seek refuge in the cavern. Grigori wouldn't dare penetrate the black wolf's lair. If he found her in her dreams, so be it. At least she wouldn't have to be helpless under his actual physical touch.

This time, Elena brought her flashlight and a handful of spare candles she'd found in a drawer in her room. Without the sapphire's glow, the cavern would be too dark.

She tucked them in her backpack, along with her book and her last energy bars and bottled water. She had no idea if Romanov would even be in the cavern when she got there, but, if he was, she had no intention of winding up in his arms.

She struggled for nothing.

The cavern was empty when she arrived except for

the bedding Romanov had carried there the night before. When she sank down on the furs and blankets, she tensed because the scent of roses and winter came from the soft bed beneath her. Romanov's skin and hair always held the scent of evergreen and fresh snow. But he had another headier scent that was purely masculine—a combination of wood smoke, leather and heated muscle.

She couldn't avoid his scent on the bed they'd shared. She breathed it in and accepted that it was mingled with her scent because their bodies had mingled perfectly together.

Elena had told herself she would resist her desire to be with him tonight, but, now that he wasn't here, memories rose up swift and hot to claim her. She shifted, still tender between her legs where they had thrust so hungrily for connection. Her body had already responded to mere recall by becoming hot and wet. She gathered the quilts and furs and held them close beneath her in substitution for the hot thighs she'd prefer to straddle. The bulk of the blankets were nothing compared to the solidity of the man. She missed his hard muscles and the heat of his eager erection.

Elena moaned softly as she undulated against the bedding that smelled like the man she desired. She hadn't come to the cavern for refuge. She'd come for Romanov. She admitted it now that she'd found him gone.

"I tried to stay away." The voice was almost a growl from the mouth of the tunnel that led to the lair.

Elena stilled, and a hot flush washed over her skin in response to the grit of desire in his tones and to being found in the grips of the sensual memory of riding him.

She pushed herself up from the ground and waited on her hands and knees as he approached. The fur beneath her knees protected them from the hard stone. Nothing protected her from the raw hunger her position inspired. She saw it in Romanov's eyes as he slowly stalked toward her. Their emerald depths reflected the candlelight, as did the mica all over the walls. The candle's glow was warmer than the sapphire's soft blue. Tonight, the mica looked like thousands of flecks of gold.

"I went to find you when night fell. I was going to send you down here alone, while I kept watch outside," Romanov said.

"I was going to keep my distance," Elena said. "If you don't want me to have the sword, then you don't want me."

A harsh, raw laugh erupted from Romanov's chest. It reminded her more of a rumbling growl than an expression of humor.

"I've never wanted anyone or anything more than I want you," he said. But it wasn't a proclamation of love. It was a tortured confession.

"You can't have me without the sword. We've become a package deal," Elena said. But she didn't rise. She stayed as she was, and her body tightened and moistened as he stepped closer and closer.

"You can't have me without the wolf," Romanov said. He was close enough to drop down on his knees on the bedding in front of her. He dropped, but he didn't relax. He towered over her, even on his knees. "I've tried to deny it, but the wolf is part of me. We've been a 'package deal' all along. And the Ether only makes us wilder."

She gasped when he reached for her hair. He plunged his hands into the silky waves on either side of her head, and he held her head in place when he swooped down to kiss her. She whimpered into his hungry mouth, but she didn't pull away. Even if he hadn't held her so tightly, she wouldn't have moved. She was held as much by anticipation and need as by his strong hands.

If wilder meant that Romanov would finally give in to their connection so that they could truly be together, in every sense of the word—physically, emotionally, partners against the Dark—then wilder was what she craved.

She sought the deep recesses of his mouth with her tongue and gloried in the heat and velvety friction she found. His tension softened. His elbows gave. She was able to press forward as they kissed and climb onto his bent legs. He took her slight weight easily—leaning back to give her a place to sit on his hard thighs. She wrapped her legs around his waist and buried her hands into the mane of hair that had always seemed to reveal the wildness he tried to suppress.

She had never been very attracted to soft, sophisticated gentlemen. Now she knew why. Her heart had held out for a legendary shifter as wild and fierce as the black wolf he could become. She was a warrior. A civilized and polished partner would never do.

His hands left her face and fell to cup the globes of her bottom and pull her even closer against him. He pressed her heat to his already swollen erection. She undulated against him.

"No chance I would stay away. None," he groaned against her lips. His face fell to her neck, and she threw back her head to give him access to the sensitive pulse point he sought. His lips were hot, even hotter than her flushed skin. He nipped and licked his way to her cleavage, and then he indulged in slower sucking kisses on the swell of her breasts that rose above the low V of her T-shirt.

Elena moaned as the different textures overwhelmed her with sensation—the tickling strands of his snow-scented hair, the rough stubble on his jaw and the soft but firm swell of his lips. The moist velvet sweep of his teasing tongue caused her nipples to peak into hardened nubs that pressed against the fabric of her T-shirt. She sought to satisfy their throbbing urgency by rubbing them against his hot, muscular chest as she continued to rock against his erection.

But it wasn't enough.

Her body knew what it was like to be filled by his heat and naked against his skin. It would never be satisfied fully clothed again.

She reached between them to undo the crisscrossed laced fastenings of his leather pants. Her fingers fumbled, and he pressed her away to make room for his own hands. She slid down his legs and waited with her knees on the fur and her hands on his thighs. His more practiced movements were able to undo his pants and press them open and slightly down. His underwear came slightly down with the pants and she could see the prize she'd sought. His erection was fully engorged.

Elena took over from there. She grabbed the edges of his fly and opened it farther so that his erection fell free. She looked from the shaft she craved up to his shadowy green eyes. The golden light brought out the flecks of gold in his irises. They matched the mica in the walls. His lips were swollen from her kisses. His hair was mussed. The color in his pale cheeks was high. His flush matched his passion-darkened mouth. But it was the intensity in his expression that seduced her the most. He didn't avoid her perusal. He met her eyes and allowed her to see all that he felt in that moment. His wild need was as obvious in his eyes as it was in his body.

He wanted her and he'd come here to be with her. Not to protect or reject her. He wasn't here as a champion or as a cursed man who had to refuse his needs. He was here to mate. She'd returned to the black wolf's lair to do the same. This was about the oldest enchantment that existed between a man and a woman. No *Volkhvy* magic required.

When she leaned down to slowly take him in her mouth without breaking the connection of their eyes, he cried out. He grabbed for her hair, but he didn't stop her or manipulate her movements. He simply held on softly, with trembling hands. He was salty, sweet and fiery hot against her tongue. His mouth fell open to allow heavier respiration to come and go between his swollen lips. His eyelids drooped to half mast, but he didn't close his eyes. Neither did she. She held her breath and took him deep with a harder suction and she watched his pleasure.

"Elena," he breathed. It sounded like a prayer.

She pulled back to the head of the shaft she suckled. She held its base with her hands and licked its swollen head.

"What, my wolf? Why do you call my name?" she teased.

"I let the wolf have my heart. I thought he would keep you out. But he is me, and we must have you," Romanov said.

"I'm here. I'll always be here. The Ether won't take me away. And neither will Grigori," Elena vowed.

She rose up to reach for his tunic and he reluctantly allowed it. His hands slid away pausing only briefly on her face. She pulled his shirt from his large frame, revealing his perfectly sculpted muscles, inch by impressive inch. He'd spent every waking moment over enumerable Cycles fighting Dark *Volkhvy* and training to keep himself sharp. He'd held the Ether madness at bay all alone for so long.

The candlelight and the reflection from the walls painted his skin with gold.

She leaned to press soft kisses over his hard flesh. On his shoulders. On his arms. On his chest. "I'm here," Elena repeated against his hot skin. "I'm here."

He trembled beneath her lips, especially when she kissed over the planes of his lean stomach. His erection wept and she throbbed with the desire to mount him. She stood to quickly pull off her clothes, but the intense gaze that followed her movements caused her to slow down. As she had taken her time with the revelation of his chest and arms, she slowly worked her own shirt off, exposing her stomach inch by inch and then her naked breasts. They were heavy with need, and her nipples were swollen into tight buds, pink with passion against her porcelain skin. She arched her back and stretched her arms over her head to remove the shirt. Then she met his eyes again. She dropped the shirt at her feet making no effort to be modest.

Still on his knees, he reached for her. His calloused hands wrapped around the two soft mounds she'd brazenly displayed for him. He cupped them and weighed them. He gently brushed over her nipples with his thumbs and forefingers, lightly pinching.

It was her turn to breathe out his name like a prayer.

He responded by tracing his hands down her sides until they got to her waist. He continued on the downward track only after he'd grabbed the waistband of her leggings. He pulled them down. Not suddenly. Not impatiently. But, following her lead, he inched them down. He exposed her skin a little at a time until she was trembling as he had done.

Only then did he use the material he gripped to pull her closer. He tugged her to his face. Her quivering intensified when his hot breath tickled over her stomach. Then she cried out because he followed his breath not with the kiss she expected, but with the fiery heat of his moist tongue. He licked her stomach as the jeans continued to come down. When his movements had revealed her hipbones, he licked those and suckled beneath them. Arcs of heat penetrated deep and rushed lower from his teasing tongue to her throbbing mound.

And still, slowly, slowly he worked her jeans down until he reached the top of her panties. His fingers softly gathered the edges so that his movements lowered her panties with the jeans until he revealed the curls they'd covered.

This time when his tongue teased the trembling flesh above those curls, she cried out. But seconds later, when his tongue delved into the curls to find the moist slit at the V of her legs, she silently grabbed the back of his head to keep herself from falling.

He teased in and out with his tongue, mimicking the thrusting she craved and her cries became cries of release. He held her hips and pressed her close to lap up her response with his hungry tongue.

She had to crumple then. He slowed her descent, but allowed her to fall. Once her body was on the bedding, Romanov pulled her leggings off her legs one by one. She thought he would settle between them once she was naked. She tried to reach for him, but he was still on his knees. He caressed her hips and thighs as she recovered from the climax he'd given her with his tongue. Softly, gently his fingers teased.

Elena's hands gripped the bedding beneath her as her body began to hunger again. She arched her back and closed her eyes. Her legs opened. He rewarded the silent request with a thick penetrating finger. Her eyelids flew open and she saw that he watched her heated reaction to his touch.

"I don't want to frighten you. But this is only making me wilder," Romanov said gruffly. She could feel the tension in his hand even though he kept his touch gentle. Too gentle. She wanted more.

"Don't mistake me for delicate, my wolf. I train to appear graceful, but there's strength behind the grace. You know that," Elena said.

She thrust her hips up to increase the penetration of his finger. And her sudden impatient movement was all the encouragement he needed. He withdrew his hand, but only to place it on her hips to roll her over. A thrill of surprise washed over her, but it quickly turned to a thrill of desire when he spread her legs and teased his finger back into her from behind. She undulated against the furs and came again. Her body pulsed around his finger.

"You're so beautiful when you become lost in your pleasure. I could spend eternity watching you come again and again," Romanov groaned. This time, he didn't wait patiently for her to recover. He lifted her hips and she found herself on her hands and knees, as she'd been when he'd first stalked into the cavern.

"I've never been so easy to please. You hardly have to touch me. I'm wet when you enter a room," Elena confessed.

"That you're always slick for me...it makes me ache," Romanov said. He illustrated his words by pressing behind her so she could feel the hot length of his erection against her.

"I like to make you ache," Elena said. "I like to drive you wild."

"Done," Romanov said.

And he claimed her with a single thrust from behind.

Elena cried out his name and the cavern echoed around them. He held her hips so she didn't collapse as waves of pleasure shook her body. And then he used his hold to rock her forward and backward for his penetrating thrusts. She had to depend on her good knee to help him, but the soft furs cushioned the other so she felt no pain.

Even from this position, she wasn't a passive lover. She arched her back and pressed her bottom against his stomach, again and again. Even as he thrust with powerful, frenzied strokes, he matched the rhythm she set with her athletic, muscled movements. Only then did the sword awaken and join the golden glow on the walls with its sapphire blue.

But this time, Romanov didn't pull away.

And his acceptance of the sword's glow brought her to a shuddering release. Her body pulsed around his shaft and she cried out his name. He held her hips as her body tried to collapse. He buried himself deep and hard and came at the entrance of her womb.

When she woke in the wee hours of the morning, Romanov was gone. But the sword still glowed faintly. She used its light instead of her flashlight to walk quietly down the tunnel. The mica shimmered on the walls as she passed. Romanov must have known when she entered the main body of the cavern, but he didn't say a word. The light from the sword didn't reach the high cathedral ceiling, but she saw a deeper shadow and recognized the broad shoulders of her lover.

He stood, a silent guard at the outside entrance to the cavern.

Elena went back to the empty bed.

He was still determined to protect her even though he knew she could protect herself. The curse would stand between them forever if she couldn't convince Vasilisa that it was time to forgive the Romanovs. What she must accomplish at the Gathering wasn't humanly possible, but she had to try.

For Lev, who was determined to die.

For Soren and the young woman he watched over every night.

For poor Patrice and all the other inhabitants of Bronwal.

But mostly because Ivan Romanov could not continue to stand alone. He was the last Romanov, but he couldn't continue to punish himself for what his father had done. He deserved peace and happiness. He deserved reprieve. Maybe she couldn't give him those, but she could give him a partner.

If only he would relent and accept it was her decision to brave the Ether.

The cool night air didn't soothe him. He wanted to go to Elena when she slipped from their bed to check on him, but he held himself back instead. She didn't speak. Once she saw him, she stood for only a moment, silently watching, before she went back to bed.

The Gathering was tomorrow night.

All the Dark and Light *Volkhvy* would come to dance in the power of the Ether that Bronwal radiated and to bask in the humiliation and subjugation of Vasilisa's curse.

Ivan fisted his hands. They were still warm from the memory of touching Elena. If he closed his eyes, he could see her pleasure, but he could also sense the intensity of his feelings for her.

He'd denied the wolf for so long. He'd denied any and every emotion. He'd had to turn away from his heart to go on and on and on. Earlier, when he and Elena had made love, he'd let go of that control.

The resulting connection had shaken him to his core.

He had never been the stoic ruler of Bronwal. He'd been pretending all along. He'd always pined and longed and hungered for something more. Elena was the answer to his hunger. She fed his wolf and his human soul.

And he could never experience that connection again, not if he was going to succeed in letting her go.

She deserved to be free from Grigori and also free from him and the Romanov curse.

Chapter 22

She polished the sword until it gleamed. The stone had continued to glow, not as brightly as it had ever flared, but it was definitely not dead. Now, the scrolling silver on its hilt and the steel of its blade also shone.

Bell had sent servants up to the tower with a formal scabbard tooled of red leather and decorated with thorny vines and roses, along with her dress and shoes. It was as if her hooded cloak had been remade into a belt for her sword. The dress had been aired outside and its chiffon held the scent of winter snow. The shoes were white leather ankle boots with solid square heels and sharp pointed toes—artfully designed and also practical. She could appreciate both.

She'd carried her own bathwater this time. The effort dispelled her nerves and kept her busy during a day that might have dragged otherwise. She hadn't seen Romanov since the dawn. She washed her hair early and dried it by the fire, combing out the long thick strands of pale blond until they were smooth. Then she braided the thick mass into one long plait that began on the left side of her head, curved to the right and ended over her right shoulder midway down her chest. Ringlets of loose curls extended from the bottom of the plait, where she'd bound it with an elastic band. She wanted her hair to be as artful and practical as her shoes.

She belted on her sword and found that her hair was perfect. Her right hand was free to draw from the scabbard that hung on her left side. Only then did she open the wardrobe to use the full-length mirror in its door to check her appearance. She hadn't packed formal makeup. Bell had loaned her the bare minimum of old-fashioned rouges and kohl. She'd managed to line her eyes and darken her lashes and lips. She hadn't bothered to contour her cheeks. The last few weeks of power bars and stress had given them natural contours no powdery tricks could match.

Above the soft white feathers on her breast, her skin was porcelain pale. Her sword, lips and eyes stood out vividly against the white. She was surprised how closely her eyes matched the sapphire gem's glow. She did go back to the tiny glass pots Bell had loaned her then to add a touch of color to her cheeks. The woman reflected in the glass was too pale.

Even with the added rouge, she looked less a warrior than a waif. She was afraid she'd miscalculated. She'd wanted to reclaim the swan princess Grigori had stolen from her, but she was afraid she would only reinforce his desire.

But there was no time to choose another dress.

Besides, she might look graceful and delicate in the swan gown, but the truth could be seen in her eyes. They matched the sapphire in intent as well as color. She was no waif. She would enter the ballroom as a swan, but not as Grigori's swan. She'd make sure all who attended would see the difference.

The enchanted castle was sprawling. Since she'd arrived, she'd searched and explored through many rooms and levels. But she'd never been to the rooms that made up the grand ballroom and its adjacent withdrawal chambers. The doors had been locked. Bell had assured her there was nothing inside but dusty chandeliers and wide-open spaces.

Tonight, she wound down the tower staircase alone. She walked through dozens of deserted corridors until she arrived at the massive arched double doorways to the ballroom itself.

The sun had set. The Cycle was almost over. Tomorrow Bronwal would return to the Ether and Ivan Romanov and all of his people would disappear one more time.

Unless she could change something tonight.

This time, when Elena tried the doors they pressed open beneath her hands. They swung inward easier than she had expected on a whoosh of displaced air. The expansive space revealed to her eyes made her pause outside the door. Her stomach tightened and her breath caught in her throat. It seemed a million candles illuminated the room, suspended from the ceiling in dozens of elaborate crystal chandeliers. The candlelight bounced off the multifaceted crystal beads, causing the very air to glimmer with reflected light.

The whole room was empty.

Save for the shadowed silhouette of one man.

He turned toward the doors as they opened, and Elena was drawn toward him in spite of his silence. Even the giant, empty room didn't make him appear smaller. If anything, he seemed even taller and more intimidating as the focal point. The sheen of his tuxedo both absorbed and reflected all of the light until he seemed a living shadow come to life when he stepped to meet her. It was the first time she'd seen him in more modern clothes. The tuxedo was still vintage, only slightly less out of time than the man who wore it, but unlike his cloak, leather and furs, the suit rode his muscles in tailored perfection as he moved.

He hadn't tamed his hair.

It was a wild mass of black waves all around his face and shoulders. And she was glad. She was also glad when she was close enough to see the emerald of his eyes. He wasn't a living shadow. He was a living legend. Her legend, whether he was fully ready to accept it or not. It didn't matter what he wore. He wore it well. And he wore it with the same wild energy she'd been drawn to from the start.

"They'll arrive closer to midnight. It's always been so. Lev and Soren stay out of sight. They would be too tempting a trophy for the Darker *Volkhvy*. For many Cycles I've watched and waited alone," Romanov said.

"Not tonight," she said. Unspoken was the promise that he'd never have to wait alone again if he would relent. "I'll wait with you."

"Grigori will not stay away. He'll brave the black wolf to have you," Romanov warned. He reached to trace the side of her face. His touch was soft; barely the pads of his fingers skimmed her skin. And still she released a quavering sigh as gooseflesh rose and her nipples tightened. "Don't be emboldened by the sword's glow. Let me handle Grigori. That's why you came."

"I climbed the mountain for help, not for salvation.

I didn't need to be rescued. I needed to be reinforced," Elena said. "The legend of the Romanov wolves brought me here, but I heard the sword, as well. I answered its call."

"The Ether can't have you," Romanov vowed. He lifted his other hand to join the first. He cupped her face and her chin lifted in response. She met his eyes. She hoped he would see what she'd seen in the mirror— determination and the power of the sword beaming from some place inside of her. "Even if it means I can't have you either."

"You will always have me, Ivan Romanov. Because you are mine and I am yours. We belong to each other. And nothing and no one will come between us once we've decided to stand together," Elena said.

He leaned to kiss her then. Not because he agreed. She could feel the tension in his shoulders when she moved to hold him. He kissed her because they didn't have much time. There was desperation in the flick of his tongue. She wished he believed her. There was so much to overcome—Vasilisa, Grigori, the curse and the Ether. But she believed they could do it because she'd always believed in the stories her grandmother had told her, and her grandmother's stories always ended well for the legendary wolves.

Music began somewhere in the distance.

Romanov pulled away from her lips and she allowed it, although her heart was breaking. He wouldn't kiss her again once the night progressed. He would be too preoccupied.

One thing was certain: he couldn't be allowed to shift to save her.

She had to stop Grigori before Romanov thought the black wolf was needed. He'd said Lev and Soren stayed away from the Gathering because they would be tempting trophies for the *Volkhvy* that came to the ball. There would be no greater trophy than the black wolf's head.

Luckily, tonight, the black wolf had a defender.

Romanov broke their kiss, but he didn't step away. He pulled her into his arms instead. Like his tuxedo, the waltz was after his natural time, but Ivan Romanov had lived through many different ages. Modern life had managed to touch Bronwal every time it appeared. It was only as the curse dragged on that Romanov had become more and more isolated. He hadn't been truly alone until she'd found him, this Cycle, after all of his loved ones had disappeared.

He waltzed as well as he fought. She wasn't surprised. He was large, but athletic. He could move with speed and grace. He easily whirled her around the large empty room beneath the chandeliers and she allowed it. The layers of her skirt floated away from her bare legs as she stepped quickly to follow his lead. The downy feathers on her shoulders fluttered as if she'd taken flight.

And that's how the Light *Volkhvy* queen found them when she entered the ballroom.

The music stopped.

Romanov continued to circulate around the room until they came to the entrance. He made the queen wait for their audience. He made her watch them fly. And then he effortlessly caught Elena's momentum and brought them both to a halt directly in front of the queen. Only a powerful partner could have executed such a complete stop without a stumble or stuttering step. Without thinking, completely directed by instinct, Elena dropped into a low curtsy. She balanced on her good leg, but her injured knee screamed. No one watching would have known it.

After all, a prima ballerina danced through pain. It was her primary skill.

"Lovely. I've never been greeted by a swan princess and her cob," Vasilisa said drily. But a hint of a smile curved one corner of her perfect lips. She was in purple again. Like Romanov, the clothes she wore never seemed to be static to one time period. Elena had seen her in Victorian. Tonight, she wore a Tudor court gown with an elaborate brocade underdress crafted of silk. It was covered in a velvet gown that split down the front to show off the brocade, in contrasting shades of plum and violet. The violet brocade had a square neck, and the plum velvet had wide bell sleeves embroidered with the perpetual thorns and roses.

On Vasilisa's head was a Tudor cap with two horns crafted from quilted black satin. The horns rose up from her temples and curved back and around like a ram's horns until they ended facing forward beside both of her high cheekbones. From the back of the cap, steams of violet silk flowed behind her in a long train.

Elena's dress was simple and natural in comparison, and she was suddenly glad of it. The queen was charmed by her delicate grace, but when she rose from her curtsy she knew the savvy witch could see the glow in her eyes.

"A swan that wears the sapphire sword," the queen continued. Behind her, a crowd had formed. Elena was certain that they appeared one by one out of the Ether that couldn't be seen. It existed in and around Bronwal. The better to take the enclave when it was time.

"Will you dance, Your Highness?" Elena asked before Romanov could say that he still rejected her.

Vasilisa seemed taken aback for the first time.

"He's a graceful partner. And I've had plenty to compare," Elena said with a smile. She was terrified. The crowd behind the queen had swelled into a hundred witches or more. And the Dark *Volkhvy* hadn't even begun to arrive. If Grigori came and if she couldn't defeat him herself, Romanov would shift in a ballroom full of hundreds of witches who wanted him dead.

Was Vasilisa as vengeful as the curse made her seem? Was there any hope she would decide to fight on her black wolf's side?

Something about the purple garb the queen favored niggled at the edges of Elena's mind. Until she understood the queen, she couldn't truly understand where they stood against Grigori.

"And what does the cob say about this invitation?" Vasilisa asked. "He's never asked me to dance before."

Elena held her breath. Romanov might well stiffen and walk away. He had many reasons to hate the Light *Volkhvy* queen. Her curse had cost him everything and doomed him to centuries of struggle. She was the one who had used her enchantments to change the Romanov genes. She had created the wolves without once pausing to consider what the shift would mean to men.

Air released from Elena's lungs when Romanov extended his hand.

The queen stepped forward. The music began again as invisible musicians followed her unspoken cue. None of her entourage dared to question her decision, although many of them gasped, whispered and stared. They had come with the hopes of a wolf hunt after all. Time and time again they had arrived at the Gathering hoping for Romanov's fall, led by their queen's anger to hate the wolves they'd once depended on to keep their Dark brethren in check.

Elena gripped the hilt of her sword and stared them all down, one by one, while the queen and Romanov began to waltz around the empty ballroom floor. As each witch lowered his or her eyes, they melted away to pair up and join their queen in the dance. Soon, they had all flowed away like water released from a dam. Elena watched them dance. The other *Volkhvy* were also dressed eclectically. Every time period she could imagine was represented, from wide skirts to flapper fringe. The men wore everything from tights, to kilts, to tuxedos in every style, but one thing common in all the men and the women was extravagance.

As Bell had said, the witches tried to outdo each other. In her simple gown, Elena shone like the candlelight that illuminated the ballroom. In the middle of a shifting rainbow of brilliant fabrics, only Elena wore white.

And only she wore one of the queen's enchanted swords.

She turned to follow the queen and Romanov with her eyes as they whirled around the floor. She doubted if anyone else present would have been strong enough to handle the queen's heavy skirts, but it was obvious that Romanov's muscles propelled the witch with ease. Elena had experienced the swoop and swirl herself, moments before. She wasn't surprised to see the Mona Lisa smile tilt higher on the queen's face. Even in the midst of pain and loss, there was joy in the dance.

Pain and *loss*.

Purple, like black, was the color of mourning.

The Light *Volkhvy* queen was in mourning for someone she had lost.

Elena took two steps toward the dancing couple before she caught herself at the edge of the dance floor. Did Vasilisa mourn Vladimir? That seemed unlikely. He had betrayed her and her affections. Their relationship had been a sham he'd used to try to steal her position.

But if not her Romanov lover, whom did she mourn and why?

As Elena's mind struggled with this new piece of the puzzle, the music stopped once more. Every couple on the dance floor paused as if their moves had been choreographed. Except Romanov and the queen. He ignored everyone else to whirl the queen around to where they had begun as he'd done with Elena. This was his castle. He was the last Romanov. He ended the dance when he was ready to end the dance and no sooner. Every eye in the ballroom followed their graceful waltz.

Including every eye of the Dark *Volkhvy* horde that had arrived. Elena had been watching the dance. Its graceful circular motions had almost hypnotized her. When her eyes focused on the horde, she was startled. They had arrived silently because they'd arrived from the Ether. One minute the spot where they appeared was empty marble. The next it was filled with Dark *Volkhvy*. Others, like Elena, noticed the horde with sudden horror. Gasps and murmurs of dismay rose up around the room, but then hushed as if the guests were afraid vocalizing their fear would only gain the attention of the Dark witches.

An unnatural hush fell. The atmosphere vibrated with expectant tension.

Romanov and the queen seemed to have no care. Other than the music ending, which must have been silently ordered by the queen, there was no other indication by the couple that they'd seen the Dark *Volkhvy* arrive.

When they stopped in front of the man leading the horde of Dark witches, Elena held her breath. Romanov was a man, not a wolf, but the black wolf gleamed darkly from his eyes.

"Well, this is a surprise. The doomed man dances with

the one who has doomed him. Surely you would rather rip out her throat?" the man said. His voice was charming but oily. It seemed to ooze against Elena's skin in the same way that Grigori's oozed. His syllables seemed to reach out and touch the listener in intimate ways without permission.

She shuddered. Romanov and the queen simply stood. Romanov didn't drop the queen's hand. In fact, Elena thought he might have held on tighter to keep from attacking the man who spoke of their centuries-old conflict as if it had been staged for his entertainment.

"King Josef. We all come to dance while Bronwal stands. Each Cycle might be its last. There is no better waltz than a poignant one, I find. And there's never been a better partner for that than Ivan Romanov," the queen said.

Romanov stood proudly beside her. He hadn't dropped her hand. She was the one who let him go. He brought his released hand up to join his other behind his back. Only Elena saw the white-knuckled grip she knew so well as he held himself in check.

"Better than Vladimir?" The man laughed, and the horde laughed with him. It was an exaggerated show of deference that told her the man must be the Dark *Volkhvy* king.

Elena looked at the king who had fathered her darkest nightmare. He tormented a man quadruple his worth.

"Be careful, Josef. Don't test the limits of my hospitality," the queen replied.

Elena's hand had inadvertently pulled on the hilt of her sword. She'd partially brought it from its scarlet scabbard. The movement and noise in the silent room drew attention. Every eye, including the king's, moved her way.

And then the light in the sapphire died.

Her fingers went numb before she noticed the slight blue glow was gone. She froze. The Dark *Volkhvy* horde seemed to draw in a collective breath. Unlike the numbness in her hand, the numbness that claimed her body wasn't caused by the loss of magic. She looked down at the dull, dead stone and then she immediately sought Romanov's face.

He still stood tall and straight beside the queen.

He refused to meet her eyes.

Her stomach fell in one sudden swoop, but it found no bottom to the pit that sucked it down. Dizziness claimed her and she ground her teeth against it. She braced her legs even though the move pained her knee. She stiffened her spine.

This was the ultimate rejection in front of their worst enemies. He had severed their burgeoning connection with a force of will that staggered her with its finality. It didn't matter that he'd done it to protect her. The loss was sharp, then devastatingly hollow. She accepted that she was meant to be a warrior and now that choice was taken from her. By the man she loved. He'd also made a decision. The dead sapphire gave him away. He was going to shift if Grigori came to the Gathering. He was going to sacrifice everything to try to save her rather than allow her to risk the Ether to save herself.

"Queen Vasilisa, the Dark *Volkhvy* have never depended on the Light's invitation to this Gathering," the words came from a silky voice that caused Elena's numbness to jolt away. The witchblood prince stepped from behind his father's retinue. "We come to dance at our pleasure. And, you must know, we come to watch and wait for greater pleasures."

She'd dreaded the moment when Grigori would arrive, but he'd already been here all along.

Grigori met her horrified gaze. A smile like she'd never seen curved his lips. It was feral. At complete odds with his quiet, civilized appearance. He wore a tailored black suit that was ruthlessly cut to his lean masculine shape. His shirt and tie were also unrelieved black, as were the onyx gems in the lobes of his ears. His sleek black hair fell straight to his shoulders. Its oily sheen reflected the candlelight when he moved with liquid grace to his father's side. His obsidian eyes matched his smile. Those eyes took in her appearance with the ease of possession. He skimmed from her head to her toes, and his gaze seemed to leave a smudge on her skin that sank to her soul.

That's when she saw the feathers.

The queen had called Romanov her cob, but it was obvious that Grigori had stolen that designation without her permission. Black feathers protruded jaggedly from his neck in a shiny ruff. More feathers protruded from the back of each hand, making them look like wing tips when he gestured as he spoke.

His hungry black eyes echoed the hollow in her stomach. She was still falling. She would never stop. There was no sword to catch her. No partner in this fight. Romanov's sacrifice wasn't a salvation. It only dug the pit of her despair deeper than it had to be.

"My swan," Grigori purred. There was no softness in the endearment. It was as slickly used as a sharpened knife against her skin, and he intended it to cut. He wanted to draw blood.

Elena forced her hand to release the sword. She trembled. The numbness had fled. In its place was an adrenaline rush with no outlet. She stood, helpless, as Grigori smiled.

"You're mistaken if you think the curse is evidence of

my weakness," Vasilisa replied. "You have no idea what I'm capable of doing for the ones I love."

"Be still. You distract me from my moment of triumph," Grigori said. It was a sharp shout that rang throughout the ballroom and echoed off the distant ceiling and walls. Elena jerked, startled.

But the rest of the room, including the flickering flames in the candles, went perfectly still. Only she moved when Grigori approached. She took one single step away only to come up against the Light *Volkhvy* dancers who had paused when the Dark horde had arrived, but now stood frozen midstep because of Grigori's shouted spell.

She'd known he was a powerful witch. But seeing his control of all other witches in the room caused her heart to race. She couldn't help it. She looked to the one man who might be able to save her. She didn't court his sacrifice, but instinctive terror caused her to seek him out.

Romanov was frozen too. He stood like a statue beside the queen. And for a split second she was struck again by his stature and his legend. Neither seemed to intimidate Grigori as he ignored everyone else in the room to zero his entire focus on her.

She pressed back against the dancers behind her, but there was no escape from Grigori's advance. She'd meant to boldly reclaim the swan as her own. But Grigori's lascivious gaze negated her efforts. In his eyes, she was his, and her dress was only a preview of the dark pleasures that were to come. With his black feathers, he made them into partners. He stepped into the spot Romanov had vacated by her side.

In the same room was too close. By the time he'd slowly walked to face her, she could barely take in enough oxygen to survive. She risked hyperventilation because the quick intake and exhale of her panicked respiration didn't fuel her lungs. When he suddenly leaned to speak against the vulnerable pulse point behind her left ear, her breath held without her permission. "I've waited for this moment for too long. I hardly know where to begin," Grigori said. The rush of his whisper against her skin caused gooseflesh to rise. She swayed as her oxygen-deprived system caused her head to go light.

Grigori saw her distress. He straightened. His smile tilted higher. He liked her fear. He courted her pain. But he was a connoisseur. There was no rush in his movements as he reached to pull her into his arms. The music had stopped when the queen had stopped dancing. Grigori began to hum as he pulled her into mimicry of the waltz he had witnessed between Romanov and the queen. His moves were more savage. He jerked and pulled. She struggled to keep up. His fingers dug into her skin.

She still had the sword. It wasn't glowing with power, but it could still stab and slash. She wasn't sure what good it would do to try to attack him if he could simply freeze her as he'd frozen the whole room of witches, but she would try. She would never be too afraid to fight him.

But, as she decided to spill his black blood, their dance became something more dizzying and horrible. A frigid atmosphere enveloped her with an unrelenting vacuum so that she was forced to hold on to the man she despised rather than be sucked away. Her vision faded to gray and her body seemed to disintegrate like a vapor into the freezing air.

And then she was back to herself once again as Grigori laughed maniacally.

He continued to spin her around the ballroom, weaving in and out of the other couples who were frozen in place.

"Others fear the Ether. I dance in its shadows. Come, dance with me, pet. Tread on forbidden pathways. Dwell with me on the edges of oblivion," Grigori taunted.

The Ether.

The cold vacuum claimed her again and again. Her tormentor forced her to desperately hang on to his arm and neck in order to survive. He played with the Ether that Romanov had rejected her to help her avoid. Only now did she begin to know what Romanov had done.

She hadn't understood.

The Ether was the absence of everything and it was always hungry for more.

Each time Grigori teased her into the nothingness, she cried out, but her screams were lost as the sound waves were eaten away. Each time they rematerialized, Grigori laughed at her frantic grip.

"Your tears are as delicious as I knew they would be." He suddenly stopped in the center of the room. Elena held on to keep from falling to the floor. Her knee throbbed. The very atoms of her body seemed disjointed and slightly loosened, as if she would never recover from the disembodiment he'd forced her to endure again and again. Grigori viciously pulled her against his chest and he leaned down. She recognized the blackness in his eyes now. *The Ether is inside of him.* He'd toyed with its power for too long. It had eaten his soul. The entire orb of his eye had gone black as he played. Elena shuddered in revulsion as he slowly extended his tongue and licked the salty moisture from her cheek.

But her revulsion wasn't his only reward.

He couldn't move. He couldn't breathe. He thought that even his heart had stopped midbeat. But his love for Elena couldn't be halted by Dark *Volkhvy* magic.

He'd tried to deny it. He'd tried to protect her from the Romanov curse and from the savagery the black wolf brought to his nature.

To no avail.

The sapphire blade had known him better than he knew himself.

He'd been made into an enchanted champion by Vasilisa while he'd still been in his mother's womb, but it wasn't Vasilisa's enchantments that had caused him to fall in love with the woman Grigori currently tormented around and around the dance floor.

She'd fascinated him from the first moment he'd seen her determined limp up the icy mountain pass and his fascination had grown into something much more binding since then.

She didn't need protecting from a wolf who loved her. She didn't need shielding from a curse they could face together.

The sword simply recognized a soul-to-soul connection that would have been forged if she'd been a baker with a warrior's heart and he'd been a chimney sweep with a wolf's teeth.

It was that savage love that finally broke through his last reservations about claiming their connection. Not a timid one. Not a gentle one. But a love that accepted and freed the part of him he'd always thought he needed to deny.

As he stood frozen in place by Grigori's power, the alpha wolf inside of him no longer threatened to consume his humanity. When the witch held her close and licked the tears from her cheek, there was only one man the black wolf intended to consume.

The floor began to shake beneath their feet. It was Grigori's turn to hold on. He gripped her tightly and looked around to ascertain who had so rudely interrupted his gross celebration. Elena thought she knew. She wasn't distracted by the *Volkhvy* who had begun to move around them as if they slowly woke from a trance. Her eyes were drawn to only one place in the cavernous ballroom.

The last Romanov had been the first to break from Grigori's powerful spell.

He had somehow managed to begin the shift while she was flickering in and out of the Ether. The chandeliers swayed now. Wax rained down in hot, fragrant spatters and the candlelight jumped crazily all over the walls. Romanov had completed the shift while she endured the slick brush of Grigori's tongue.

She'd glimpsed the final moments of his transformation, but it wasn't horrible to her. The change from human to wolf was beautiful compared to the sucking emptiness of Ether in Grigori's eyes.

The black wolf was surrounded by hundreds of *Volkhvy* who were eager to kill him. But the roar of his first howl violently shattered thousands of crystals above their heads. Broken glass tinkled down like a sudden ice storm. Elena shielded her eyes against the dangerous dust as others ran and screamed.

It was one thing to fantasize about killing a legend. It was another to suddenly face him.

"You're going to die," Elena said. She whispered the words. They weren't for the black wolf.

Because the sapphire stone had blazed into glorious life.

The candlelight had been mostly snuffed out by the chandeliers' destruction. A few flames still flickered here and there. The bright blue glow from the gem in her sword was vivid against the shadows. Even more so when she jerked away from her captor and freed the blade. The

Romanov sword. Her sword. Because she was the black wolf's mate. The sword had called her and she'd been brave enough to claim it.

And now the legendary shifter claimed her in return.

Her sword had never blazed so brightly. Grigori backed away from her. His hands were held up defensively as she advanced. But she was momentarily distracted by the Light *Volkhvy* queen. Vasilisa stood behind the black wolf as he met attack after attack. Her back was to his tail, and Elena recognized the defensive strategy she'd been taught. The queen was helping Romanov against Dark *Volkhvy* as they came for his head. Energy shone from her hands and her lips moved with words Elena couldn't hear.

Grigori tried to take advantage of her distraction. He stepped forward as if he would grab her again. She knew it would be a mistake to allow his touch. He was too connected to the Ether. He'd learned to use it even as it ate away at him inside. He'd been too greedy for power and for the pain of others.

He'd danced at the edge of the Ether, but now it could have all of him, with her compliments.

Elena pressed the tip of her blade to Grigori's throat and he froze. She didn't need a magic spell to make him freeze. She had a warrior's heart. Another howl ripped through the air and Elena saw the Dark *Volkhvy* king go down under the black wolf's attack in a torrent of black blood. A few of the Light *Volkhvy* had fallen before they realized the intent of their queen. Now, they fought against the Dark witches rather than the black wolf. With the king's death and Grigori's capture, the Dark *Volkhvy* began to disband.

From outside the ballroom, Elena heard more screams and growls. Reinforcements had arrived. Her endless fall had stopped, but her insides were still hollow. Lev probably wasn't fit to fight and Soren wasn't as big and strong as his alpha brother. He was quick and clever. Much faster and brighter than the brightest natural wolf. But he risked his life to fight on her behalf.

"If Queen Vasilisa hadn't decided to stand with the black wolf, you wouldn't have stood a chance," Grigori hissed. As he spoke, his throat moved an infinitesimal amount, but ribbons of black blood trickled down his feathered neck as a result of the unrelenting pressure from her sword. She didn't waver. His eyes were still completely black. She was certain he couldn't change that. The Ether dance had taken him over an edge he'd skirted for too long.

"I don't stand with the black wolf. I stand with my warriors. I always have," the queen said as she approached. She was covered in steaming blood too black to be her own. It sullied her perfect gown, but she was regal still.

"If you stand with me, then you stand with my mate. You can't separate us in your affections," Elena said.

The queen paused, brought up short by the intensity of Elena's declaration. Then she resumed her steps.

"It wasn't until the sword called you that I began to understand my mistake," Vasilisa said. "I'll never forgive Vladimir for his savagery, but he and I are the only ones to blame."

"Too late. Far too late. You hurt the ones who loved you the most," Elena said. "Madeline and the baby…"

"All is not as it seems," Vasilisa replied. "But there'll be time for explanations after we deal with this Dark prince."

Grigori had lowered his hands. He stood with them fisted at his sides as his blood continued to soak into his shirt and coat. He didn't cringe when the black wolf reappeared from the corridor where he had chased after the escaping horde. The arched double doors were barely big enough to allow him to enter without ducking his head. To Elena's relief, he was followed by a red shadow and then a white. His brothers flanked him on either side as he stalked into the room.

And a smaller figure in green.

"Bell," Elena breathed. She tightened her grip on the sword when Grigori attempted to turn.

The other woman was wearing the green gown. It fitted to her curves and revealed that her petite size was no indication of her age or maturity. Elena had been right. Bell had loved the dress that had been made for her long ago. She must have decided to wear it to the Gathering in hopes of waking the man in the red wolf she loved. Elena's heart squeezed when she realized the dress was stained with black blood. Bell hadn't arrived in time to dance before the fight. Now, she would never have the chance.

"Oh, I see. The red wolf has also inspired someone to stand for him," Vasilisa said. She turned from the wolves to face Elena once more. "Vladimir was an aberration. He didn't deserve the powers he was given. He abused them. I allowed his actions to blind me to the truth. I must stand with my wolves and the women who love them. We all must continue to stand against the Dark."

"Together," Elena said. She said it to the approaching wolves and to Bell, who had paused halfway across the room as if she didn't deserve to approach the queen. There was no fear in her face. Only resignation. Elena didn't know what had become of the third sword, and it wasn't her place to determine which woman it would call to stand with Soren.

But she did know who had been standing with him for centuries. The resourceful orphan stood now as if at a loss on how to proceed. She was more used to devoted service than fighting witches, but she'd been fighting the Ether all along. Bell was a survivor and more importantly she helped others survive. There was no finer quality in a warrior than that.

"You'll forgive me if I don't linger," Grigori suddenly interrupted. "I have no interest in meeting your black wolf. Goodbye, my swan. I'll see you in your dreams." Elena thrust with her sword, but it was too late. The man with Ether in his eyes had slipped easily into the vacuum. His body disintegrated from the head down, and her move met nothing but particles of dried blood left to float away in the air.

But the black wolf was more practiced with the Ether than she was. He knew to pounce for the witchblood prince's feet. Elena shouted a warning, but it didn't stop Romanov from clamping his teeth down over Grigori's boots before they, too, began to disappear.

Elena's horrified gaze met a familiar pair of emerald eyes. Her lover, her Romanov, had leaped to grab the prince before he could escape into the Ether. Had he known he would be taken into the vacuum Grigori manipulated at will? As the mighty wolf's black body disintegrated into the air and disappeared, Elena screamed.

Chapter 23

The tip of her sword clanked onto the floor once it was no longer lodged in Grigori's skin. Soren and Lev had leaped too late. They both whined and snuffled the floor where Grigori and the black wolf had stood. Lev limped, but he wasn't slowed down by his injuries. He snuffled and whined as urgently as the red wolf. Maybe more.

"He warned me how bad the Ether was. I didn't understand why he was so determined to spare me from it even if it meant losing himself," Elena said.

"He's strong. He'll come back. He always does," Bell said. She had run forward to catch Elena before she crumpled to the ground. The small servant was much stronger than she seemed. But Elena had known almost from the start. Like calls to like, and they had been fast friends because they saw each other better and more clearly than others saw them.

"I'm sorry. The Ether is seductive. The Light *Volkhvy*

resist its allure. I used it to curse Bronwal. This is all my fault," Vasilisa said.

"You always wear purple. It's the color of mourning. Who do you mourn, my queen? You didn't do this because Vladimir betrayed you. There's a secret behind your greatest pain. One deeper than your love for Vladimir Romanov," Elena said. She leaned against Bell. Her friend took her weight without protest.

The queen looked from Elena to Bell and back again. But then her gaze was drawn to the petite servant in green silk. Her eyes traced the bellflowers embroidered onto the stained gown.

"Vladimir killed my daughter, Anna. I had placed her with a mortal family for her protection. I knew something was wrong. Vladimir had begun to act strangely. I was afraid he would betray me, and I wanted her well away from danger. But I never imagined my greatest champion would murder a Light *Volkhvy* princess in cold blood," Vasilisa said. "He destroyed the whole village of Sovkra. No one survived. It wasn't until then that I realized he might have killed my consort, as well. My prince died in the same battle as Vladimir's wife. The Dark *Volkhvy* had managed to surround them and the gray wolf never reinforced them." Tears streamed down her perfect pale cheeks. "I didn't know. I turned to him for comfort only to receive an even greater betrayal." And still she didn't blink or look away from the bellflowers on Bell's dress.

"He didn't kill your daughter," Elena said. Anna's story was too similar to Bell's to be a coincidence. Sovkra had been Bell's home. It was only the ending of the tale that Vasilisa had gotten wrong. She straightened. Bell's hands had fallen away from her shoulders.

"No," Bell said. "It isn't true."

The curse had traumatized Bell for centuries. The

queen was the devil in her eyes. No better than Grigori was to Elena. A tormentor. A horror.

Her eyes tracked the movements of the red wolf as they always did. But, at her agonized denial, he stopped and stared. He whined. Elena reached out to Bell as her friend's face petrified into a look of disbelief.

"He didn't kill your Anna," Elena said. "He brought her to Bronwal. Maybe he thought her presence would shield them from your wrath once you knew he'd betrayed you. He didn't stop to think that you might not know she'd survived his attack on the village."

"Dark witches killed my family. The gray wolf saved me," Bell said.

Soren whined. He took one step toward the girl he'd protected for centuries.

"The gray wolf killed them all. He didn't save you. He kidnapped you," Elena said. The puzzle was finally complete. "Vladimir was darker than the darkest witch." She looked at Soren when she said it. "I'm sorry, but it's true. He risked you all for a power grab that failed. He killed his wife, Naomi, and the prince consort by delivering them to the Dark *Volkhvy* king and then refusing to come to their aid during the battle. He seduced Vasilisa. She was vulnerable. She had lost her warrior, her husband and the father of her child. But when she began to suspect Vladimir wasn't what he seemed, he kidnapped the baby she'd hidden. The only reason he didn't kill Anna was that he thought he could use her. When his whole plan failed, he gave himself to the Ether rather than face the consequences of what he'd done."

"My…daughter?" Queen Vasilisa said. "I remember the fields of bellflowers. It seemed a safe place, a happy place to shelter her."

She reached for Bell, but the shocked girl jerked away.

She stumbled back from Elena's supportive grasp and from her mother.

"I could never forgive Vladimir for murdering my daughter. Even when I realized I needed to free his sons from my wrath. Now, the curse is broken. I'm sorry. I'm so sorry," Vasilisa cried.

"I put on this dress because I wanted to claim a place in Bronwal. I've been an orphan and a servant most of my life. Scrambling to survive. But I was wrong about needing to claim a place. I had a place. And a wolf by my side," Bell said.

Soren had backed away from them. His legs were spread wide and, when Bell took several steps toward him, he growled deep and low. Lev limped to join him. His ferocity had always been tempered by Soren's civility. Now, his growl rumbled up from his chest to join with the red wolf's. Both of them looked fully capable of turning on the Light witches they'd been fighting for seconds ago.

"She can't help who her mother is any more than you can help who your father was," Elena said. But the red wolf didn't relent, and Bell lowered her hand.

"I didn't know," Vasilisa said.

"But you did know that abusing the Ether's power was wrong," Elena said. "And you sacrificed Madeline and Trevor because you thought Vladimir had killed your baby."

"No," the queen said. She blinked and pulled her attention from her daughter. "They have been protected from the Ether all this time. They sleep on my island home. I protected her and her baby even though I thought no one protected me and mine."

"Madeline isn't gone," Bell said. She spoke as if she begged the red wolf to hear her, but Soren and Lev had edged farther and farther away from the witches their animal instincts obviously warned them not to trust. They were almost out the door and Bell couldn't follow. Not when both wolves had their teeth bared against her. But she held back from her mother. She stood, all alone, deserted by her wolf and claimed by a Light *Volkhvy* queen. Elena wondered if Bell would ever feel at home at Bronwal again now that she knew the truth. Or if the others would welcome her, as a princess, or at all.

"Romanov should be back by now. Where is he?" Elena suddenly asked. Long minutes had passed since the black wolf had disappeared into the Ether. She couldn't follow him. She didn't know how. Like Lev, she was left to watch and wait for her love to return.

"Grigori was nearly consumed. I saw the Ether in his eyes. The only way he could have defeated Romanov was to devour him in the vacuum. He would have to sacrifice his life to kill the wolf," the queen said.

"He would do it to hurt me," Elena said. "If he can't have me, he would destroy me instead."

The sapphire in her sword still glowed. It was the only sign that she had any hope of seeing Romanov again. She refused to sheath it. The Light *Volkhvy* were tending to their injured and sending the dead into the Ether. Elena looked away from their rituals and their pain. The Dark *Volkhvy* had all vanished without ritual. They had fled, leaving their dead and injured behind. Those that had been left disintegrated. Either they traveled through the Ether to the place they called home or they were consumed.

Elena didn't care.

She waited for the black wolf to return with her sword drawn and ready.

Romanov couldn't disappear. Not when their connection was finally causing the sapphire to shine, brilliant and strong.

Even though secrets, revelations and reunions took place all around her, her attention was riveted on the spot where the black wolf and Grigori had disappeared. No one tried to move her. They wouldn't have dared. She was finally the warrior who truly wielded the sapphire sword.

And she would watch and wait for her mate to return for an eternity if need be.

She willed him back to her with every beat of her heart and every breath that passed through her slightly parted lips.

When the air wavered in front of her eyes, she raised the sword. But instead of the black wolf she expected, it was Ivan Romanov who appeared. He held a struggling Grigori with his powerful hands clasped around the witch's chest from behind. The witchblood prince had a black viscous liquid running down his cheeks from his obsidian eyes. Elena didn't think it was blood. She thought the energy from the Ether had filled him to the brim and now it overflowed. He screamed and cursed incoherently as he fought the man who held him.

"I brought him back to you," Romanov said. His legs were widely braced and his muscles bulged, but it wasn't physical power that he fought against. Grigori was weaker in muscles and form. It was the Ether. Grigori caused them to flicker in and out of existence as he'd caused Elena to do during their dance. It was the disintegration Romanov fought. Tendons strained in his neck and his jaw was clenched. He spoke through clenched teeth. "I was wrong. When I saw him torturing you with the Ether, I knew that standing between you and the sword's call was wrong. I will stand with you forever, as the black wolf and as a man, but you must fight this fight. He is your demon to slay."

As Romanov spoke, he and Grigori flickered in and out of existence again and again. Every time, Elena's heart seemed to follow Romanov into the cold. But it was the frigid memory of Ether in her chest that told her what to do. She lifted the sword and braced the back of the hilt against the palm of her free hand. She timed her thrust against the flicker of here and gone again to be sure she penetrated Grigori's heart while it was materialized. The sapphire blazed, and Romanov let go of the witchblood prince. Her legendary shifter remained solid in front of her as the evil *Volkhvy* who had stalked her since she was a young teen disintegrated in a sudden implosion. Every molecule of his body was sucked into the black hole of Ether her sword had unleashed from his corrupted heart.

The bright blue light of the sapphire's glow wrapped around her and Romanov. It held them tight in this world until the black hole that had been Grigori disappeared in on itself with a hissing pop.

And, after, the glow continued as her lover stepped toward her. She lowered the sword so he could take her into his arms. They were solid and real. She pressed into his chest to absorb his heat. She placed her cheek against him so she could hear the steady beat of his heart. He'd always been more than a story. The sword had called her to his side, but it had been the legend that had awakened her to the sword's call.

"I've loved you longer than I realized," Elena said. "I heard the sword's call because I loved you before we'd even met."

Romanov held her as if she anchored him in this world. He didn't yet know that the curse had been lifted.

He would have to be told about Lev and about Bell. There was good news and bad to share. For now, she shared her embrace and her heat. She shared the modern world she'd brought to him and her dancer's strength.

"I think I knew when I first saw you climbing in the snow. I hadn't felt so alive in ages. I had to go to you. But I couldn't accept the evidence of my own eyes when the sword first glowed. It's too cruel. The Ether…you don't deserve that fate, Elena, my love," Romanov growled.

"No one does," Elena said. "Except maybe those like Grigori who court its darkness."

She pulled back to look up into Romanov's emerald eyes. They were haunted as they always were, but there was a new light in them too. Maybe it was the sapphire's glow influencing the gold flecks in his irises, but she decided to call it hope.

"Bronwal is free," she said softly. His eyes widened. Only then, did he look away from her to see what had been happening while he was fighting Grigori. His hands tightened on her back when he saw the queen and Bell standing side by side. His brothers were by the door, alive even if they weren't quite well.

"You came to us for help, but it's you who saved us all," Romanov said.

He looked back at her, and Elena wrapped her free arm around his neck. She pulled him down to her mouth and their lips met in a kiss that was long and leisurely. They'd fallen in love as a ticking clock counted down their last moments together, but every moment from now on was theirs to enjoy.

"I was afraid to call the wolf, but I didn't let that stop me," Elena said, when they finally came up for air.

"I was afraid when you picked up the sword, but that didn't stop me from loving you with all my heart, even when the black wolf ruled it," Romanov said. "He is me and I am him. Can you love an enchanted shapeshifter after all *Volkhvy* magic has forced you to endure?"

"My mother's sacrifice taught me that the greatest power is love. She bought me time to find my way to you. And now our love is more powerful than *Volkhvy* enchantments. We'll fight for the Light together with the sword and the wolf," Elena said. "There are still difficulties ahead. Bell is Vasilisa's daughter. Your father kidnapped her for leverage. The queen thought he'd killed her. That's why her rage was so long and deep."

Ivan Romanov stiffened at the news of his dead father's further treachery. He looked at the queen and her daughter. Elena followed his gaze. Their reunion wasn't warm. In fact, Bell looked as if she'd rather be swallowed up by the Ether.

Soren was gone. He and Lev had slipped away once Romanov was safe. The white wolf didn't know that his wife and baby had been found. He might be too far gone to ever know. Soren was his lost brother's only hope and yet the red wolf had his own heartbreak to face.

"Bronwal stands," Romanov said. His attention came back to Elena.

"And whatever comes as we recover from the curse, we will fill this castle with love," Elena replied.

Epilogue

Vasilisa left without a word. Her entire entourage disappeared. What could she say to the black wolf she'd almost killed? It wasn't until Elena went searching for Bell that she realized her friend had disappeared too. Her aviary was abandoned. All her magpie collection was gone.

Except for the trunk of male clothes that Elena had helped her drag up the stairs. It was open at the foot of Bell's bed. On top of the carefully folded and preserved garments was the boy's hat Bell had always worn.

Elena lifted it from the trunk and blinked against the moisture in her eyes. Soren had growled at Bell when he'd heard the truth about her parentage. He had lashed out at the girl who had kept a silent vigil for his return for centuries. The hat must have been Soren's. She was certain of it. And the trunk was probably full of his clothes, as well.

The dress Bell had worn to the Gathering was abandoned on the floor. She wouldn't be able to abandon her feelings for the red wolf as easily. Had she gone to live with her mother to escape the wolf who had always protected her? Elena already missed her determined smile, even though she realized now that it and the hat she'd always worn hid much of her true feelings. Bell…Anna… had persevered through it all. She'd shouldered much of the brunt of her mother's curse and she'd survived, in large part, because of the debt she thought she owed the Romanovs for saving her.

Only to find out it was all a lie…

There was nothing she and Ivan could do to repair the damage his father and the Light *Volkhvy* queen had done. They could only work toward a future where Bronwal thrived once more. Romanov was already consulting with the people who had reappeared when Vasilisa lifted the curse. There were more survivors than they'd known. Patrice was in the thick of things. By her side was a man who called her "my wife." It seemed her long-lost husband had been looking for her for many Cycles. She'd been looking for him too. Much of her distraction was caused by that search, not by being Ether-addled after all. Most of the survivors decided to stay and reclaim a life with others who were also like time travelers in a strange new world.

The Dark *Volkhvy* had lost their king, but they were still a threat that had to be controlled. All of Romanov's plans included empowering his people to continue to champion the Light. The training courtyard would be full once more. The halls would be lit and alive and full of people with purpose. Now that Bronwal wasn't coming and going from the Ether, he planned to update and modernize their home. For that, they would need to reach out to the queen for help. Their location was inaccessible without her abilities.

They had time.

Currently, her head was full of more sensual plans.

She'd brought her grandmother's book with her to the castle's roof. She lit several candles that had been left in the aviary, but she sat on one of the openings in the ramparts to open the book beneath the stars. The illustrations sprang to life in her hands, but they were nothing compared to the reality of Ivan Romanov when he came to her side. She looked from the book up to the man. He was larger than life as he always was—tall, broad and handsome. This time there was an added thrill though, because he was also hers.

Finally, she and Romanov were alone.

Her swan gown was rumpled and dirty, but she didn't care because the look in Romanov's eyes was one of desire and appreciation. She stood to meet him. As usual, her head came only to his chest. She had to lift her chin to watch his face. His eyes were highlighted in the soft glow of stars, candles and the sapphire's gleam. He reached for her belt and she placed the book on the wall in order to raise her arms out of the way. He unbuckled it slowly, never once breaking contact with her gaze.

The stars above his wild hair reminded her of the mica in the cavern, but the cold breeze and the distant expanse of snow-capped mountains reminded her that they were free. She didn't have to seek refuge in the black wolf's lair.

"Every time we've been together, I've resisted our connection," he said. The belt came free, and Romanov placed the sword in its scarlet scabbard carefully on the wall beside the book. "I'm not resisting anymore. And every second away from you tonight has been torture."

"We're free. I don't have to be afraid to sleep or to dream. I don't have to be afraid to show you how I feel," Elena said. "And you don't have to be afraid of our connection."

"You were always the braver of us. I was afraid to allow myself to love you. I didn't want to ensnare you in the curse," Romanov said.

"Your strength and control were a siren's call. I'd been relentlessly pursued. I'd never been given a key and told that I could say no," Elena said. "Of course, with you, I wanted to say yes. Again and again."

"You killed me when you refused to use the key. I thought I would die from wanting what I couldn't have," Romanov said. "But every kiss, every sweet sigh only brought me back to life."

As they'd spoken, he had found the fastenings beneath the feathers on her shoulders and he'd unhooked them. The top of her dress slid down her chest revealing her naked breasts to his intense perusal. Her nipples peaked in the chilly air, but the rush beneath her skin that caused gooseflesh to rise was all warm anticipation, not cold.

There was a fireplace in the aviary, but Elena didn't want to lose the stars or the wide-open sky above their heads. She wanted to see the mountains she'd braved to find her alpha wolf and the legend that called her home to his arms.

"You're shivering," Romanov said. He reached for her waist and pulled her against his chest. Her breasts were crushed against his loosened shirt. Sometime after the fight, he'd shed the jacket of his tuxedo and his white silk shirt had come untucked. His tie was long gone, and his buttons were unfastened all the way to his rippled abdomen. This was her lover, a man from a less-civilized age who had survived through the centuries to come to her.

"I hadn't even noticed," Elena said. Her attention was fully caught by the man who held her. She buried her face in his neck when he leaned down to scoop her up into his embrace. As always, he was careful with her injured knee when he arranged her in his arms. She held around his neck and breathed deeply of his wintry, evergreen hair. She wanted to go back into the woods with him soon. She wanted to see him, there, among the trees when nothing was trying to kill them. She knew from the worn trails and the scent on his hair and skin that he walked there often.

"I wanted to kiss you the first night you carried me to the tower," Elena confessed. "When you gave me the key. When you explained that you weren't locking me in. I began to desire you at that moment."

"I needed you to lock me out. I knew I wouldn't be able to stay away," Romanov said. He nuzzled the top of her head as he carried her into the aviary.

"I'm glad I didn't hide in the tower," Elena said.

He placed her on the bed and turned to start a fire. She watched him lay the logs and strike a match. There was no rush, but she thought she saw a tremble of anticipation in his hand. The flame on the match danced more than it should have before he tossed it on the logs.

"So am I," he said as he turned around.

He unfastened the rest of his buttons while she stared transfixed by the hardened body he revealed. He was so unlike the other men she'd known, but some part of her had always known she would need to leave the ballet and Saint Petersburg. The legend had called her long before she'd felt the sapphire's call. The fire caught behind him and its golden glow illuminated his muscular form. Elena rose to reach for his waistband. She helped him loosen his pants and, as they fell, her body tightened in response to what they'd revealed.

He was hard all over. From his head to his feet. But some parts of him were even harder.

Romanov reached for her skirts, but the bodice of her dress had fallen over the fastening at her waist. She gasped when he tore the chiffon rather than patiently burrow for the means to release it.

"I've been waiting too long to do that," he said.

Elena stood nearly naked in the firelight. Her silk underwear was translucent and so were the gossamer stockings on her legs. She kicked off her shoes, but that was all he allowed her to do before he pushed her back onto the bed. Her legs embraced him. She cradled his stiff erection at the moist juncture of her thighs. She wound her arms around his muscled back.

"Don't wait. Not any longer," Elena whispered urgently.

She moaned when he tore the fabric of her underwear to slide it out of the way. She raised her hips to meet his thrust when he joined his body to hers. She was slick with need and she only got slicker as his shaft filled her. She cried out when he began to rock. Their bodies moved together in perfect rhythm.

"I don't know how I didn't carry you to the lair and keep you there from the moment you arrived," Romanov growled against her ear. She gloried in his hunger. She undulated beneath the urgent movements of his hips. Her body tightened around him. The cold mountain breeze whistled around the shutters, but it didn't cool the perspiration that had risen on her skin.

"You were too used to being strong and alone. You didn't know we could be stronger together," Elena said. She punctuated her words with a push, and Romanov allowed her to roll him over so that she could straddle his hips. Her knee protested, but not too much, because other parts of her body were too pleasured to be interrupted.

"You're so small and yet so fierce," Romanov groaned. His head arched back on the pillows as she braced her hands against his broad shoulders. The position gave him total access to her depths. She cried out as she was stretched wide and the head of his penis found the entrance to her womb.

"The better to take my black wolf to the stars," Elena said.

They didn't need the mica cavern or the sky. They didn't need the sapphire's glow. On the wall outside, it beamed its light alone. They only needed each other. When Romanov came, he cried out her name and it sounded very like a howl she'd once heard in a distant wood. His release caused hers, and she joined him in shouting her pleasure to the mountains.

Their pleasure rang out to echo down Bronwal's lonely halls. Their love dispelled the castle's curse as a lone red wolf tucked his tail and ran far away.

* * * * *

LET'S TALK
Romance

For exclusive extracts, competitions
and special offers, find us online:

f facebook.com/millsandboon

◎ @millsandboonuk

🐦 @millsandboon

Or get in touch on 0844 844 1351*

For all the latest titles coming soon, visit
millsandboon.co.uk/nextmonth